Producer & International Distributor
eBookPro Publishing
www.ebook-pro.com

Deadly Ties
Aaron Ben Shahar

Translation from the Hebrew: Guri Arad

Contact: bsaaron28@gmail.com
ISBN: 9798636836766

DEADLY TIES

AARON BEN SHAHAR

"Logic will get you from A to B. Imagination will take you everywhere."

Albert Einstein

Prologue

The prime minister was sitting at the head of the table with the minister of defense to his right and the science minister to his left. The chief of IDF general staff was sitting next to the defense minister, and next to him sat the intelligence affairs and strategy advisor. The head of the Mossad was sitting left of the science minister, and next to him sat the head of the General Security Service (GSS). This was Israel's top echelon.

The meeting was taking place in room X, whose exact location, four floors below the basement of the Mossad building on a hill north of Tel Aviv was known to precious few. There was a small antechamber right at the front, accessible only by an elevator, with an entry code known only to the head of the GSS security department, who had led the group into room X earlier.

Prior to their entry into the room, each of the participants, without exception, was asked to leave his cellphone with the head of the GSS security department. The cellphones were disconnected from their batteries and placed into the safe at the lobby.

The door leading from the antechamber to room X featured

hidden magnetometers that monitored the participants without their knowledge. The room itself comprised a unique electronic system constructed by a select team of electronics engineers from the GSS operations department. This system foiled any means of gleaning information on the goings-on in room X through wiretapping, taking images or any type of surveillance.

The participants were all seated when the prime minister began. His message, like those of everyone else, was not recorded, but rather taken down by the GSS security department chief in his own hand. He later filed the protocol in a specially dedicated safe whose combination was known only to him. A backup code was kept by one of the members of Israel's security community, who was chosen jointly by the head of the Mossad and the head of the GSS.

"Gentlemen," the prime minister began, "we are gathered here today to discuss one issue and one issue only, namely – the removal of Iran's Islamic Revolutionary Guard Corps commander. I now call upon the head of the Mossad to provide us with a short briefing."

"We've had IRGC Commander Mehdi Mohammadi in our sights for many years now," the head of Mossad began his review. "Mossad began compiling a file on him back when he was a junior university student in Thessaloniki, where he was also an operative for Iranian intelligence. He rose in the ranks all the way to the top thanks to his unique skills, uncanny ferocity, and extraordinary valor.

"At some point, Mehdi caught the attention of the CIA, who soon discovered it was he who had shot dead point-blank one of their top agents in Europe. MI 6 also initiated a file on him, a little belatedly, after they found out it was Mehdi who was behind the elimination of one of their own, whose body surfaced in the Bosporus.

"Our own security services have a bitter score to settle with Mehdi. He had one of our best field commanders, whose name is still a secret, eliminated. On top of that, he masterminded numerous operations against Israeli targets worldwide.

"Today's meeting was called urgently when we received accurate intelligence according to which he is planning a major terrorist attack on one of our important embassies in Africa.

"Our joint efforts with the GSS Operations Department led to the conclusion it is high time we rid the world of this mass murderer."

"Now that we have heard from Mossad," concluded the prime minister, "the concise message of the head of Mossad brings this matter before your approval. I would like your vote on the removal of the commander of Iran's Revolutionary Guard Corps by a show of hands."

Everyone present raised his hand.

PART ONE

Chapter One

"Surprise! Surprise!" Estée heard Claudia's lively voice over the phone. She was her cousin on her mother's side of the family. "You thought you were going to get married and that's it, nothing else?"

Claudia lived in Thessaloniki, where she worked at a travel agency. They knew each other since childhood, but the year before, after spending six nights with Claudia and her girl-friends in Thessaloniki's ouzo bars, where the staff poured and poured, and the playful music added further gusto to the festivities, Estée felt their bond grow stronger.

"What are you up to, Claudia?"

"We're throwing you a bachelorette party!"

"Who's *we*? What's the plan?"

"*We* is us two and Celia, remember her?"

"How could I forget?"

Celia, Claudia's best friend, was as breathtakingly beautiful as she was petite. A real chatterbox, she left an unforgettable impression on Estée. Celia knew all the Greek tunes that were playing there, filling Ladadika, Thessaloniki's main entertainment district, with mirth to accompany all those wonderful seafood restaurants that catered to local and foreign thrill seekers alike. How was it that Claudia referred to Celia in a moment of elation? "*The* lioness of Thessaloniki's roar of life."

"I am getting excited already," continued Estée, and added, "So what's the plan?"

"I found this great spot in Sithonia," replied Claudia. "It's one of those treasures Greece received as a gift directly from the gods. An hour and a half's drive south of Thessaloniki. An eight-room boutique hotel. You're gonna love it. Celia took it upon herself to take care of all of our culinary delights. She's promised us an experience like no other."

Estée, a mere bank clerk from Haifa, who had never tasted seafood until the year before, got fidgety. "Everything sounds great, but isn't all this a bit too much?"

"What is up with you?" Claudia was her usual confident, joyful self. "You don't get married every day. Don't worry. I've got this."

One quick phone call, and Estée found out that there wasn't a direct flight from Tel Aviv the day she and her girlfriends were going to meet.

"Claudia, it's me," Estée called her up. "I am pushing my flight up to Monday, the day before we meet. The idea of having a day all to myself appeals to me. That day is on me. No point arguing. Just update the hotel and have them book me a room for another day prior to your and Celia's arrival."

"Got it. Don't worry about the room. We're arriving at the end of the tourist season, so we're going to be the only guests in the entire hotel. I'll arrange everything with Maria, the re-sort manager. See you in paradise."

***

The red-eye flight from Tel Aviv to Thessaloniki took two hours. On arrival, Estée boarded a local south-bound bus serving local commuters from Thessaloniki to the Sithonia Peninsula. After a bumpy two-hour drive, she finally arrived at the hotel, where she met Maria in a modest room that served as the reception. Maria handed Estée her room key. A few short steps, and there was Estée's room.

The moment she got it, she threw what little luggage she had on the single armchair and immediately fell asleep on the comfy bed, where she slept soundly for three hours.

Estée woke from her dreamless slumber, took a shower and got into an Arab *galabia*. She had picked that robe up on a trip to Jerusalem's old market. She was now ready to explore this place her girlfriends got her to.

The views and sights were amazing. The front of the hotel had an infinity pool with waters that seemed to merge with the blue bay yonder. This bay stretched across from the Sithonia Peninsula to the nearby Athos Peninsula.

"If you're thinking of trying to get to the Athos Peninsula, forget it," Maria told Estée as she came out of the kitchen, while offering her a glass of ouzo, her first for that day. Maria was about forty, as beautiful as she was kind, with a pair of piercing eyes. She poured Estée and herself a glass of ouzo each and downed hers in one gulp.

"They call the Athos Peninsula 'the Island of Men' as well," she told Estée. "It has dozens of monasteries and women are prohibited. There are no roads, so the only access is by ferry. Besides, what business does a pretty girl like you have there? The monks are celibate, isolated from civilization. They don't even allow TVs and cellphones. Owning them is strictly prohibited."

"I really have no business going there," agreed Estée, smiling.

"Take the path down, and you'll find what you are looking for," Maria winked whimsically.

'*How could she know what I was looking for?*' Estée asked herself. '*I wish I knew myself,*' she grinned slightly and went down to the beach.

'*Amazing!*' was the first word that occurred to Estée as she got to the cove that was right next to her hotel, but she immediately purged it from her vocabulary for seeming too small, too bland to capture the scenery for, to her, the inlet seemed like a droplet of azure that had dripped from the Creator's pallet at the moment of creation. Round and surrounded on three sides by cliffs, the bay's eastern side opened up to a wide mouth. The bay itself consisted of tiny patches of islands that formed a zipper-like line. Soundless sailboats traversed these tiny islands in search of a path to the open sea.

The Athos Peninsula lay across, on the other side of the cove. Towering over its southern tip, the mountain it was named after, in honor of a giant mentioned in Greek mythology, stretched all the way to the edge of the peninsula, where white cliffs dropped in a magnificent angle right to sea.

Lying on a comfy chair, her must-have glass of ouzo in one

hand, Estée watched the sea's changing hues right before her tear-filling eyes as the day went by and as the sun cast the cliffs' shadow around the bay.

The deep blue of the cove turned into a crimson. All the different tones seemed to be produced by this huge crystal ball. Responding to the color of the white cliffs above and to the sandy bottom of the bay, the water seemed to turn clearer every now and then. The water was so clear, she could count every grain of sand.

Evening was drawing nearer, so only few holiday makers remained at the beach now. Perched on her chair, Estée was considering whether to take off her galabia, the only thing she had on, and go native. Rather than join the other bathers and lie naked, she let her laziness prevail. Clad in her robe, Estée downed her third glass of ouzo that enchanted afternoon, right after the teenage waiter catering to the guests at the beach had served it to her.

As she lay there, marveling at the mighty Athos that dominated the view in front of her, she watched the sun setting down, filling the mountain range with dark, heavy brushstrokes. The scenery grew grayer, their lighter shade fading, succumbing to the tenderness of dusk.

Suddenly, the whole world seemed to grind to a halt. The Athos mountain range turned black, while the summit, far and lofty, remained golden in the distant sun, lighting the world like a huge lantern.

Then, transfixed, Estée saw the Lord turning the summit off as well, all the way from the foot of the mountain. It took several minutes, and then, in a split-second, the mountain gave off one last flicker before descending into indulgent darkness.

'*Time for my fourth ouzo,*' Estée whispered to herself dreaming, as though in a daze. The beach was now lit by dim lanterns. Estée finished her glass of ouzo along with the Greek salad she had ordered, bid a heavyhearted farewell to the beach and made her way back to the hotel. Euphoric and saturated with ouzo, she strutted to the small chamber that Maria used as the hotel reception.

'*She isn't here. But who's this?*' Estée spotted a tall, dark, blue-eyed man with flowing curly hair all the way to his shoulders. '*Is this Athos?*' she wondered to herself. His presence dominated the room and caused Estée to go silent. She couldn't even utter her room number. All she could bring herself to do was raise three fingers of her left hand. Athos, or at least the person she thought was Athos, didn't utter a single word either as, with his long fingers, he handed her the key to room three.

Estée crawled to her room, opened her door despite her quivering hands, removed the key and replaced it on the other side of the keyhole, from inside the room, but as she proceeded to lock the door, her hand slipped and she sat on the bed, catching her breath.

A few seconds passed, and then she heard a knock on her door.

In came Athos.

Estée knew.

He took his blue t-shirt off, and before he removed his shorts, Estée had already removed her robe. All at once, their bodies clung to each other. They moved over to the bed, embracing. Estée could not tell whether this took a moment or whether this lasted an eternity.

Not a word was uttered, not a sigh was sounded.

Athos disappeared suddenly, much like that mountain that vanished along with the sun.

Estée was a beautiful young woman. A bit short, clear-skinned and sporting a pair of shining blue eyes, she was one of those teenagers who find it hard to come to terms with their own beauty, repressing it from their minds. Until Athos came along, that is. Before he turned up, her sexual experience had been scarce and sparse: the odd hand over her breast there, fingers fumbling, lips pert, and her virginity lost in some summer trip she took to the desert with a classmate. Oh, to be sure, she and her girlfriends spent a great deal talking about sex but actually had very little of it.

Estée had spent her compulsory military service out in the desert, in a completely desolate spot, with nothing but fellow women soldiers around. But for a chance encounter with Avram, a soldier she met at a hitchhiker's stop right before his own military service was drawing to a close, she had had no sex at all. Avram was of average height, his black hair was combed to either side, showing off his soft brown eyes and prominent chin. He was hardly the leading man type. Nothing about his outward appearance could make Estée boast about him or even consider showing his picture off to her friends. Nevertheless, his inner peace endeared him to her, and the attention he bestowed on her appealed to her. More than anything else, she loved his home back in the valley, amid fragrant orchards and green fields. They began having sex shortly after their first encounter. Nothing thrilling, though. Satisfying and regular was the most she could say about it.

Nothing of all this had prepared her for the tumultuous, earth-shuddering, unworldly time she had with Athos. Their torrid romp filled Estée to the brim, leaving her in a daze of passion and pleasure the like of which she had never known. He vanished just as suddenly as he had appeared. Estée was still lying on her bed, weary to the point of falling asleep, suddenly recalling an experience she had a few years back.

One day, she had gone to the beach by herself. After a short swim, she had decided to go home and had waited for a good strong wave to carry her back to the beach. Then, this great swell had suddenly grabbed her by the back, thrown her up and slammed at the back of her neck to the bottom of the sea. She lay there, motionless, under the water, unable to count the seconds. She felt her mind was going blurry, she was losing control.

This powerful experience stayed with Estée her entire life. She marveled at how she could still accurately retain so many details of what had happened despite her daze and partial loss of consciousness. She recalled a seashell she had seen on the sea floor, the tones of the water that had forced her down and the color of the swimsuit strap twirling about her neck.

The experience with Athos reignited the memory of Estée drowning. The same daze and sense of blur came back, along with the memory of several details she knew she would always remember. The muscles on his back felt like living beings under her quivering hands; his long fingers, dark skin, well-defined thighs, going up and down over her so amazingly… She remembered it all in and of itself, and above all, she recalled his scent, so much like that of the sea itself. Estée kept feeling his touch and the weight of his body all through the night, long after he had gone. Not wanting to lose any trace of this, she did not take a shower.

Estée did not sleep a wink, either. She spent the entire night daydreaming. First thing in the morning, she went over to the reception desk to meet Athos, but he wasn't there.

'*Oh, here's Maria*'.

"Good morning, did you have a pleasant night?" Maria then added, in that same congenial tone, "Your breakfast is ready."

"Simply wonderful. I'll go grab something, but please tell me, where's the guy from yesterday? He promised to give me an address in Thessaloniki."

"I don't know," answered Maria.

"May I have his phone?"

"I do not have it."

"So how do you get in touch with him?"

"Well, I do not. I do not even know his name."

The look of disappointment on Estée's eyes was plain as it was clear.

"This address in Thessaloniki must be very important to you," Maria added, "but I am sorry to disappoint you, I do not know anything about him. A student from Thessaloniki comes every now and then to stand in for me and my husband and take over our evening shift. He called me yesterday afternoon and said he had to return to Slovenia, some family urgency. I do hope everything is fine. He assured me everything was OK, and that he would send a friend of his to fill the shift, an Iranian fellow, a med student. He promised me he was a serious, responsible person. Well, I had no choice, so I agreed to the switch. I left this med student my key and went back to Thessaloniki with my husband. We had to attend my niece's wedding. I never saw this guy, so I do not know who he is... He did leave me everything neat and tidy. He truly is responsible. If I manage to get hold of this student, I shall ask for his friend's phone number. In the meantime, have something to eat. You seem like you could use a long espresso too."

Estée went down to the breakfast buffet, grabbed a large coffee with milk and went over to a pool chair facing the sea. A short while passed, and the phone rang.

"We are running late. There was a traffic accident, and the road is blocked. We will let you know," Claudia said sweetly, "but don't worry, everything's fine."

'*Oh, that suits me just fine,*' Estée thought to herself. She went back to her room and got the good sleep she was in such need of. Three hours later, she awoke to the sound of her friends clamoring about her joyfully.

"What happened, are you fine?"

"Yes, some Iranian dude," replied Claudia.

"No, a Persian," Celia corrected her. "He lost his mind, drove in the opposite direction and hit a few cars. It was so scary. I nearly fainted."

"How do you know he was a Persian?" wondered Estée.

"A policeman who was at the scene of the accident passed between the cars and asked if there was anyone who spoke Farsi," Celia explained.

"Or Iranian," Claudia stood her ground.

"Ok…" Celia replied, "We're here to have fun, not argue about an Iranian of Persian descent!" Let's go, we've got one hour to get it together and hit the beach!"

The bay was teaming. The girls just barely found a spot. Celia immediately took the top of her red bikini off, as Claudia and Estée kept theirs on.

"You mermaids," Celia sneered, laughing her head off.

A few hours of idle chatter later, complete with several glasses of ouzo each and fantastic sights, Celia excused herself, said something about stuff she had to do and scurried off back to the hotel.

**

Estée heard a knock at seven, only to find her two best friends all dolled up and smiling, lighting up the room as they walked in. Claudia, tall and slender, had a long white dress on. Estée noticed the Greek embroidery in gold and azure. '*It really brings out her dark, lovely face and lovely, black, long wavy hair*,' she thought. Celia, short and bouncy, had this high-cut bright red top baring her belly. '*It somehow matches her nose piercing and Havaianas flip flops.*' Estée also liked Celia's rolled up bun, despite the messy way she wore it up.

Estée wore a turquoise galabia that complimented her curvy figure. '*Pity I didn't have time to do my hair,*' she thought, while inspecting her friends' hair.

Celia and Claudia each took her by the hand and led her to the edge of the pool, where Maria was expecting them in her long blue dress; her husband, Nicholas, sporting a tiny mustache and tanned face, stood next to her in his white clothes. Both had a glass of ouzo each, same as always.

"And now, for your surprise!" Maria announced.

They followed Maria and Nicholas to the restaurant at the front of the hotel, right at the edge of the cliff, where the three young ladies were seated at a wide table, decorated by a bright white cloth strewn with small flowers. Other than that, the table was bare.

Marveling at the bay, the three friends saw the moon lighting the waves and exchanging secrets with the mountain yonder. Proud Mount Athos watched over, taking the day in.

Then, the whole commotion began. The light went on, tiny candles appeared on the table and a procession, led by Maria, followed by Nicholas and Ahmed, their faithful assistant from Afghanistan, sent out from the kitchen. They were carrying bowls of mussels of different sizes and seasonings and set them on the table along with select local white and red wines. Then, out came Margie, the chef, bestowing on them another lavish bowl of bright red *moules marinière* and white tzatziki.

"A toast to your happy marriage!" Claudia and Celia greeted Estée.

"May you have as many kids as there are mussels here!" Margie added, right before rushing back to her kitchen. Soon followed the most sumptuous dishes, taking even Celia aback, for all her expertise on the local cuisine, which quite naturally made her in charge of the culinary side of the celebrations.

One by one, the kitchen sent over plates of fried scorpionfish, baked seabass, then shrimp and calamari in various forms, lobsters, oysters and crabs, followed by fresh anchovies and sardines and *lakerda*, brought all the way from Istanbul. Alongside came Greek delicacies such as local salads, zucchini and much more.

"Let's take a short pause," Maria asked. "I would like to tell you about the dish Margie just sent over to our table, vine leaves filled with octopus pâté. This was prepared by the monks who live up in the mountain monastery. The monks pick the vine leaves right before dawn and catch the octopus at sundown. They are the only ones who know the secret of this dish, so we only serve it on special occasions."

Estée was delighted, ecstatic, even. *'What do all these wonderful sights and scents have to do with me? How in the world could a simple girl from Haifa like me possibly have anything to do with Athos? What was that? The hand of fate? Divine intervention? Mere coincidence?'*

She helped herself to another glass of ouzo Claudia poured her and, setting aside her thoughts, rejoined the culinary orgy, now in full swing.

It was approaching midnight when our three young ladies trotted, alcohol-saturated and sated, to their rooms. Come morning, Maria had to pound quite hard and long on their room doors to get them up and about. They hardly touched their sumptuous breakfast – a cup of black coffee each sufficed – before getting into Celia's car and making their way back north, to Thessaloniki. At the airport right outside town, Estée and her friends embraced and kissed.

"See you at the wedding," they parted.

***

The wedding took place about a month later at the main community hall of Avram's village. It was a genuinely festive event. All the young folks, both the locals and Estée's friends from the nearby town danced, delighted in the folk dances and sang national songs. At the height of the evening, two guest singers climbed onto the wooden platform that served as a stage, and, much to the crowd's delight, swept the guests in a medley of Greek songs. They couldn't get enough of Claudia and Celia and joined their Greek dances too.

***

Three months after the wedding, Estée recalled the date very accurately, she was sitting with Avram in their living room.

"I went to the doctor today," she told him.

"How is he?"

"*He* is fine. He told me I was pregnant."

"What a wife, what a wife!" Avram got up, excited, and gave her a loving kiss on the forehead. He then returned to the kibbutz receipts and went over the accounts.

***

"I'm in labor," Estée told her husband. "It started early. Take me to the hospital!"

Avram sat by her side, genuinely attempting to help out and ease her pain. When the baby wasn't emerging, he asked her permission to step out and return to his accounts. A devoted accountant for the Israeli labor movement, this was typical of him.

The baby was delivered the moment Avram was out the door.

"What a beautiful boy!" the midwife called out. She picked it up and held it in front of Estée.

'*He has such long fingers. He has such brown skin,*' Estée immediately noticed.

She watched him and knew. Oh yes, she knew all too well when she looked at him.

Chapter Two

The tractor, which was as old as its faded red, was dragging the flat cart. Normally, it was used to carry animal feed to the pens, but now, it was carrying Avram Fiddlemann's coffin.

A banged-up Toyota kept its distance behind the tractor. Bonnie, the deceased's son, was driving, along with his mother and younger sister in the back seat. He pulled up near the village synagogue at the end of the main street. Four men placed the coffin down and laid it on iron slabs which normally served to carry the milk containers.

The synagogue was built about a century earlier, along with the dozen houses erected by the village founders, who had collected large, black galilee rocks and stones from the surrounding hill. The synagogue had survived, thanks to having been declared a building meant for preservation by the village committee. Two additional original buildings had also remained intact, having been turned into storage houses over the years.

The funeral was set for six o'clock, right between the end of field work and milking the cows. Every village member attended. Some of them had enough time to change into clean clothes, sporting their Sunday best, and others simply put on their blue-collar work shirts, kept clean and neat in the closet especially for this occasion. Everyone wore open sandals with leather straps about their ankles.

Those among the villagers, who could not hurry home in time, came straight from the field, still in their muddy, sweaty, faded work clothes, a blue or khaki *kova tembel,* similar to a bucket hat, over their heads to protect them from the unrelenting sun. In addition, they had quintessential work boots on, to protect them from snakes and scorpions.

A few among the womenfolk put on short shorts, exposing their tanned legs. The more elegant of them had on long dresses that hid their figures. Vera, the mythological village chief, a woman of no age, came straight from the village HQ in the satin and cotton tunic she was always wearing.

"When does she ever manage to get it cleaned?" One villager asked her fellow villager.

"If ever…," her friend replied.

Vera produced a piece of paper from her bosom and began reading it out in her confident, commanding voice.

"Dear Estée, Bonnie and Michal, all of us, the members of Moshav Tel Broshim, are grieving over the sudden death of our friend Avram."

"We have not forgotten that only five years and two months ago, Avram closed down his cow shed, but we hold to his credit the memory of his late father, Feibel, who was a founding member of our moshav."

"We also recall that only four years ago, three years and eight months ago, if you allow me to be absolutely accurate here, Feibel let his plot run completely dry and went to work for the farming cooperative, but then again, it is to his credit that he helped the village secure a loan from the cooperative when our barn caught fire…"

The cows' moos in the distance reminded Vera to keep it brief.

"On behalf of myself and the entire village, I offer you our condolences. We hope you shall find solace in the thriving valley. Long live the People of Israel!"

Four men lifted Avram's coffin and circled the synagogue en route to the adjacent graveyard. It was right next to a grapefruit orchard the villagers had planted many years before. The first settlers, a merry band of optimistic young pioneers, had not considered death and had never planned to have a cemetery. It had not occurred to them to allow for one within their village.

Nevertheless, as reality had unfolded, they were in for a rude awakening. One day, Yodel, one of the founding pioneers, lifted a bale of hay and a snake that was lurking there bit him. Yodel was rushed over by a horse-drawn cart all the way to the Scottish Hospital in Tiberias, but the bumpy road only hastened the venom's spread throughout his body, and so he died on arrival.

The villagers convened urgently and voted that, on the grounds of efficiency and saving time, the cemetery they were to have would be situated close to the synagogue. They had to pull out three grapefruit trees to make room for the village's first grave.

Additional grapefruit trees had to be pulled out over the

years. Fever, the odd clashes with the nearby Arab villagers, Israel's wars and the toll of the passage of time had all claimed their dues, and additional graves had to be prepared, much at the expense of the grapefruit orchard. The graveyard expanded northwards as its membership increased.

Now with dozens of gravestones, the cemetery was well-kept, cultivated and spacious, as the graves were, after all, still few and far between. Three of its sides were delineated by a row of cypresses, lending further calm and respectability to the place.

"I would die to die in such a place," one of the few non-villagers who attended Avram's funeral told his friend.

Avram's freshly dug grave was situated at the edge of the cemetery, not far from two recently dug out grapefruit trees. Bonnie stood over his father's grave in his sandals and slightly oversized khaki pants and old gray t-shirt, for he was forewarned he would have to tear his shirt, as was the old Jewish custom for mourning one's immediate relation. Bonnie's sister and mother were still in shock over Avram's sudden death. Estée, Avram's widow, Bonnie's and Michal's mother, stared blankly. She had not yet uttered a single sound since she walked into her husband's study the night before and found him slouching on his desk, bereft of life.

The regional rabbi stepped forward, keeping his reverential albeit disapproving distance from Vera, the village chief. When the rabbi saw that Bonnie had no yarmulke on, he took his own off and gently rested it on Bonnie's head. After the ceremonious tearing of the clothes, the rabbi placed a plastic laminated cardboard with the Jewish prayer for the dead in

Bonnie's hand and beckoned him to recite the *Kaddish*.

The coffin was soon thereafter lowered into the ground, and each villager covered it with earth. A wreath of sunflowers locally picked in advance by the village women was laid over the fresh grave. Several doctors and nurses from the regional clinic, adjacent to Bonnie's veterinary practice, laid a wreath they had purchased on their way to their colleague's funeral.

"May we never have to dig more grapefruit trees out," the villagers greeted one another as they dispersed.

Chapter Three

Bonnie was sitting in the middle of the modest living room in his parents' house, surrounded by ten of his late father's friends, men in their sixties and seventies, whom he had asked to come one evening during *shiva*, the customary Jewish week of mourning, so that he might share intimate memories of his dad with them.

The guests, country folk weary from a life spent toiling away in the sun, all came over after yet another working day out, each in his field, cow shed or orchard. Customarily, they took their cold showers at the end of their hard work, put their clean shorts and sandals on, grabbed a spotless t-shirt, and off they went to pay their respects.

"I know that were I able to consult with dad whom to have over to mourn him, he would have picked each of you. He always told me how he admired his fellow villager friends and envied them for sticking with farming, contrary to him, how they never let their aching backs, white hair and kids who abandoned farming, to keep them away from the field, not for one day."

"Whereas we," retorted one of the guests, "always envied

Avram. We always thought that he, with his shining car, nice clothes and easy, cushy job uptown would eventually bury us all, but look what happened…"

"No, don't get me wrong," countered Bonnie, "not a day went by without my father telling me how he longed to get back behind his tractor, to milk the cows, get the eggs and get up before dawn and pick the avocados."

"Such a shame," Avram's friends told Bonnie in reply, "but we needed among us someone from the big city to give us the latest gossip, the real deal…"

The newly widowed Estée walked in carrying a tray with tea and snacks. "I'm sure that would never have happened had he continued working on the farm." Teary-eyed, she handed each guest his teacup, added two spoons of sugar each and retired to her room.

"I've got a surprise for you all," Bonnie began, "but before I tell you about it, please try and tell me what you make of this: 'the purchase of an item of clothing recalls the value of the toil it took to obtain it,'" he read out of a cardboard sheet he was holding.

His father's friends look at each other. They had no clue.

"Let me give you another clue," Bonnie added with a touch of mystery. "In what context was the following said: 'clothes for work'?"

"Quit joking," Shaikeh, one of Avram's friends, cut Bonnie off. "We came to talk about your father, our pal, and you're giving us this quiz…"

Bonnie left the room to go to his father's study. When he returned, he threw a pile of blue-colored work outfits all over the coffee table. "Do you know what these are?"

The men came over to the heap of clothes and uncovered a blue triangular tag attached to one of the pants.

"Blue jeans work denims!" cried Shmil. "I've been looking for one of those for years! Where did you get 'em?"

"You wouldn't believe it. Michal and I went through dad's personal effects and put them in order. We got to the storage, too. Once we went over the lot, we found this box in one of the corners, an old carboard box covered in rags. No one even touched it for years. We carried it out to the porch, opened it up and discovered all sorts of old things that used to belong to grandpa. These pants were at the bottom of the box. They had these ads of some blue jeans factory. I remember from dad's stories that Pops used to work there. Still, I have no idea how they got to be in his storage. Do you have any idea how?"

"That's quite a story," Moishe interjected. "I know, from those stories, that after they set up that factory, long before all of us were even born, every time money was tight, or in winter, they would go to work down at the jeans factory for some extra cash, what you might call, 'supplement their income.' But what's that got to do with these denims?"

"Maybe your Pops stole 'em?" Haim asked cunningly.

"There you go again with your foolish crap," Shmil exclaimed. "We're in mourning, not out looking for thieves."

"So where did he get them jeans from, eh?"

Shloimeh, the eldest member of the bunch, who had kept silent about all this until now, joined in. "I came to the funeral in my blue jeans. Shmil took me aside when they were lowering the coffin into the ground and asked me where I got them from."

"No, I didn't. Only after Avram was buried."

"Before, after, what does it matter? What's important here is the question, which I couldn't answer. I went back to Feige and asked her, seeing as here in our village, it's the women who are in charge of the clothing. At first, she could not recall. She's been a bit senile recently, you know… Anyway, she got back to me after some time and said it came back to her. She told me that her dad once told her that anyone who worked at the jeans factory got a pair of pants for Passover as a gift on the occasion of the holiday. The pants I was wearing, well, her dad got them. He gave 'em to me as a wedding present when I married Feige. So there."

"That was your entire dowry?"

"No. I also got a kova tembel."

"How many years did your Pops work at the factory?" Ronny, another member of the gang, asked him.

"I don't know exactly, but there are nine pairs here, so do the math…" Bonnie replied.

"Why did he keep them?" Ronny insisted.

"Not everything has an answer," Shmil cut the discussion short. "Gotta leave some room for suspense in life."

"So be it. Anyway, I haven't any need for work clothes, so I would like each of you to have a pair. A gift. In my dad's name."

"But there are only nine pairs here…"

"No sweat. Haim will wait until my Pops steals another pair."

Chapter Four

Bonnie seldom walked into his father's study. He revered and respected him and never went through his papers. Avram, in turn, was proud and loving. Even as a child, Avram would proudly present Bonnie, whenever he tagged along, as his tall, beautiful son, saying, "As luck would have it, Bonnie here's got his mom's genes rather than mine."

In the evening of the fourth day of the shiva, once the last person who came to offer their respects had left, Estée, Michal and Bonnie were sitting together in the terrace facing west, which was always windswept and drenched during winter and all the more beautiful for it, tender in the glow of sunset in the fall.

"We need to get into dad's study and tidy up," said Bonnie.

"Count me out," Estée immediately exclaimed.

She had this terrified look. All during shiva, she sat as much as she had to with those who came over, biding her time till they were out the door. When each day came to a close, she and her two kids took their seats in the big porch, spent and exhausted from all those stories and guests. Bonnie and Michal were keen to hear new anecdotes and tidbits about their father. Estée, in contrast, was all too familiar with the stories, and whatever was new had gone through one ear and out the next.

"I keep seeing Avram sitting on his chair, his head lying on his desk, his open eyes gazing at the door. Helpless. I'm not getting in there," Estée concluded.

That terrible day, Estée had walked in to ask Avram whether he would like some tea. Upon seeing her husband in that state, she had begun shouting. Next, she had called in Bonnie, whose house was right next door. Bonnie had laid his father on the floor, called for an ambulance and begun his own attempt to resuscitate him. The ambulance had been quick to arrive, and the paramedic had quickly taken over from Bonnie and rushed Avram, still conscious and hooked up to an oxygen mask, to the hospital, siren sounding and everything. Bonnie had driven right behind, Estée by his side.

Bonnie and his mother had waited in the emergency room with Michal, whom they had called away from her home in the nearby town. The three had heard the sound of the fight the medical team was waging over Avram's life. As time went by, the noise had subsided, until they could no longer hear the doctors or the nurses, not even the respirator or life support machine. Silence.

"I'm truly sorry, we didn't make it," the manager of the emergency room had put his arms around Estée, shaken Bonnie's and Michal's hands, and off he had gone.

***

They finished their sweet tea and Bonnie said, "We have to. It can't be helped. We're going in."

The room, silently conveying the fight for Avram's life, was an absolute mess. The chair was thrown back, papers scattered all over the floor next to it; disconnected from the socket, the lamp had fallen, too. There were piles of plastic sheets in the corner.

Bonnie and Michal proceeded to tidy up without a word. They laid the paperwork back on the desk, set the lamp back up, lifted the chair and opened the windows to let the air back in.

"I suggest you return tomorrow morning," Estée said quietly, her eyes blank.

"You're right, mother. It's difficult to be here." Bonnie left to return to his nearby residence as Estée laid her sheets out on the living room couch, as she did throughout the mourning week.

The following day, after they had had their morning coffee, Bonnie and Michal went back into Avram's study as their mother went in the kitchen. The night air had let in a pleasant, fragrant breeze and aired out the stuffy room, with a window, facing a magnificent view of the fields, on the northern wall. The bookcase that stretched on either side of the window consisted of wooden shelves and iron stands. It was packed with rows of books.

"I didn't know dad has so many books," Michal told Bonnie.

"I actually do remember all these children's books, Michali," Bonnie replied, marveling at his favorites, those copies of books by Israeli children authors, his series of *Tarzan* books, old copies of children's magazines, and so on. "Who was he saving it all for?"

"Grandkids, probably," Michal answered.

They looked at the disarray of the shelf above the children's books. Encyclopedia volumes, all sorts of poetry books, Passover Haggadah, *History of Modern Hebrew Literature*, albums of photographs of the Six Day War, books by 19th century Hebrew authors, etc.

"I didn't know he took an interest in teen psychology." Bonnie pulled out one of the books. "What shall we do with them? I don't think I would find an interest in any of them."

"I don't care for them either, but I don't think we should come to any decision right now. Perhaps we'd better talk it over with mom when she's feeling better."

The study also had its fair share of paintings, mostly reproductions of works by Rembrandt and Van Gogh, a family photo pf Avram, Estée and the two kids, and an old photo of Avram's parents, who were among the founders of Tel Broshim.

"Michal, let's move over to the desk."

Avram's desk stood out as the most curious and unusual item in the entire room. Contrary to the bookcase, the faded curtains and old couch, the desk conveyed some intriguing respectability, with its shiny mahogany and handcrafted woodwork which augmented its general air. The desk featured a four-drawer left cabinet one could extend out using four polished ivory balls.

"Dad once told me that Pops bought this desk. Our grandfather had picked it up at the old flea market in Nazareth and bought it for a song. With an army friend of his, he had it restored. They came across the original sign of the craftsmen, a real artisan from Istanbul, while they were busy with the renovation. The sign attested to its authenticity and origin. Apparently, a Turkish pasha bought it and had it brought over to his summer palace in Nazareth, which is how it ended up being sold off, until it finally made its way to the *suk*. I would like to have it someday," Bonnie concluded.

"But in the meantime, it's Mom's. let's go through the drawers, Bonnie."

The top drawer comprised ten-year-old bank statements, old checkbook stubs, pay slips and the like. Bonnie and Michal left the most recent bank statements and pay slips and put everything else in a large bag.

The second drawer was yet another treasure trove of old bills. "There's not a single receipt dad has not kept," they remarked, rifling through old electricity bills, village taxes, a receipt for getting the cow shed roof fixed, for veterinary payments, old bus tickets, a subscription to the encyclopedia, a ten year old receipt for staying at a sanatorium at Zichron Yaakov, a dentist bill, old cinema tickets and dozens of other receipts for all sorts of things.

They threw the drawer's entire contents into the trash can.

The third drawer contained their father's personal papers: end of year report cards from the regional school, his army card, some faded commendation for heroics dad had performed. It was signed by a major. Dad kept his discharge papers when his army service was up, his and Estée's marriage license, a complaint he had made to Tnuva, the food and beverage company for damages caused by a late milk collection, a framed distinguished service award Avram received from work, and dozens of similar items, which neither of Avram's children was at all impressed by.

"I do hope my kids will find more interesting stuff in my drawers someday," Bonnie joked.

They set aside the documents they'd decided to save, tied them in a string and put them back into the third drawer.

The last drawer consisted of photos: old pictures of Avram's elementary school, childhood trips, the summit of Masada, the beach at Eilat and other childhood photos they could not recognize.

"Dad never told me whether he had any girlfriends before Mom," Bonnie quipped.

He and Michal skimmed through their parents' wedding photos, their own childhood photos, pictures of the old cow shed and other equally interesting memorabilia.

"Let's leave it all to the kids we'll have someday. It'll make for a nice family tree project for them…" Michal and Bonnie agreed as they slammed the drawer shut.

Chapter Five

IDF Chief of the General Staff Lt. General Shauli Aviram announced his resignation. It was a sudden move that was met with great surprise. His private meeting with the minister of defense focused on his telling the minister he felt he had exhausted his interest and ability in office, so he had decided to retire and embark on a new course.

"What are you going to do?" the minister asked.

"I am going to be a farmer. Cows."

This reply took the minister by surprise. Lt. General Shauli Aviram was the minister's senior commander. Nevertheless, he knew all too well that "Shamrock" always had the last word and there was no point arguing. He gave him his blessing and wished him all the best.

Shauli, or 'Shamrock,' as everyone who knew him called him, went and bought himself a cow shed. He got a dairy farm with 32 milk cows in the Jezreel Valley from a farmer whose age and failing health kept him from holding on to the farm.

No one knew how the nickname Shamrock stuck to Shauli. His own father swore he did not name him Shamrock at birth, but apart from Shauli's parents and Shauli on the dotted line, no one knew him by any other name. He was Shamrock.

The first step in this new chapter in his life was to improve the state of his dairy farm and give each cow *her* own name. Getting to know each of them on a first name basis, he thought, would lead to a personal connection with the cow, boost productivity and improve the quality of the milk. Shamrock named his first nineteen cows after the girlfriends he had had in the course of his life. He asked his wife to provide him with the name of her own female friends, but she only gave him five. The remaining names he obtained from his fellow army friends, all of whom were generals. Each had come to see for himself whether the rumors were true, that their illustrious commander had indeed turned farmer. Not so long ago, he was a demigod to them, their promotion was totally dependent on him, and now... he has opted for cow dung instead of a general's baton.

Shamrock treated each of his former subordinate officers to a personal treatment the likes of which he never bestowed on them before. He took them on a personal tour of the farm and even engaged in gossip, a rare occasion as he was famed to be sparing in his use of words. He succeeded in delightfully getting them to tell him the names of their wives. Seeing as none of them ever returned to the cow shed, they were none the wiser about his unique commemoration of their spouses...

Ida, the new cow farmer's wife, could not be happier with this change. Short and silver haired with an occasional white streak, she had kind eyes. A devoted wife and mother, she would always tell their three children she wasn't actually married to "Shamrock" for thirty eight years, as the official documents attested, but rather three measly years, if you were to subtract the time he was never around. Come to think of it, she continued, his total net stay at home between wars and drills amounted to three years, but two and a half years out of that he spent sleeping in their marriage bed, exhausted as he was from chronic fatigue and constant lack of sleep, the main trait of his military service throughout his tenure.

"Even now, I'm still puzzled as to how we ever found the time to have three kids…," she always told her children genuinely perplexed.

As part of their new lives, Ida set up a small dairy farm right next to the cow shed, where she made exquisite yoghurt and cheeses. She sold some and gave most of the produce as gifts to their relatives and numerous visitors.

***

Several months after his father's passing, Bonnie received a phone call. General Shamrock was on the other end of the line.

"Hello, Shamrock here. I got your name from one of the neighbors. It's about Mathilde, my cow. She's having a difficult labor, so I need your help."

Bonnie received the call with palpable excitement. Shamrock had been his much-admired commander during his military service in the parachute brigade. Shamrock was as creative as he was brave: strong, with eyes like a hawk and rare leadership skills. His soldiers had looked up to him and worshiped the ground he had walked on. He used to keep them at a distance, so any conversation anyone had with him was as rare as it was a real treat and a powerful experience.

Hearing his old commander took Bonnie back to a horrific memory of an event from eighteen years before. He was called to him on some business, but rather than raise his right hand in salute, Bonnie accidentally saluted with his left.

"Circle the parade ground ten times! Run with your full combat gear, complete with your steel helmet and gun. On the double!"

That was Shamrock for you. The punishment always came down hard and without delay.

The weight of this trauma still lingered, and, genuinely concerned he was about to be summoned in full combat gear to circle his veterinary clinic running, Bonnie rushed for his medical kit, shut his clinic, put up the "Be right back soon" sign and hurried over to the general turned dairy farmer.

The calf was delivered safe and sound and everything went well. Also an avid reader, Shamrock named the calf 'Chekov.' The subsequent calves were named 'Victor' and 'Hugo.' He knew they would be sent to the slaughter within six months, so he was thrifty with their names.

With the successful labor over and done with, Shamrock asked Bonnie to come and sit with him on the porch, where, seated by the natural wood table the retired general built single-handedly, he offered the vet a plate of homemade cheese. They got to talking, and Bonnie did not neglect to mention how much he admired Shamrock when he was his commander. At the end of their pleasant meeting, they parted wishing to meet again under auspicious terms.

But the general's cow shed had nothing but troubles. Two weeks after Mathilde's labor, the general called the vet again, this time to treat Suzy's sprained leg, which she sustained due to a crack in the floor of the pen. Bonnie bandaged her leg and promised the owner a complete recovery. This time, the assortment of cheeses went down with four bottles of beer Bonnie had picked up at the local grocery in the small mall that housed his clinic as well. The two friends discussed politics, corruption and the state of the Middle East.

But the troubles that plagued the cow shed wouldn't go away. The general called Bonnie to complain that the new heifer wouldn't suckle Miri, her mom. Bonnie, ever the skilled vet, applied sugar syrup onto Miri's udders. Problem solved.

At their usual table, the general informed him of a new problem. Tova, a young fatted cow, recently took up a new hobby, every time they would milk her, she would kick the full bucket, spilling the entire contents.

"Don't worry," Bonnie reassured him. "I know some folks who do the same."

On his following visits, which grew longer as their friendship prospered, Bonnie brought along six bottles of beer, and Shamrock supplemented the now traditional cheese platter with a bowl of his own pickled olives from the trees that grew nearby.

While they were enjoying the cheese and the beer and spitting pits over the fence, Bonnie turned to Shamrock and said, "We keep complaining about politics in this country, about the spread of corruption and leaders who only care about themselves. Maybe the time has come for us to do something about it instead of bitching about it?"

"What do you mean?"

"Election is coming up in a matter of a few months. Why don't we join, form a party and run?"

"Us? Start a party?" Shamrock laughed out loud. "Who would vote for us?"

"What have we got to lose? Let's give it a try."

Smiling as ever, they said their warm, friendly goodbyes.

A few days later, it was afternoon when Bonnie was treating a poor dog that got run over by a tractor. An urgent call. "Come this evening," Shamrock requested. "There's an urgent matter I would like to discuss with you."

That evening, Bonnie came by without the bottles of beer, excusing himself. "The minimart was already closed…"

"You owe me one," Shamrock replied and proceeded to the business of the day. "Today, I would like us to discuss not cows but rather something of greater importance. I spent a few nights considering what we've said and decided to embrace your idea. Let's try and get this country back on track."

By the time their meeting ran its course, it was past midnight. They concluded to form a party and even came up with a name: "The Milky Way Party."

The next day, Bonnie called on his friend, a professional attorney, and asked him to handle the newly founded party's registration for the election. Even prior to that, Bonnie and the attorney approached eight of their acquaintances and received their consent to join the new party. "The Milky Way Party" soon became the joke of that election. They were met with contempt and ridicule on all parts of the political spectrum, much to the derision of the media too.

When the election was over, the entire public tuned in to watch the polls. The results were no less than astonishing. The commentators had to eat crow and swallow their hats. The voters themselves were in shock, and the papers tripled their circulation the following day of election. It turned out that the new party succeeded in getting all of its candidates elected to the Knesset, Israel's parliament. A huge swing in favor of change and something new and different translated into many people casting their votes in favor of the new party. So much so, they had more votes than their actual candidates for Knesset members.

After the official results went public, the political negotiations didn't take long. The government that ensued included three ministerial posts for The Milky Way Party. Shamrock was appointed Minister of Internal Security and Bonnie, Minister of Science. They were both also appointed to the Knesset's prestigious and important Foreign Affairs and Defense Committee.

Chapter Six

Estée's funeral was a very different affair compared with Avram's, three years earlier. The neighbors said she died of a broken heart. Nevertheless, Bonnie knew it was cancer. The faded black hearse was ordered especially all the way from Haifa. Two employees of the orthodox funeral service were clad in brand new outfits that were clearly bought especially in honor of this particular occasion. They were sitting on either side of the coffin.

An official government car, driven by a chauffeur, followed suit with Bonnie and Michal in the back seat. Although he knew all too well what was about to befall his shirt, Bonnie still had a brand-new white shirt on, along with black trousers and shiny black shoes. Michal herself put on appropriate, reserved attire.

The official hearse pulled up in front of the village synagogue. Four moshav members, in white shirts and khaki pants, took the coffin out and placed it, as instructed by the master of ceremonies, on the wooden platform out front. Bonnie and his sister Michal stood right next to the coffin. Bonnie's bodyguard, a stern-faced, stocky man in a dark suit, stood at his side. He had an earpiece. The platform had a specially prepared stand with the Israeli flag at half-mast.

"The government secretary will deliver the government's respects," announced the master of ceremonies, cordially summoning the official, who soon rose from one of the chairs on the platform and proceeded to the stand. He approached the microphone that had been placed there in advance.

"His excellency Minister Binyamin Pladot, esteemed family members, I am deeply honored to express the government of Israel's heartfelt condolences for your loss…"

The government secretary kept to the written statement prepared by the government spokesperson's office. Bonnie took the time to survey the crowd surreptitiously, noticing that only one minister besides himself, out of the government's twenty-three ministers, took the trouble to turn up: none other than Shamrock, the Internal Security Minister. He was seated at the podium next to the government secretary and the family. Early on, he handed Bonnie a note, apologizing in advance that he could not stay long and would have to be going soon on urgent state business.

Bonnie used the time, and the fact that his eyes were lowered anyway, to look for other familiar faces. Aside from his own close employees in the minister's office, he could not quite recognize most of the persons who turned up to his mother's funeral in their shiny cars. '*Probably government officials,*' he told himself. Shamrock and the government secretary kept glancing at their watches, barely biding their time before taking their leave. '*I wonder how many members of government would have put on an appearance at the Finance Minister's funeral*,' he continued his musings.

The moshav members, excited by the official attendance, stood together in a separate bunch. They've never seen a government minister in real life before. Vera, tight-lipped and blank-faced, was standing in their midst in her old, all too familiar tunic.

Bonnie did notice two doctors and several staff members from the nearby clinic. He also spotted some school friends of his, who had attended the regional school along with him. Next to them, he saw another group. Michal later told him these were her old friends from school days.

The funeral procession made its way to Estée's final resting place. There, the crowd dwindled. The honored officials were gone. Bonnie's secretary at the Science Ministry was standing by his mother's grave, along with a junior employee who was holding the government wreath, obviously barely containing his eagerness to return to the office back in Jerusalem.

Bonnie recited Kaddish for his mom. He was more adept now. The rabbi, sporting a new hat, delivered the customary prayer. They lowered the coffin next to Avram's grave and everyone dispersed.

Back home, Bonnie's secretary told him about the telegrams of condolence he had received at his office and showed him the official obituary notice the government had run. "According to protocol, the government may only publish it in one paper," she explained. She also passed on the prime minister's apology and that of the other ministers for not being able to come and pay their respects that week due to their tight schedules.

Bonnie's secretary asked whether he needed her for anything, and he graciously told her she was free and also excused her from coming to shiva.

***

On the sixth evening of shiva, after the last guest was finally out the door, Michal and Bonnie went into their mother's bedroom where, in the corner, next to her makeup table, stood an elegant little dresser.

Back when she was still a young girl, Michal used to creep up into her mother's room whenever she wasn't around and apply mascara to her eyelashes or use her lipstick. Nevertheless, she knew the dresser was off-limits. "Every woman needs a place of her own, something that is entirely hers," her mother had said.

They sat by the dresser, aware that this time, sorting everything out was not going to take long. The top drawer contained their mother's elementary school yearbook. Both crying and smiling, they leafed through it.

"*One great king and tiny Snow White through the looking glass, you're the prettiest girl in the entire class,*" a fifth grader wrote fellow fifth grader Estée, whom he had adored. The following year, one sixth grader was more daring: "*Roses do wither, glasses may break, but our love shall forever reign. To thy own country be true, do your parents proud!*"

Come seventh grade, this student, Itzik, proved quite the poet: "*Limerick for Estée: What shall I write you? / What feat to do? / Favor thee with a fable, a poem or a tale? / So better bear this and hope I won't fail. / To wish, may the good Lord always watch over you!"*

At the bottom of that drawer, they found an envelope with the inscription "*personal*" in her handwriting. Moved and curious, they opened it, but it was empty. Clearly, someone had already removed its contents. The bottom drawer contained photo albums. Tuning one page after another, they found a photo obviously taken in Haifa on her high school graduation day, featuring their mom with three of her girlfriends. Young Estée had had a long skirt on and blouse with puffy sleeves. She wore a white ribbon around her head. She was so demure: the picture of innocence.

"That was one year before she married Dad," Michal told Bonnie.

"What a person our mother was. I'm sure Dad was her first guy," Bonnie added.

"You can go over the last drawer by yourself, Bonnie. I need to go home. Tell we tomorrow if you found anything of interest."

Alone in his mother's bedroom, Bonnie sat next to the bag filled with paperwork he and his sister had decided to cast aside. He emptied the last drawer and added its contents to the bag. He took a second to consider what to do with her fifth-grade report card, which noted her mother was poor at Bible and Israel studies. It soon found its way into the bin too. The same fate befell a brochure on stretching and shrinking shoes, and an ancient booklet with discount coupons and similar leftover matter.

When he was done surveying the drawers, Bonnie asked

himself whether it would be fair to suggest to Michal that she would have the dresser and he would take Dad's mahogany desk. But then he noticed something funny about the dresser's bottom drawer. Though the same size as the others, its volume was much smaller. Upon closer inspection, he realized its bottom was unsteady and soon found the cause: it was partitioned by plywood. He lifted the board and found additional paperwork, including a telegram dated October 22nd, 1979, to the Hypocratio Hospital in Thessaloniki. The faded paper read as follows:

Attn. management, Hypocratio Hospital, Thessaloniki,

Please be so kind as to provide me the details of your patient, admitted on October 17th following a car accident on the road from Sithonia to Thessaloniki. I would like to forward him a personal item he left with me.

Thank you,
Esther Navot

Attached to this old telegram was the hospital's reply:
Dear madame,
We regret to inform you we are not allowed to provide any personal details of our patients. We can nevertheless neither confirm nor deny we have a patient answering the description you gave.

Yours faithfully,
Hypocratio Hospital

Bonnie saw four more similar telegrams from the same date, addressed to four other hospitals at Thessaloniki, with the same replies attached to each.

Something felt strangely upsetting. He placed all the paperwork from 1979 back in the envelope and shoved it into his shirt pocket.

The last item in the drawer was a long, white, untouched envelope that read as follows in his mother's handwriting:

To Bonnie – personal

To be opened only after I am dead

Bonnie decided to open the envelope at home.

Once he was home, the envelope resting on his trembling knees, he sat on his old, much loved armchair, the one his grandfather once bought at the flea market in Haifa. He was terrified. He tried to calm himself and somehow slow the pace of his heart, for it was beating so ferociously Bonnie felt he was about to burst. Somehow, he knew opening this envelope was going to change his life.

Bonnie and his mom were close. She had always been there throughout his life. She knew how to pet him in childhood, cope with him when he entered the terrible teens, guide him through adulthood and lend a hand when he had to make tough calls. He and his father were on good terms, but Avram was such an introvert, always keeping to himself and his work, they could not form an attachment akin to the one between mother and son.

"*What am I to make of this sealed envelope?*" he asked himself, aware how much this shook him to the core. "*After all, she never kept any secret from me, so what could it be?*"

The fact that the letter was addressed exclusively to him was also troubling. He and Michal, his younger sister, were close. After the necessary "who's the boss" period in which he took advantage of being the older brother by beating her to submission, they had become firm friends and even allies. They were a family like so many others, with both children treated the same. "*What then? Why did she address it to me in private? Why isn't Michali a part of this too?* "

Somehow, the envelope felt heavier than iron. He rested it on his desk and went over to his little bar in the living room to pour himself a drink. "*Yes, double scotch, that should do it.*" Suddenly, it did give him strength. The events of the funeral and the week-long mourning all vanished from his mind. He even forgot about his anger at his fellow ministers. "*What shall I do with the letter, then? What is about it that's so scary?*"

Bonnie was famous for being fearless. His commanders and subordinates alike knew him to be a gifted decisionmaker. But faced with that envelope, white and rectangular and sealed, he was perplexed.

But then, the whiskey lent him the courage he needed, as did the full knowledge he simply had no choice. "*Can't be helped. Now, where did I last leave the letter opener?*"

Still, it took forever to tear.

Bonnie produced two yellow pages, which his mother had torn out of some notebook, right before scribbling all over them, filling them with her all too familiar, crammed, handwriting.

***

My dearest Bonnie whom I love so dearly,

Come on, open it up. I can see you from up here, the envelope in your left hand and the letter opened in your right hand. You're so helpless.

I wanted to tell you that my lifelong agony is over. No more dilemmas. Thirty-seven years I spent thinking what to do, questioning, constantly deliberating, by day and mostly by night.

I never worried about my illness. The pain never bothered me. Quite the contrary, it was my refuge. The pain only served to help me find solace and calm for my torn and tortured soul. The pain allowed me to decide whether to take my terrible secret to my grave or whether to share it. With you.

Is my secret not your secret? I am even allowed to keep it from you. Is it a good thing or is it a sin to tell you that which you deserve to know?

I remember how one night you found me, staring on my hospital bed, my eyes clouded, detached, completely wrapped up in a totally different experience. You looked at me like you've never done before and you began to fear something. You did not dread my approaching death but rather something so powerful you could not put it into words.

It's a good thing that you've opened this letter, my love. So good of you to do so, dearest. It was on that very night that I finally decided. It was right before you walked into my room at the hospital. A second earlier, I asked myself what you would have done in my place, and then I saw that frightened look on your face, and I knew that fear is courage. Only he who is afraid of the truth can handle it.

So, I've made up my mind. I am writing this letter from the bottom of my heart, confident in the knowledge that you would rather know the truth, even if it is hard as steel and weighs heavier than a rock.

I know not what you might do with the truth. I only know what I would have done, but that I shall not tell you. I probably could have helped you, but I won't, so as not to influence your decision. Know this: now that I am resolved, I couldn't be calmer and at peace. I am ready to take my leave of you having shared my secret with you, a secret which is now yours too.

So know this, my love, that the father, who loved you so much and admired you so much, is not your biological father.

This is where my secret ends, and I have nothing else to share with you beyond that.

I love you dearly, from here to the moon,
Mom.

PART TWO

Chapter Seven

The great revolution was something Mehdi Mohammadi experienced from afar. Several months prior to the events, he enrolled as a medical student at the University of Thessaloniki. He arrived there a few months before the academic year was due to begin in order to enroll in a Modern Greek course the university provided to its non-Greek students.

The revolution caught him in the middle of his first freshman term. He was extremely concerned for his family back home in Tabriz, northern Iran. Even prior to his leaving Iran for studying overseas, the city's streets were a flurry of discontent, and the great bazaar was buzzing with resentment. The people were tired of the corruption, dictatorial regime and the harsh economic conditions, but no one expected that millions would converge on the demonstration in Tehran and there would be a great revolution that ousted the Shah and ushered the return of Khomeini.

Mehdi believed Iran was desperate for change and sided with the demonstrators' demands for integrity, democracy and economic relief. Once Khomeini assumed power, he considered dropping out, returning to Iran and being part of the Islamic revolution. Mehdi had long talks with his father Suleiman and his two brothers, but they all persuaded him that for the time being, it was for the good of the family for him to continue with his med studies. His family set his mind at ease and told him Tabriz was relatively calm compared with the other major cities, and they had found a way to cooperate with the new regime.

Collaborating with powers that be was part of the family's DNA. They had always believed that maintaining good relations with whomever was in power and cultivating this relationship was paramount to doing good business. They firmly believed that a sympathetic ruler would allow them the utmost leeway, citing their old family maxim, "no power is without capital."

This saying came with a cost. One day, prior to the Islamic revolution, Suleiman, the head of the family, was called to visit the Shah's royal palace, along with other provincial businessmen. Upon entering the lavish reception hall, the guests were seated on padded armchairs across from the Shah's throne, which was decorated with a golden peacock. Despite the exhilaration of waiting, Suleiman could not help noticing the carpeted floor was slightly worn, so he resolved to make a gesture. '*The Shah's birthday would make a good opportunity. I shall present him with a special present,*' he said to himself, '*a carpet especially made for this hall.*'

Back in Tabriz, Suleiman consulted with his mother, Suheila, who was in charge of weaving, and it was decided to have the Shah presented with a unique carpet, featuring a pattern exclusive to the family, a pattern Suheila cherished as a secret that was handed down by one generation to the next. The weaving itself was entrusted to the factory's best artisan, under Suheila's direct guidance and supervision, for she alone remembered the pattern.

Suleiman had Ali, one of his sons, whose position in the family business was purchasing raw materials, acquire the special ingredients this particular rug called for: exquisite, rare silk from Sichuan, China, soft sheep's wool all the way from Lhasa, Tibet, cultivated by priests, and golden threads custom-made in India by renowned artisans.

For two whole years, the weaver confined herself to the special room she was allocated, focusing on the task at hand. The carpet was stunningly colorful. Its dyes were made by the factory's experts, who used only natural substances. The red dye was made from a special plant, blue came from indigo, yellow was made from saffron, and scarlet was produced from a special worm.

The carpet, 144 inches by 107, was completed ahead of the Shah's birthday, quite close to the actual date. Suheila's unique signature was woven into it.

But then, the riots erupted.

A few days after the mass demonstration in Tehran, attended by millions, and the seizure of power by the Islamists, the revolution came to Tabriz as well. Revolutionary Guard officers captured the local government bodies and the imam of the city's Blue Mosque was declared the supreme local religious authority.

***

"*Hazrat* Imam," the head of the Mohammadi addressed the imam, taking care to use the safest honorary title, not too exalted, so as not to appear too obsequious, and yet adhering to the figure's authority. Suleiman was granted a meeting two weeks after Khomeini's triumphant return. "In keeping with the appreciation and respect our sacred teaching deserves," Suleiman continued, "with complete accord with the principles of the revolution, and in great deference to your holiness greatness, whom I have had the privilege of knowing these many years, my family and I would like to bestow our humble gift to the mosque."

The imam was wary of persecution during the time of the Shah, for the regime went after many a religious figure, whether they posed an actual threat or merely an imaginary one. He had adhered to strict modesty and reserve throughout the Shah's reign, lest he incur the regime's wrath. He replied to Suleiman as follows:

"In the name of Islam and our exalted leader, I happily welcome this present of your modest and respectable family, a centuries-old part of our city. I would like to take this opportunity and share with you the news: after many years of oppression, we have decided to renovate the mosque at a cost of five million rial."

The very next day, four burly men appeared at the Blue Mosque, so named for the mosaic stones that comprised its floor. The men proceeded to replace the old rug at the center of the main floor with the new carpet Suleiman had brought forth. The carpet's splendid colors and blue motifs matched the mosaic perfectly.

The following day, Suleiman Mohammadi arrived in the imam's chambers with a large envelope containing five million rial in cash.

"On behalf of my family and myself, I would like to offer you our thanks for accepting our humble contribution."

"*Moteshakeram*," the imam thanked him and proceeded to count the banknotes.

A month after this, Tabriz city hall hosted a ceremony, officiated by the imam himself and attended by the heads of the Revolutionary Guard, honoring the Mohammadi family as champions of Islam and the revolution.

***

Specializing in handwoven carpets, the Mohammadis were among Tabriz's wealthiest and most respected families. Three hundred years of practice and tradition had made their wares renowned the world over. Their items always fetched the best prices, as they were the most sought after. As the years went by, they amassed a great fortune and their bazaar stalls expanded into several stores and then into a commercial compound known as *khana*, whose reputation as the best, most prestigious and fairest held fast. This was no small feat for the Tabriz Bazaar, stretching from the Blue Mosque to the Jameh Mosque, was considered one the world's three largest markets.

The Mohammadis' khana was a large-roofed complex specifically built around a central yard, surrounded by a two-story property where the first floor comprised stores and the second was reserved for living space. In days of old, the top rooms housed illustrious traders from all over Iran and other countries, who had come to purchase the famous family carpets or to sell the family the raw material for the carpets. These merchants often shared accommodations with tourists and other visitors who came to bask in the magnificence of the historic bazaar, famous for its intense sights, sounds and fragrances.

Over the years, some of the top floor rooms had to be converted to weaving floors where dozens of women worked tirelessly. The Mohammadis, citing the family tradition, "they haven't the fine fingers and patience for such delicate work. They are too coarse," never hired men as weavers. "Besides," the rationale continued, "any expert easily can tell the difference between a carpet woven by a woman and a one woven by a man."

The ground floor consisted of stores, some of which, serving hundreds of prospective shoppers each day, were also open to the general public, all of whom marveled at the magnificence and fine workmanship of the wares, but only some daring to make a purchase, as the least expensive Mohammadi carpet was still priced at a senior bank clerk's entire annual salary.

The sale of the Mohammadi wares was an art in itself, the quintessential "Persian bazaar" that any "Turkish bazaar" could hardly keep up with…

The venders, who were as seasoned as they were driven, were all skilled salesmen who knew their entire catalogue by heart, the quality, the faults and the history of each and every carpet. They had their sales targets and commission, their expertise.

Each carpet had a pre-set minimum price that reflected its cost and desired profit, so that the basic price was one hundred and twenty percent of the target price. Their very first lesson during training was dedicated to learning that the first price quoted was the hook, greatly impacting the final price.

***

"Afghan, ninety by sixty, hand-woven with silk trimmings, one hundred and twenty thousand rial!" shouted the salesman as his young assistant showcased the carpet before the crowd that pushed closer.

"I'll get it for forty thousand," this young man told his wife proudly, and then raised his voice, high above the crowd that gathered there. "Those vendors won't fool me!" he promised her.

"One hundred and ten thousand. No less. This one has a unique design. There are only nine others like it!"

A crowd of curious bystanders watched the unfolding match with mounting attention.

"Not a single rial above fifty!"

"If he isn't budging, I'm in for sixty, then," one spectator interrupted the eager husband.

The salesman noticed the disappointed look in the young man's wife's eyes. "Thank your wife. I am willing to go as low as one hundred in honor of her beauty for this beautiful carpet."

Half of the crowd that gathered was certain this was a

great bargain. The other half suspected some trick was being employed.

The spectator from before intervened again. "I'm willing to pay seventy."

The salesman noticed the wife nudging her husband. However slight the movement was, he nevertheless saw her elbow. "Eighty then. That's my *last* price."

"Sold!" The husband shouted back.

The salesman's assistant rolled the carpet as his boss quickly crunched the numbers. '*Good sale. Fair commission. Even after the bonus to my man in the crowd*,' he thought, while taking in the cost of the guy's assistance in driving the price up.

Further deep into the Mohammadis' khana lay other shops, the realm of the real pros, where only the greatest were allowed. The center of the room had a round table with two chairs. The task of constantly serving the vendor and the merchant sweet tea fell to the hands of one of the boys, as another would present the guest with hundreds of carpets, one after the other. Each item was numbered. The buyer quietly kept to his notes atop his padded armchair. When the parade of carpets concluded, he would call on those he liked, kicking off the haggling.

Contrary to the loud, theatrical negotiations between everyday shoppers and salesmen, which followed the traditional, customary social ritual of gesturing and raising one's fists and voice as the sums hurled back and forth, the inner rooms were the backdrop of a calm scene of minute nuances. Fully aware of the quality and value of their wares, the Mohammadi vendors would not easily budge from their unique carpets' true prices. Likewise, the buyers sought a reasonable profit after their worthy commissions.

***

The Mohammadi family carpet factory was run by Suleiman, the paterfamilias, aided by both his sons. His two daughters were responsible for weaving and for preserving the rich heritage of patterns. Nevertheless, the most important woman in the family business was none other than Suheila, Suleiman's mother. Her vision, leadership and personality were the key elements of the factory's uniqueness and its singular stature as a leader in the industry. An age-old tradition, down the generations, decreed that the women were the keepers of the tradition, preserving the range of exclusive patterns and passing them down the line. Thus ran the chain of family tradition, conferring continuity and venerated customs.

Suheila was a legend even during her own lifetime. Any person even remotely connected with the carpet industry knew of her. From the holy city of Qom through Nain out in the desert and Esfahan, the city of bazaars, all the way to the ancient city of Kashan, everyone exalted in Suheila's feats and incredible skills. They said of her that she could weave no less than three thousand knots in one tenth of a square inch of a silk carpet, whereas an experienced weaver could barely tie one hundred knots, while the most seasoned weaver might reach as many as one hundred and fifty. The tales surrounding her also said she retained in her wondrous memory each and every pattern sample of the factory's three centuries of carpets.

Each carpet Suheila wove bore her own woven signature, affixed in silk and gold tassels. Such carpets were so rare only museums and lavish palaces could afford to showcase them. At some point, the Shah of Iran considered declaring her carpets a national heritage, but other, more influential carpet merchants dissuaded him.

At sixty-two, Suheila would no longer weave by herself, but she was nevertheless the undisputed queen bee. She inherited the rich tradition of exclusive family patterns and passed them on to only unique, highly skilled, women members of the Mohammadi family. Handpicking a fresh class each year, she would convene the new disciples of weavers, tell them about herself and how fortunate and privileged they were to have the great honor of working at the family factory and of learning from her.

As early as he was six years old, Mehdi would surreptitiously sneak into the great weaving hall to listen to Grandma Suheila teaching the new girls. He would secrete himself among the bales of carpets, a single man among the all-female class, his attention focused on the queen.

"*Khosh amadid*," welcome, she began. "*Bismillah*," in the name of Allah.

The girls were transfixed. Fully aware of the honor that befell them and the rare fortune that smiled on them, they quivered with excitement. Only precious few were accepted to Suheila's class, and only the most skilled among them were asked to stay on and work at the factory.

"I was your age, maybe even younger, when I was first introduced to the wonders of weaving."

Their legs crossed, the girls who were seated around were aged twelve, the optimal age for starting a career as a carpet weaver. The advantage of their tender age was having thin and supple fingers that could handle the highly intricate knots that formed the basis of each carpet.

"I never had a dull moment in my entire life since I began weaving," Suheila told her young admirers. "My gift is from Allah. I learned the glory of creating lovely things and what gives life its purpose. Weaving, let alone becoming a successful weaver, calls for talent, skills, physical attributes, perseverance, patience and complete and utter dedication to the work," she taught them.

"Once, there was a time when even six and seven-year old children would weave, for only their exquisitely thin and lithe fingers could tie the most delicate knots." Child labor was only stopped when teachers complained. "In the rarest of cases," she continued, "when a uniquely intricate pattern was called for, a special permit from the imam had to be obtained for children to be brought in, and even then, at least one of the parents would have to be present during the child's work."

The girls hung onto her every word, all the more determined to excel, for passing Suheila's workshop successfully meant high pay, equivalent to one dollar fifty a day rather than one dollar, which was the average pay in the carpet industry. The girls' elevated position would mean upward social mobility and better chances of marrying well to a husband with good qualities.

"Best of luck to you all, and may Allah be always in your favor," Suheila concluded the short introductory meeting with her new trainees."

***

Mehdi was the youngest child, younger than both his brothers and both sisters. His two older brothers were clearly destined to become managers in time, as they were trained to follow in their father's footsteps from a very young age. Suleiman, who knew the importance of a good education, saw to it that they attended the best private schools in Tabriz. When the two boys graduated high school, they went to the University of Tehran to study business management. They spent their holidays at the family carpet factory in Tabriz, learning the ropes firsthand, including all the family business secrets.

Mehdi's sisters were not so fortunate as far as their education went. They were enrolled as weavers right after graduating elementary school, literally tying ropes and weaving knots, keeping up the family tradition by learning the secrets of the trade.

Early on, even as a mere child, Mehdi was different from his brothers. He loved playing hide and seek throughout the khana, the family complex and running around there. Whenever he would grow tired of everything and everyone, he would dive into a stack of carpets, hide himself so expertly no one was the wiser. He also loved escaping into the silkworm farm adjacent to the factory. Most of the factory's silk threads, save for a small quantity of Sichuan silk, came from there. The Mohammadi family's silk farm produced the most unique and exquisite raw fibers. Mehdi used to follow each molting stage along the larvae's metamorphosis with great curiosity. When he was so disposed, the foreman allowed him to handle the cocoons with great care and comb them using a special instrument that was designed to produce the long silk fibers.

Mehdi's favorite thing to do was to listen to his grandmother recount her exploits. One day, he quickly seized the rare occasion of her taking a break from weaving and asked her, "how come your eyes are blue, grandma, how did you come by this color?"

"From the Yezidi tribes high up in the mountains," Suheila replied. "That's where. They also gave me another pair, which I gave you as a present."

"And why does everyone fear you?"

She laughed. "Who?"

"Everyone," he replied. "Even Dad."

"Do your fear me, too?"

"No! I am not afraid of you."

"Listen, you only get respect if they fear you." She patted him on the head and continued with her weaving.

Mehdi was a beautiful boy. His blue eyes were not the only thing that set him apart from his brothers and sisters. His character was very different to theirs. He was talented, daring, courageous, decisive, and also, much to his parents' lament, belligerent. They often had to berate him for abusing his brothers, who were too timid to strike him back, however bigger and older they were.

One day, when he was eight, he came, all excited, into his grandmother's bedroom. Only Suheila and Mehdi had their own private rooms.

"*Maderbozorg*," he called her as he entered. Mehdi was the only one who called her *Grandmother*. Suleiman called her

Mama and the rest of the family turned to her saying, *Khanom* (lady or Mrs.).

"What is it, *pesare aziz*? (dear boy).

Mehdi exchanged an azure glance with her and said, "I would like to become a carpet weaver."

Suheila watched him with pride. "That's not possible, *azizam*" (dear). "You know that only women are given this job of weaving. Besides, you will have better things to do. You were born for greater things in life. You were born for Allah and for our homeland. *Duset daram*" (I love you).

She kissed him on his forehead and sent him on his way.

He took to skipping school but was nevertheless knowledgeable, even learned, in many fields. He did not attend religious classes and yet knew entire suras (verses) in the *Quran*. He only had to pass by a class where a history lesson was being taught, his teachers told his parents, to know the entire history of the Persian kingdom from the time Noah's ark landed on Mt. Ararat.

That said, Mehdi's teachers also came to know his dark side. During one break, the headmaster saw the children playing soccer in the yard. He noticed Mehdi kneeling in the corner. As he drew closer, he saw the boy tearing a live frog limb from limb.

"What are you doing?!" He shouted.

He did not await the boy's reply. '*Those glistening eyes. Such cruelty. I'd better call his father in*,' he thought.

"Why are you being so cruel to animals?" Suleiman asked Mehdi.

"I enjoy it," came the boy's reply, leaving the father

astonished and anxious.

Mehdi would never cry. He never did. Not even as an infant, let alone as he grew older. At six months, his mother Fatimah took him to the doctor, the pediatrician Dr. Morhabi, a renowned figure in Tabriz and a close friend of the family.

"He never cries," she complained.

"Do you feed him well enough?"

"Constantly. Daily. I have enough milk to nurse him."

Dr. Morhabi glanced at her full breasts and set his own mind at ease.

"Do you change him regularly?"

"All the time, even when his diaper is dry."

"Do you shower him with love and attention?"

"All day, doctor. I hug him and pat him all day. Suleiman says I am spoiling him…"

Dr. Morhabi patted the boy's belly, turned him over and tapped the back, and proceeded to tell the anxious mother thus, "He's getting all the food he wants, you keep changing him, you always walk with him out in the park, like you've told me, you're giving him all your love, so what does he have to cry about?"

Suleiman, Mehdi's father, both admired his son and feared him, having recognized the boy's enormous talent, his aptitude for making contact with people, his great intelligence and leadership skills. And at the same time, as he grew into a teenager, Mehdi also exhibited signs of cruelty and a domineering nature. Whereas Suleiman, like his father, grandfather and ancestors before, were brought up to work well together with others within the confines of proscribed rules and norms,

Mehdi would have none of it. He broke with the education he was given, unlike his brothers and sisters.

It took Suleiman no time to notice that his youngest son's unfolding character consisted of individualism, leadership and internal toughness that did not conform with teamwork. '*These qualities may put the family business at risk someday*,' he feared.

One time, Suleiman had an old Greek friend over. The merchant had the concession for the family's carpets in the whole of Greece. The two firm friends had lunch together in Berkeh, one of Tabriz's most famous restaurants, where you could only get *halal* food, in line with the strict dietary laws of Islam.

Dining to their hearts' content in *Gondi* (dumplings), *horshet sabzi* (beef stew with herbs – *sabzi* means *herbs* in Farsi) and other delicacies the Persian and, in particular, the Tabriz cuisine is renowned for, they could be said to have been sitting at the Shah's table, or better yet, as the Shah was gone by now, the imam's table. They also had *falooda*, a famous Persian sweetened drink. Then, it was time to discuss each other's families, as old friends do. Suleiman talked mostly about his children.

"I'm only concerned about my youngest," he confided to his guest. "I am not sure he's cut out for work in the family business and even less so that he has any interest in weaving. If this isn't what drives you, it isn't for you."

"Why don't you send him off to medical school, then?" suggested his old friend. "Look, Thessaloniki, where I come from, has a fine med school with a special class for overseas students."

Astonished, Suleiman Mohammadi fell off his chair. "Are you crazy?" he asked his guest as he stood. "Mehdi? A doctor?"

"Go ask him. What have you got to lose?"

A few days later, Suleiman did ask his boy, in jest, telling him of his Greek friend's idea.

"Dad, that suits me fine," Mehdi replied in an instant.

Only Mehdi's lightning response kept Suleiman from falling of his chair yet again. a few days later, Mehdi enrolled to learn Greek at the Thessaloniki School of Medicine.

Chapter Eight

Med school began in October. All the classes were in English, which Mehdi had learned back in Tehran. His high aptitude for languages also came into play when he quickly picked up Greek during the summer preparatory class the university offered ahead of the academic year. Mehdi shared his room at the dorms with Ali, a fellow student from Tehran, who studied economics.

Suleiman paid all of Mehdi's expenses. On top of the steep tuition fee, he also financed his son's rental payment and added a generous sum in the form of a monthly bank transfer.

In 1979, with the advent of the revolution that ousted the Shah and feeling support for its ideals, championing adherence to Islam, equality and fighting corruption, Mehdi decided to stand on his own two feet and pay his own way. He told his father he would no longer receive his support and that he would fend for himself. Suleiman, who always made sure his children would want for nothing, was very proud of Mehdi's declaration of independence, despite the constant worry this caused Mehdi's mother.

"What will he live on?" she complained to her husband.

"He'll have no food on the table..."

But Mehdi made ends meet. Determined and resolute, he would not shy away from any paying job. He gave English lessons, joined Ali whenever he went to do some gardening at homes of the wealthy or as a doorman in high rise apartment buildings. When money was tight, he did not shirk from cleaning the premises at the small mall that was not far from his dorm.

***

Mehdi was homesick. He missed his parents and his siblings and most of all Suheila, his grandmother. He also missed the new Iran very much and followed the news closely in complete accordance with the new regime and the principles of the revolution. He considered going back home for the summer break, but then the school announced a special summer class for non-Greek students, so he changed his plans, concluding he would rather not disrupt his studies. '*Iran would have to wait for another time.*'

His fellow med student Samir turned to him one day and asked, "I need a favor, please. I promised Maria, the one I've told you about from the hotel by the island, to show up for a shift on Monday night. She and her husband have an appointment in Thessaloniki, so it's my chance to help up at the reception desk. But then, I received a call saying my mom is ill, so I have to go see her urgently."

"I wish you and your mother the best of health, but what can I do but pray for her with all my heart?"

"I would like you to pick up my shift. Stand in for me."

"What? How? What do I have to do?"

"Don't worry. There's practically nothing to do there. Maria told me that during the middle of the week, there's only one guest in the entire hotel. All you have to do is show up. Just be there so that the guest who is staying there will not feel he is there all by himself. You have to get there by evening. Maria is expecting you. She will explain everything. Don't worry, there is very little to go over."

Samir smiled, lent Mehdi his car and gave him the directions to the hotel and added, "Don't forget to collect your pay, one thousand drachmae."

The following day, Mehdi climbed into his friend's worndown Skoda and began driving to the hotel at noon, following the directions to hotel Kallithea (Greek for "the best view") that was out at the Sithonia Peninsula. As he climbed up the hill, Mehdi already knew he had arrived. '*The hotel's name really lives up to the scenery...*' Atop this marvelous cliff, overlooking a spectacular bay, it seemed to proudly announce "Here I am."

The hotel consisted of eight rooms, each with its own balcony overlooking the breathtaking bay and Athos Peninsula on its other end. Another structure comprised a kitchen, and adjacent was the hotel restaurant, boasting a spacious veranda with a view to the sea. The small room that constituted the hotel's reception desk was no more than twenty square feet. It was situated all the way at the end of this complex.

'*This woman nervously tapping her heels out there must be Maria*.' Mehdi relied on his friend's explanations. Next to her a man was seated in the only parked car in the middle of a small lot. '*Indeed. Not another soul in sight.*'

"Are you Samir's friend? My husband and I have been waiting for you for very long."

Maria proceeded to show Mehdi where the power switches were, then the alarm system and the main water pipes. "This should do," she concluded. "The kitchen is closed, and we currently have only one guest. This is where she's staying," Maria pointed at the rack where only one key hung. "She went down to the beach."

Underscoring her heartfelt wishes he would not have to use it, Maria gave him an emergency phone number, and left, not before telling him she and her husband would be back by nine the following morning.

"You do not have to wait for us. Simply leave the key in the potted bougainvillea plant by the entrance, and you may return to Thessaloniki."

Maria rushed over to the car but stopped in her tracks, ran back to Mehdi and gave him a bunch of rolled up banknotes. "This is your pay, according to the arrangement with Samir," she said and ran right back to her husband, who had already started the engine.

Left to his own devices, Mehdi had nothing to contend with but silence. The small office had a wooden desk, an armchair padded with a Greek pattern and two chairs. He sank into the armchair, but, feeling a bit boxed-in, he carried it outside.

Facing east, he saw a large pool with clear waters rivaling those of the cove. The pool seemed to extend into it. He felt calm and at peace, as if his tension, pressure, bad energy and troubles suddenly all went away by a miracle and were supplanted by an unshakeable smile. Sleep soon got the better of him.

The view was different when Mehdi opened his eyes again. The sun no longer shone brightly, and the deep blue of the sea was likewise gone, both having given in to a soft twilight. The inlet was gone, but he could make out the distant lights of the far-off monasteries. He took in the large moon over the bay, beyond which he could hardly see the stars.

And then, lo and behold! What a woman!

Coming up the stairs from the pool to the reception desk, the beauty of the scenery, and perhaps his own imagination, made him believe that the princess of the bay was riding the waves toward him. '*Such lovely blue eyes. Face like marble.*' She looked at him, motionless and silent.

She eyed him, and he her. They both said nothing. She stretched out her left arm and gestured with three upright fingers.

He got up from his chair, walked in, and, almost buckling, reached for the key rack. He laid the key to room three in her open hand, avoiding any contact with her bare skin. She, in turn, made her way to her room, her lovely, curving back getting farther away from his gaze.

It was as though the moon guided him. Mehdi rose to follow her. Something told him her door would not be locked. He opened the door.

Rising from her bed, she undressed, letting her galabia fall to the floor without a word. She awaited his own naked flesh.

The room was lit by nothing but the moon. Her milky skin

glistened by the dim glow the fell through the windows, but he could still somehow make out her breasts and arching belly. Transfixed by her light blue gaze, he could barely believe this was real. '*More lovely than the mid-day sun on a blue spring day.*'

As he took off his shirt, he could feel his shorts falling to the floor on their own. Their bodies merged.

Not a word was uttered. Not a sound was made.

Next thing he knew, he was out the door again. But the moon was gone by now, as were the dim, distant monastery lights. The darkness, slightly alleviated by the stars, guided him back to his reception desk. '*I'll never forget thee, princess of the bay…*'

But the night was not yet over. Mehdi found no rest. He kept quivering.

Tormented, he finally shut the door behind him in the morning, leaving the key where Maria had instructed him. He got into the car and made his way back to Thessaloniki.

***

Meeting the 'princess of the bay' shook him to the core. A tall, well-built man, Mehdi was a striking man with a pair of piercing blue eyes to boot. Though handsome, his sexual experience nevertheless amounted to few encounters with the opposite sex, as he had attended a boys-only school and had never encountered any girls his age aside from his sisters.

"Never let any Tabriz girl trap you," his mother, fully aware of the attractive figure he cut, had warned him. "They are only after your money and our family's name. Let me get you a bride. I will find you a suitable wife from Tehran, or at the very least, from Esfahan."

Mehdi smiled back to his mother. "Don't you worry about it, *madar*," (Mom). "I'll find my own mate, whom I am sure you'd approve of."

He did have a short fling with the sister of a friend of his. She would never put out, though, always insisting they would progress "after we wed," She was a good Muslim girl from a good family, after all. Her strict upbringing saw to it they never did anything remotely amounting to full intercourse.

One day, he decided he would at least make an attempt to break through the confines of tradition, norms and conservative values. On one of his trips to Tehran, he stole into a lingerie store and asked the saleslady to discreetly pack something for him. He barely contained his excitement at the prospect of seeing his girlfriend put it on for him. He asked his friend, her brother, to pass the parcel on to her. Needless to say, he was careful not give away its contents.

The following evening, when he put on his best clothes, made sure every hair was in place and spent extra time in front of the mirror, he told himself he should not forget to ask his friend to let him and his girlfriend spend some time by themselves. But when the door to his friend's house opened, his girlfriend was furious. So much for the loving smiles he was expecting.

"You sick bastard! I thought you loved me! Get out of my sight! I never want to see you again!"

She shut the door in his face, cursing inaudibly through the door. Astonished, he caught sight of the door opening again, only to see her throw the bra he bought in his face "Get your own mother a D-size bra, you scum!"

She slammed the door again. '*What's gotten into her?!*' Her slurs, not to mention invoking his mother, meant that he was over and done with. He left the house and went back home to finish packing for the flight back to Thessaloniki.

***

The road to Thessaloniki had been renovated not long before Mehdi drove on it to Sithonia. The project had been designed to help promote tourism to the three inlets. As the tour guides say, the area boasted three small peninsulas, each about thirty miles long, that stretched into the Aegean. The two-way road cut through low hills, often covered by orchards and olive groves. But Mehdi saw none of this. Still dizzy with last night's exploits, not to mention tired, he could barely pay attention to the road ahead. He knew he had better stop by the side of the road and steady himself before driving on, but before he could get a chance, a huge truck came crashing in.

Luckily for Mehdi, he managed to veer to the right in a split second. The car flew into a deep ditch that broke the fall.

When he woke up in the hospital, the police told him the accident was caused by his drifting into the opposite side of the roads, straight into the incoming traffic. They also told him he was brought in unconscious. He had his Iranian passport on his person, so they had left word with the Iranian consulate in Thessaloniki, informing them about the car accident.

Chapter Nine

Professor Inusias Siasu was instructing his group of eight med students, five of whom were young women, at Thessaloniki's Hypocratio Hospital. This was his clinical training class, one of the additional duties there, on top of serving as deputy manager and faculty member. Joining his class was the ultimate dream of any fourth-year med student there.

The professor led his excited pack through the corridors, until they reached orthopedics, where, in room 19, they were greeted by Sandra, the attending nurse.

"Good morning," he returned her greeting. "Let's begin with the patient's medical file."

"The patient, Mehdi Mohammadi, a foreign national," began Nurse Sandra, "was rushed to hospital after sustaining injuries in a car accident. When the ER examined him, they found three broken ribs, a ruptured spleen, a broken nose and several bruises of varying degrees of severity all over his body. He was then admitted to surgery for a splenectomy," (an operation to remove the entire spleen) "after which his broken nasal bridge was attended, and he was then admitted to the internal medicine ward. His last checkup established he was doing fine. He might be released home for a full recovery and complete rest in a couple of days... Professor, shall I move on to the prognosis?"

"No, thank you, Nurse Sandra."

The professor then turned to his students. "If you think I've brought you here for three broken ribs, you've got it all wrong. My intention is completely different. I wish to introduce to you the hospital's policy concerning its patients. We shall come back to this point later. In the meantime, we have Professor Dionysus, who will tell us about the case's continued treatment."

Professor Dionysus, deputy head of the hospital's genetics department and a much sought-after lecturer at the med school, began his short review.

"Two days ago, I was asked by Dr. Supiniades to come down to ER, where I met the patient, who was undergoing various tests and treatments. The ER doctor alerted me to a lesion, about one-inch square in size, under the patient's armpit. Having obtained the patient's consent, I ordered the lesion be surgically removed and then analyzed. A histological test was made on a sample. The results proved it was benign."

"Any questions?" asked Dr. Supiniades.

"Yes," one of the students braved a question. "What does the hospital lab do with the results of the histological test?"

"The results are sent to whomever ordered them. If the results are positive, they are also sent to oncology for follow-up treatment. In either case, the block of paraffin containing the sample goes into the hospital archives."

"Thank you, my dear colleague. You are now dismissed to

carry on your important duties," said Professor Siasu and addressed his students once again. "Now, what do you think was the point of this lesson? If you think it was to learn how we treat the victim of a car accident or what a histological test is, you are mistaken."

The room became completely still. The professor continued, "The point was to demonstrate to you, using a practical, real-life case example, the hospital's policy when it comes to treating a patient. In this case, the hospital would have done its duty by the patient had we limited ourselves to treating him for the injuries he had sustained as a result of the car crash. But our view in this hospital is that we are obliged to make full use of the patient having been admitted, to conduct a comprehensive test and to check the patient thoroughly. These tests brought to light his lesion, which we've summarily checked. Had, God forbid, the test proved positive, we could have dealt with the findings and pursued a course of treatment as he was already hospitalized. That's it for today. Thank you."

***

"You've got another visitor," the nurse told Mehdi when the doctors finished their rounds.

The man who entered seemed to be in his forties. Short with white sideburns with occasional black patches, he had on a suit like those Mehdi had seen in the window shops of Thessaloniki's main shopping district, which featured the best in menswear.

The visitor introduced himself, "Suleiman Tehrani,

Consulate General of the Islamic Republic in Thessaloniki."
He took his seat on the plastic chair by Mehdi's bed. He
thanked the nurse who handed him a glass of water and continued, "I hope they're taking good care of you here at the
hospital, Mehdi. I meant to visit you earlier. In the meantime,
I received some details about you from back home and was
glad to learn about your esteemed family and its contribution
to the revolution. You are probably aware your parents are on
their way. I've arranged for them to be picked up at the airport
and brought straight here by the consulate car. Once you are
feeling better, I expect you at the consulate office. There are
some people here who would like to meet you."

Before he left, the consul left him a *Quran* bound in a green
cover decorated in gold letters, along with his business card
and the consulate office phone. The consul added his personal
number in his own handwriting.

Mehdi waited for his parents in the sitting room all the way
at the end of the hospital corridor. This was the first time he
got up and off his hospital bed since the operation and this
in itself, along with the ensuing ten-yard walk proved difficult for him, but his father's sigh of relief and the joy in his
mother's eyes were indeed worth the pain in Mehdi's ribs.
His parents, having expected the worst, saw him seated in a
big armchair, wrapped in a blue hospital gown and smiling at
them expectantly, thrilled to see them. And so, they rushed
over to hug him. Their tearful exchanges soon abated after
they met the doctor in charge of Mehdi's ward, and composure took over. Even Mehdi's mother, always concerned and
fearful of the worst, smiled calmly. Mehdi told them he was

feeling fine and took in their own stories about the family and the family business.

The following day, Mehdi bid a warm farewell to the medical staff and travelled with his father by a special taxi to the luxury suite his parents had reserved at the Excelsior Hotel, just off Aristotelous Square, right in the center of Thessaloniki. And what a surprise awaited him there! In the suite, the entire dining area was filled with bowls upon bowls of the most sumptuous dishes from home, which Mehdi had longed for. Somewhat sheepishly, his father told him how he had to bribe the Iran Airways staff to let him bring all that on board with them, and how the airline's security officer was obliged to inspect the cabin and the entire plane after some passengers complained about "the strange smells" in the course of the flight, despite the plastic containers Suleiman and Fatimah took special care to check all the food in...

While Mehdi was piling his plate up with *gourmet sabzi* (herb stew, *qormet* or *ghormeh* means *fried* in Azeri, a major local language in Iran), *polow* (or *polo*, a rice dish) and *gondi* (dumplings) brought over directly from the family kitchen back in Tabriz, his mother told him how much Suheila, his grandmother, missed him, but as much as she had wanted to go, her own doctors forbade her due to her heart condition in recent months. Fatimah also told her son how much his sisters Shahnaz and Yasmin were missing him and how devoted they were to the care of their grandmother, who was also their great weaving teacher.

Suleiman told his son about the factory. Not wishing to upset Mehdi, he kept it very general. Speaking in broad terms, he recounted how the revolution had ushered in no economic improvement to Iran's economy and that the carpet sector, too, was plagued with a decline in revenue.

A week had gone by before Suleiman had to return to the family business in Tabriz, but Mehdi's mother stayed for another week, dividing her time between preparing his meals at the suite kitchen and helping her son take short walks and cope with the pain. When Mehdi got better, his mother made him enough food to last him many days and returned to the rest of the family back in Tabriz. Mehdi, for his part, checked out of the luxury suite and moved back in with his friend Ali at the university dorms.

Prior to Suleiman's return to Tabriz, Mehdi and his parents agreed that as soon as his doctors cleared him to fly back, he would return home, where the entire family council would agree on his future. The day his mom went home, Mehdi received the following call: "Hi, this is Tehrani, the Consulate. Surely you remember me. I see your parents are back in Iran."

'How could he possibly know that?! I just hugged Mom good-bye.'

"Tomorrow at eleven am, a consulate car will bring you by. There are some people here who would like to meet you."

Tehrani hung up before Mehdi could get a word in.

The following day, Mehdi carried himself over to the front of the dorm at the appointed hour. A black car with a CC next to the license plate was already waiting for him. The driver opened the back door for him and helped him get in. It was a short ride. The gate camera IDed the car and cleared its entry. As the car slid into the parking lot at the back, a large wooden door opened, and out came an impressive, tall man in a Western-style suit, albeit with a revolutionary-style beard. He shook Mehdi by the hand and invited him in. They walked into a spacious room at the far end of the corridor.

A man in Revolutionary Guard uniform rose from behind a mahogany desk to greet them. His beard reached all the way down to the middle of his chest. "I am Iraz. The person who brought you over here is my aide, Nasser. We represent the Revolutionary Guard in Greece. We came especially from Athens to meet you, having heard all sorts of good things about you. You come highly recommended."

Iraz continued. "We're glad to see you are feeling better. We know you had a nice time with your parents at the Excelsior. We are also in the know about your doctor's approval to fly to Tabriz. He will give you the all clear tomorrow."

'*How could they know so much?*' He noticed the camera that captured everything in that room as did the tape recorder, plain for all to see, right there on the desk.

Iraz then said, "We know you're about to go on a visit to Iran. We wish to speak with you about what you will get up to once you return to Thessaloniki. As you know, the Revolutionary Guard is fighting in various arenas worldwide, as well as within Iran, to protect the revolution. We are up against many hostile elements, including the supporters of the Shah, the U.S. and Zionism."

Only a brief pause preceded the rest. "In order to win our war, we must have people like you on our side. With your consent, we shall get you in touch with important figures in Tehran, where we will coordinate the continuation of our association. I am sure you know full well that your contribution will be of great help not only to the revolution but also to your family."

Mehdi didn't even require a respite. He barely finished his glass of water before taking them up on their offer. He accepted the Revolutionary Guard representatives' proposal.

***

The building that had constituted "SEVAK" headquarters was built in 1957, back in the days of the Shah, when this organization had formed the regime's secret police. Its name was derived from the acronym for *Sazman-e Etela'at Va Amniat Keshvar*, which stood for (the) Organization of Intelligence and Security of the Country. Its main building was purposely located on the southern outskirts of Tehran after consultations with the FBI and with Israel's Mossad. All in all, it comprised hundreds of thousands of square feet and its staff was estimated at dozens of thousands.

Very few changes ensued following the Islamic revolution of 1979. The organization was renamed the Ministry of Intelligence and Security, *Vezarat-e Ettela'at Va Amniat-e Keshvar*, more commonly known by its acronym: VEVAK. Also, its insignia was replaced, and SEVAK prisoners became VEVAK jailors. Other than that, the more things changed around, the more it stayed the same: the cells at the basement were still being kept full at all times, and the gallows worked overtime.

VEVAK was placed under the command of a cleric and

divided into two wings, one in charge of internal security, and the other, *Quds* Force or QF, was put in charge of security abroad. QF was assigned handling agents worldwide, eliminating opposition, gathering intelligence and all types of 'special missions' at the behest of Iran's president.

Mehdi arrived at VEVAK HQ three days after his return to Tabriz, by direct flight from Thessaloniki. He had spent three days of utter bliss, basking in the warmth shown by family and friends when he felt everyone wrapping him with love and tenderness that knew no bounds.

Then had come the phone call.

"We're expecting you at HQ tomorrow morning. Your flight ticket from Tabriz to Tehran will be waiting for you at the Tehran Airways counter at the Tabriz airport. Do not forget to bring your ID with you."

The building was surrounded by a concrete wall over eighteen feet tall, topped by barbed wire rumored to made of steel and watchtowers about ten yards apart from each other, constantly staffed with armed guards. The front of VEVAK HQ had an electric steel gate for vehicles and another pedestrian gate.

Mehdi identified himself to the gatekeeper, who proceeded to check for his name in the ledger. He was told to wait in the nearby sitting room. A few minutes later, a man in Revolutionary Guard uniform asked Mehdi to follow him.

Mehdi was ushered into a nearby structure whose door slid open at the flicker of an automatic peephole. He found himself in a large, empty room. A voice, loud and clear from a loudspeaker in the ceiling, ordered him to remove his clothes, his shoes, too, and place them in the container by the corner. Mehdi noticed there was also a camera, capturing the whole process, in the ceiling. As soon as he removed everything, a side door opened and a man in uniform took the container and told Mehdi to wait. The man returned a few moments later and asked him to follow him to the next room, where Mehdi found his clothes next to a magnetometer at the center of the room. The man in uniform instructed him to put his clothes back on and pass through another door there.

On the other side of the door, Mehdi met a tall man who was wearing a green head band. The man smiled at him. "I apologize for the discomfort we caused you, but after the recent attempt on the life of one of our operatives, we have had to resort to the most stringent precautions in order to safeguard the revolution."

Mehdi was then led into yet another spacious room, where smiling but unfamiliar faces apologized for having inconvenienced him. The room's walls were covered with handwoven rugs. The center of the room was dominated by lavish SEVAK-era furniture. Three men were waiting for him. They rose to greet him and shook him warmly by the hand.

"*Khosh amadid* (welcome)," said a tall man with white stubble. "I am Suheil Barazi," he introduced himself. "We are members of the Quds Force. We are in charge of maintaining the revolution. You should know we have our work cut out for us. Our friends and colleagues are fighting reactionary forces within Iran, whereas we are tasked with keeping the revolution safe from any danger coming from abroad. We heard about you and your family. We've also made all the necessary inquiries and have concluded you are suitable to join our special forces."

"My name is Sallie Lakhian," one of the men seated there joined the conversation. "I head the counterintelligence desk in Europe. We have good intelligence about cells of opposition to our government that have sprouted in various universities in Europe. These cells also attract Iranian nationals. Some of them pose as students while some actually are. They are bankrolled by the CIA and the Mossad is training them. We discovered one of these cells in Thessaloniki. As you are well aware, this city has thousands of students, many of whom are overseas students from Iran."

"This is where you come in," a third person joined the conversation. "I am Suheil Murhabi. I am to be your handler in Thessaloniki. We need eyes and ears on the ground, complete with a sharp mind and a keen heart, to help us stamp out the resistance to the revolution in the city's campuses."

Suheil Barazi did not wait for Mehdi to reply. "We're glad you've agreed to join the ranks of the revolution. Go spend time with your family in Tabriz. This Sunday, come back here to Tehran and report to a weeklong basic intelligence course, after which you'll return to Thessaloniki. Thank you, Mehdi."

He then added, "I wish us all *ruze xubi daste basid* (a nice day).

Chapter Ten

VEVAK's school of intelligence was situated in a separate wing of its HQ. The school comprised a basic course of three months and an intelligence and operations school whose courses and training were six months long. Its curriculum, lesson plans and training courses were based on material dating back to SEVAK-era days. The Islamist revolutionaries had found the brochures and books neatly numbered in the classes and library.

"Mossad's operations and training staff did such a good job, it would be a shame not to use this stuff," the heads of VEVAK had told themselves right after they assumed control of the intelligence school.

In a stroke of genius, the Islamist revolutionaries changed their mind about executing the person in charge of the library and archive. Grateful for hanging on to his head, unlike most of his friends and colleagues, whom the revolutionaries hanged, the chief collaborated with his new masters and helped them internalize the array of training material and familiarize them-selves with it, no small feat, given that it comprised thousands of manuals and books filled with lesson plans. He also helped them find their way through the dozens of rooms and dungeons that were jam-packed with a never-ending assortment of training aids and paraphernalia that formerly served the operatives the Shah employed.

This time, Mehdi's visit was more dignified. They did not waive the requirement to pass through the magnetometer at the entrance to the training compound, but he was led directly to one of the meeting rooms immediately afterward.

"I am Mahmid. I will be your personal mentor," a tall, stocky man with a black beard, as black as the uniform he wore, greeted him. "I was assigned to teach you in the course of one week what other cadets learn during three whole months, so no time for chit-chat or any niceties. Let's get straight to work."

Mahmid guided Mehdi during an entire week, eighteen hours a day, often taking him through numerous guides and instructors, who taught him, among many things, the fundamentals of intelligence and combat, surveillance, how to "shake" a surveillance, how to establish contact with agents and handlers, how to conduct drop-offs, the primary method of written communication between an agent and a handler. They also taught him about transmissions and how to use code. A special guide trained Mehdi in hand-to-hand combat, whilst another showed him how to use various weapons, including an Uzi, the famous Israeli-made submachine gun, thousands of units of which the Revolutionary Guards had captured, mostly in their original shipments.

Mehdi's course also comprised theoretical lessons. "The topic of our lesson today is how Zionism has taken over the Middle East and the risk this poses for Iran," began an expert on International Relations who came to give his lecture from the University of Tehran exclusively to Mehdi. "Zionist ideology, American money and English treachery came together nearly one hundred years ago in order to take over the Middle East. In their cunning ways, the Zionists began arriving in Palestine as early as the turn of the nineteenth century. Over the years, they kept sending more and more Jews over there, and used the Holocaust in order to gain further strength and win over the world's approval for their control over Palestine. As early as 1917, the British gave their backing to the Jews, in the form of a declaration by some *Lord* called Balfour. They completed their treachery in 1948, when they conspired with the Zionists to surrender control of Palestine to them and drive our Arab brethren out."

The expert continued: "All this would not have happened without American money and Jewish domination of the global economy. The Zionists and the Americans had another goal in mind, namely, to seize control of Iran's oil, and with it, to assume control of the whole of the Middle East. They came very close to achieving this with the help of the corrupt Shah, who took advantage of his people and only cared about his own family and cronies. The blessed revolution, led by our esteemed president, has saved, right at the very last moment, Islam, our nation and our glorious people. In order to preserve the country, we must fight the remnants of reaction within, fight the Zionists and America without, and bring *El-Quds* (the holy, i.e., el-Aksa and the Dome of the Rock in Jerusalem) back to the Muslims."

Mehdi's training also included a theological lesson. A cleric, who came especially from the holy city of Qom, gave a stirring sermon about the supremacy and eternity of the *Quran*, and the holy duty to persecute all heretics.

At the end of the seventh and final day, Mehdi met with Suheil Murhabi, his designated handler in Thessaloniki. "In one week's time, you'll be going back to Thessaloniki to continue your academic studies as usual. You are not to come to the consulate under any circumstances. Do not phone them either. We know the consulate is under constant surveillance and that all the phone lines are tapped. We also know that Greek intelligence is in close contact with both the Mossad and the CIA. We will contact each other using drop-offs, signs, and written messages. The city's promenade has a white tower. Right next to it there's a tall cypress and a bench. Once a week, you will mark a white '*x*' right behind the bench's top level. This would be a sign confirming you are fine. If you have an urgent message for me, make a cross, and then I shall meet you within two hours at the archeological exhibition on display inside the tower."

Murhabi continued. "Once a month, you will compile a report on your activity. At six pm on the first Sunday of every month, I shall meet you 'by chance' by the bench. After you recognize me, and only after you will have seen me sitting down, will you walk away. Leave the report in a paper bag, which you will put inside the trash by the bench. Do not sit at the bench before shaking off any surveillance as we taught you in the course. If you sense anything is off, keep walking. We shall meet the following day, same time and place. Now, in case we need you, don't worry, we will find you. I am also giving you my personal number. You may only use it in case of emergency. Memorize it. Learn it by heart. It must not appear written down anywhere. Do not leave it around. What's your bank account number? You'll find one thousand dollars there each month. See you by the bench." Suheil got up and left without shaking Mehdi's hand.

'*My handler sure is tough*,' Mehdi thought to himself.

***

Mehdi went back home to Tabriz to see his family and told them he had decided to return to Thessaloniki to resume his studies. They all expressed their regret at his decision, but, judging by the look on his father's face and those of his two brothers, Mehdi realized some members of his family regretted his decision more than others.

Once he returned to Thessaloniki, Mehdi relished his new post and adjusted to it with great enthusiasm. Having espoused the values of the Islamic revolution wholeheartedly, he grew more devout. Ali, his roommate, followed Mehdi's transition with surprise, noting to himself with astonishment how his friend, a formerly avid student who couldn't help focusing every spare second on his studies, turned into a leading social activist among the community of Iranian students on campus. Mehdi asked the university's administrative manager for a list of all Iranian nationals among the overseas students, saying he would use it to promote the relations between the students and the university authorities, but he actually used it to form a social framework to promote his own political agenda.

Mehdi's reports to his handler were detailed, featuring a great deal of knowledge about the students and their political views. Most of them did support the Islamic revolution and identified with its principles. Nevertheless, Mehdi detected a small core student body that hated the revolution with all their heart. Some of them resented the fact that the revolutionaries had executed their fathers, and others belonged to families who had prospered under the former regime of the Shah and saw their wealth and power being taken away, often by force. Mehdi cataloged them by various groups and handed the referenced lists to his handler.

One evening, Mehdi felt like a day off. He invited his friend and roommate Ali for a few ouzos at the nearby pub. As devout as he was, he did not consider ouzo *haram*, prohibited. As the evening progressed, and after his fourth shot, Ali told him he would be absent from their apartment the following week.

"I didn't know your mother was in such a bad shape." He seemed to recall Ali telling him his mother had been ill.

"My mother is feeling better. I'm going abroad."

"Abroad? Where?"

Ali averted his eyes, lowered them, and, somewhat hesitantly, replied, "Don't tell anyone. I am going to Israel."

"What? Why? What have you got to do with Israel?"

"I've been meaning to tell you for a long time, but never got the chance. My real name isn't Ali. It's Eli, short for Eliyahu, as in Elijah. I come from a Jewish family whose members live not only in Tehran but also in Israel, so I am going to see them."

"How will you get there?"

"Don't worry about it. I am traveling via Rome, so nothing in my passport will ever disclose my having been to Israel."

Shocked to discover his close friend and roommate, his confidant, was a Jew, Mehdi took a bit of time to mull the news over. *'I've shared quite a few secrets with this guy. But then again, he's merely a Jew. He's got family ties, and surely other connections too, with our Zionist enemy.'*

The following morning, Mehdi's only thought was whether to act at once or to wait until after his dentist appointment that day. His deliberations could not be any shorter. The motherland won over. He cancelled his appointment, went straight to the bench by the white tower and made a cross on the bench with the white piece of chalk he always kept in his pocket. This was the first time he made this sign since the beginning of his career as an informant for Iranian intelligence.

Two hours later, he walked into the exhibition at the white tower, where he saw Suheil, his handler, standing in front of a large window, watching the sea, his back turned away from the general public. Mehdi walked around the exhibition hall. *'The coast is clear,'* he told himself after a while and walked over to Suheil. He watched the same view. Remembering what they had taught him, he kept his message short and to the point, as befitting an intelligence briefing.

"I have just found out my roommate is in fact a Jew. He hid this fact from me all these years. His family is still back in Tehran. What's worse is that he travelled to Israel earlier this morning and asked me to keep this under wraps. He told me he was going to Israel via Rome and that according to some arrangement he has with the Israeli authorities, they will not stamp his passport so as not to disclose the fact he visited there. You may find all the details in the pouch I hid."

The moment he was through, he was gone

A few days later, a man turned up in Mehdi's apartment. He told him he was a staff member of the Iranian embassy. "I'm here on behalf of our friends," was all he said. He gathered all of Ali's personal effects and documents and went away.

Mehdi had not heard a word from Ali since their night out at the pub nor received any word of him. '*I actually really do not care*,' he told himself. Indeed, he showed no sign of remorse or compunction. "Regret or bad conscience are for the weak," he recalled what Suheila, his grandmother, had told him.

Several months later, he heard on CNN that the leader of the Iranian Kurdish party had been assassinated in Germany along with his three bodyguards. The news bulletin further reported that three Iranian nationals were arrested as suspects, and that an international warrant for the arrest of one Sallie Lakhian, a senior Revolutionary Guard official, had been issued. He was suspected of having directed the hit squad.

Mehdi smiled proudly, recalling the occasion of his recruitment to the Revolutionary Guard by three seniors, one of whom was Sallie.

Chapter Eleven

When the Islamic revolution broke out in Iran, Kamal Mosseri was a young political science lecturer at Tehran University's faculty of social studies. Like many of his peers, he grew a beard and kept it well-groomed with the help of bi-weekly visits to his barber. He also wore Western-style suits, which were very much in fashion among the faculty staff.

Revolutionary Guard members who were on the lookout for replacements for the thousands of academics who had been executed, as well as for those who had managed to flee the terror that the Islamic regime had devolved into, soon traced Mosseri among the surviving staff members and ordered him to serve undercover as an Islamic Revolutionary Guard Corps (IRGC) Quds-Force (QF) agent. With the aid of Iran's embassy in Athens, he secured a position as a lecturer at the University of Athens, specializing in "managing international crises."

As part of his academic specialty, Mosseri traveled the globe extensively, fulfilling various tasks for Iranian intelligence in addition to his academic work. Nevertheless, unbeknownst to them, he was wholeheartedly against everything they believed in. On one of his visits to London, Mosseri contacted the CIA and quickly became one of their top agents in Europe, code-named "Olympia." He proved so important and valuable, he was assigned a personal handler, a rare and highly extraordinary occurrence.

***

"Olympia is gone," Michael Gilly, CIA station chief in Greece and a two-star general, informed the team of commanders convened round the desk at the agency's meeting room in Greece. General Gilly, a silver-haired, tall and thin man with bright eyes, had become an intelligence operative after a long career in the US Army.

"He told his handler," General Gilly continued," he was scheduled for a meeting with the security officer at Iran's embassy on the 22nd of this month at twelve o'clock. We warned him this wasn't looking good, but he reassured us and said the Iranians suspect nothing, and that he could, in the course of that meeting, glean important information."

The general continued. "Seeing as Olympia's handler received no confirmation for the latter's safe departure from the Iranian embassy, after the conclusion of that meeting, we put through our emergency protocol, 'Meteor,' into practice. It is designed especially for such cases. Per this procedure, we've had a senior Athens police officer contact the Iranian embassy and ask about Olympia. Well, they did confirm he was there, but claimed his meeting at the embassy lasted an hour and a half and that he left the building immediately after that.

"The Greeks checked the surveillance camera surrounding the Iranian embassy. The footage shows Olympia entering the embassy building five minutes to twelve, but they feature no record of him leaving.

"At our request, the Greeks checked the cameras again. It turned out there was a fuse short on the street where the embassy is located. It lasted half an hour, during which the cameras were out of commission. Nevertheless, the Greeks did not leave it at that and asked the Iranians for their own security footage, which runs on in-house embassy generators.

"The Iranians raised an eyebrow at the Greek security services interest in an Iranian national. They also told the Greeks their generators failed due to the same electric grid malfunction.

"The gist of it is that things don't look too good. The Greek security services, together with the Greek police, are trying to locate the whereabouts of this person. I assigned Colonel Norton to widen the inquiry into the matter of Olympia. Unless we receive some new information within forty-eight hours, we'll raise this issue to level four. I reported the case to HQ in Paris, and they asked us to keep them in the loop."

***

The team of commanders reconvened on the 28th for another meeting. This time, it was attended by the CIA head of operations in Europe.

"The Greek security services," reported General Gilly, "found no trace of Olympia. They said, 'It's as if Mt. Olympus has swallowed him.' I always knew they were still living in a world of myths and legends…

"The way things stand," the general continued, "we've decided to raise this matter to level four. Colonel Norton will now deliver you his report on the findings of the investigation. I would like to make an initial note and underscore that things don't look promising at all."

"As General Gilly just told you," Colonel Norton began his report, "we've raised this issue to level four priority and clearance, only one level below that of a national crisis requiring the involvement of the president. We have also approached friendly organizations, so here are the relevant facts we've managed to uncover:

"One, on the afternoon of the 21st, an Iran Air aircraft landed at Athens airport. This was an unscheduled landing. Three Iranian nationals carrying diplomatic passports were onboard. They were later identified as senior Revolutionary Guard intelligence operatives.

"Two, Mohammad Fakhlazi, deputy head of Iran's forensic pathology institute, who had attended an international conference in Vienna, suddenly left the conference, but the Austrian security service found no record of his departure from the country. It later turned out that on the 22nd, he took a night flight from Athens to Tehran on board an Iran Air jet.

"Three, Dr. Ali Corazon, a senior surgeon at the Khamenei hospital, cut short a family vacation. He just happened to be vacationing in Athens with his family. He too boarded that Iran Air flight with the three diplomats back to Iran. An inquiry with Hilton Athens revealed he checked out in a hurry, leaving two days prior to his planned departure, although the two rooms he was staying in were reserved for two days longer.

"Four, Alaa Morati, the Iranian embassy's chief security officer, has not been seen since the 22nd. He seems to be hiding in the embassy.

"Five. We received the footage of the persons entering and leaving the Iranian embassy building on the day of the 22nd from the Greeks, except for the comings and goings between the afternoon and between seven pm and eight pm. The Greeks told us the power was out again. We received permission from the Greek prime minister to look into what was causing all those power outages in Athens. Looks like someone messed with the switch."

"Six. On the midnight of the 22nd, the surveillance cameras picked up a black van with diplomatic license plates leaving the embassy's own parking lot due south.

"Seven. Very early in the morning of the 23rd, the Iranian tanker *Choral Sea* left the port of Piraeus, although it had unloaded only about one third of its cargo."

"Thank you, Norton," said General Gilly." As I told you, things don't look too good. We're continuing with our investigation."

***

Two weeks went by, and then the Turkish police released the following email:

"A small, unidentified piece of a human body was recovered

off the coast of Turkey. Please find the body's DNA profile attached. We kindly appreciate any assistance in identifying the body and letting us know immediately."

***

"Olympia has been found," Two-Star General Michael Gilly informed his colleagues at the CIA.

***

On the morning of the 22nd, Mehdi was awakened by the sound of strong thumping on his door. *'This is enough to wake a polar bear in the middle of his winter sleep,'* he couldn't help thinking as he went over to open the door. Much to his surprise, he saw his handler Suheil Murhabi on the threshold.

"Get dressed and have some coffee," Murhabi, told him. "We have a few errands to run. This morning, at ten, your will have a visitor, Rubazi, your successor. You need to pass on to him all your material so that he may take over from you. At four o'clock, they will come to take you to the airport. You will catch a flight to Athens, where you will take a taxi to the embassy. Use any taxi that may come along. Under no terms are you to take a taxi from the permanent taxi station at the airport. Tonight, at eleven, you will board an Iran Air flight from Athens to Tehran. Along with your plane tickets, I am also giving you a new passport instead of the one that got stolen from you. Now, hand over your 'stolen' passport. Now, please."

Mehdi gave Suheil his passport and they shook hands, and he then disappeared from Mehdi's life completely. A few months later, Mehdi found out that some mysterious assassin had gunned Suheil down at the entrance to the White Tower on Thessaloniki's main boardwalk.

When Mehdi opened the envelope Suheil had given him, he found flight tickets and a passport with a recent photo of his, bearing the name Saddeq Kandasi. Saddeq immediately took to his new name. It reminded him of Mohammad Mosaddeq, who had served as the Shah's prime minister between 1951 and 1953, long before Khomeini's Islamic revolution. He recalled being taught that the Shah had had the CIA and MI6 oust Mosaddeq, his own popular prime minister, who had been duly elected by Iran's parliament, over the latter's policy of nationalizing Iran's oil industry and his intentions to launch a semi-socialist agrarian reform.

After spending many hours with Rubazi, his replacement as the operative at the University of Thessaloniki, Mehdi bid farewell to his apartment, fully aware he was never to return. He went to the airport to catch his flight to Athens. When he landed in Athens, he took a random taxi as he had been told. "To the Iranian embassy, please," he told the driver.

The arrival of Saddeq Kandasi was indeed expected. On his arrival at the embassy in Athens, a hidden button was pushed as he passed through the checkpoint, and a tall, broad-shouldered man came up to greet him and lead him into a luxurious waiting room on the first floor, where Saddeq found a pot of sweet tea, a pile of sandwiches and fresh Greek salad. After he had rested from his journey and helped himself to the tea and the food, a severe looking man walked in and motioned him to follow. This man led Saddeq through a long corridor into an elevator where the panel only had one button. As the man pressed it, the door shut, and the elevator descended all the way to the embassy's basement, at least three stories, by Saddeq's impression. Stepping out of the elevator, they confronted a high steel door. His escort pushed a six-digit code. The door turned and shut immediately upon Saddeq's entry, leaving the man who had led him there outside.

It took him no more than a few seconds to adjust to the windowless room, in the center of which Saddeq saw a blindfolded man tied to a chair, his legs tied together and bent, his arms tied over his back, which was resting on the chair. Thus, the man's pose resembled a banana. Behind this man stood two men in robes tied from the back, akin to those worn by surgeons, but these men had black balaclavas that covered their faces, save for two slits for the eyes. Each man wore a pair of disposable nitrile gloves.

The silence in the room was thick and heavy. One of the men pointed at a clothes hanger and gestured to Saddeq to move where it hung in the corner of the room. Saddeq went over, took off the robe that was hanging there, identical to the one those two men wore, and put it on. He donned the black headpiece and gloves. The man pointed to the floor, and Saddeq put both feet into a pair of canvas shoes.

The man who was silent until now made a gesture signaling to Saddeq to approach. he could now see that next to the man, who was tied down and contorted, stood a narrow desk with a 9 mm Beretta and a silencer. Using only his hand, the silent man instructed Saddeq to pick up the gun and aim at the back of the tied man. Saddeq followed each command like a robot. He felt absolutely nothing.

"Finish him."

Those were the only two words uttered in that chamber of horrors.

The trigger responded softly, as the thick concrete walls and the silencer absorbed the sound. The man's head fell forward, right before convulsing and dying.

The silent man pointed at the hanger. Saddeq took the robe off, removed the hat and gloves and took off the canvas shoes. The steel door flung open, seemingly on its own, only to reveal his escort outside.

"I was asked to convey the high command's congratulations," was all he said.

The elevator took them back up, where Saddeq was once again led via the long corridors to the exit. A Mercedes parked inside the building's lot took him directly to the airport.

Air Iran's flight to Tehran took off promptly at eleven o'clock. Untroubled in the slightest by the hit he had just perpetrated, Mehdi slept peacefully nearly the whole time. '*Morals and a conscience are for the weak, not for leaders,*' he told himself. '*And I am going to be a leader.*' He slept well all the way.

***

Back at the Tehran airport, Mehdi had enough time to update his surprised parents that he was back in Iran and to promise he'd come visit the first chance he got. A black car picked him up from the airport to VEVAK HQ. This time, he was not subjected to those humiliating inspections he remembered from his previous visit there but was rather taken directly to see the commander of Revolutionary Guard Quds Force (QF). When he entered the office, he was asked to return the passport he had used to leave Athens and was given his original passport back.

"We are proud of you and are glad to have you on board," the senior commander began with a greeting. "You should know that our men spotted you and recognized your talents the very first days they got to know you. They quickly appreciated your courage and your devotion to our homeland and to holy Islam. They commended you in particular for favoring the good of the country over friendship. That is exactly what is expected of a leader and a commander.

"You have passed your final test in flying colors at the embassy in Athens, where you courageously eliminated, without any hesitation whatsoever, one of the worst traitors to our country, an American agent who worked tirelessly under the regime. His American handlers called him 'Olympia.' Based on all your achievements, QF high command has decided to appoint you chief of the special operations unit."

Chapter Twelve

Revolutionary Guard Quds Force (QF) "special operations unit," or 'Special Ops' was a euphemism of sorts for the VEVAK's hit squad. The VEVAK resorted to the harshest and cruelest means against those who opposed the Islamic regime both at home and abroad. Immediately after the Islamic revolution began, thousands of officers and leaders who had served the ousted Shah were executed. This tough policy remained in place for years. QF, in charge of Iran's security against threats from abroad, followed the same approach as the VEVAK and conducted extensive hits against numerous figures.

QF assassins eliminated dozens of people who opposed the regime worldwide. To achieve these hits, it relied on an extensive intelligence network, directed for the most part from Iran's diplomatic missions worldwide. The intelligence that was gathered served the needs of VEVAK, which, in turn, issued QF its orders to kill. Mehdi's appointment as head of Special Ops greatly boosted QF. The new commander soon consolidated all the elimination operations abroad and concentrated the unit, instead of having it scattered among QF's various forces. Mehdi's charismatic personality won him large budgets from HQ, which were allocated towards enhancing his unit with quality personnel, training and advanced technology. Under his command, the war between VEVAK and the Israeli Mossad intensified and unfolded into a genuine fight for life or death.

Mehdi was ambivalent about the Mossad. On the one hand, he knew it to be a staunch, unflinching organization that had set out to fight Iran and the assistance Iran provided terror and *jihad* organization worldwide. On the other, as a professional, he appreciated Mossad as the world's finest secret service.

During the training courses and classes he gave, he always stressed before his men the importance of decisiveness and tenacity, of pursuing the target no matter what, and cited the Mossad as an example. "For instance," he told the class once during one of his lessons, "in 1972, our Palestinian brothers carried out a heroic operation. They eliminated eleven Israeli athletes in Munich, thereby raising the issue of Palestine to the top of the public agenda. Under the premiership of Golda Meir, the government of Israel decided to have everyone involved in this courageous act eliminated. The Israelis had them killed one after the other. Nevertheless, they could not get their hands on our dear brother, Hassan Salameh, the commander of "Black September," who was in charge of the entire operation."

"The Israelis, however, did not relent. They chased Hassan Salameh for years. The Mossad chased him like a cat after a mouse, until, after years of this pursuit, they located him in Beirut and killed him. I am telling you all this so you'll know what kind of stubborn, dangerous enemy we are up against."

***

A.K., a man of average height with a pair of glasses, was a major sardines exporter. In eloquent Portuguese, he ran his business from his firm's offices in Avenida de la Libertad. But this was not the whole truth about him.

Truth be told, A.K. was in charge of Mossad operations in western Europe. He chose Lisbon, way off the beaten track of the classic world of espionage, precisely in order to avoid any undue attention, in particular that of various European secret services, which were always keen to know as much as possible about Mossad activity in their respective countries. Their Portuguese counterparts, however, were far more lethargic about the Mossad, and, to begin with, how could sardines and spying possibly have to do one with another?

A.K., whose full name remains to this day under the strictest confidence, ran a highly intricate network of agents across Europe. He gathered a great deal of information on Iran's activity in various European countries. The material was passed on to 'the hill,' Mossad HQ, where it was analyzed, sifted through and evaluated. Some of it was passed on to the relevant countries' intelligence services, some was kept for further monitoring and surveillance, and some was simply not to speak of, perhaps read about here and there. Mind you, what one reads in the newspaper is not always true...

***

Tibriz Zakiri, a well-built man who never failed to sculpt his figure at the gym, did not sport a double identity. He had a threefold identity: assistant to Iran's trade attaché at the embassy in the Hague, the person in charge, on Mehdi's behalf, of a string of secret agents in Europe, and, more to our point, he was A.K.'s informant. He apprised the sardine man about all of Iran's elimination operations throughout Europe.

Tibriz passed the information he gathered onto A.K. using secure means. The intelligence he provided was always credible, important and relevant. Only three figures were privy to his existence: the head of Mossad, his deputy and A.K., of course.

Mehdi was the first person to become concerned about the intelligence leakage from VEVAK. Many of his own hit men were getting hit. His top agent in Istanbul was eliminated by two motorcyclists at the entrance of Kempinski, the well-known luxury hotel. Another agent's car exploded while he drove on the fast lane from Copenhagen to the city's airport. The testimonies gathered by the local police included an eyewitness account by one of the drivers, who said that he had noticed a motorcycle riding very close to the car seconds before the explosion, with one of the motorcyclists attaching something to the car. Another agent of Mehdi's was shot dead while still in bed in Montparnasse, Paris. French police investigators, along with Iranian investigators who were allowed to take part in the case, could not track the assassin. They could not even figure out how the agent's killer succeeded in getting through all the apartment security measures.

Among the improvements Mehdi introduced into his organization was installing a system of control over his men and over his communication with them. He tried to get to the bottom of the explosions and assassinations that had claimed the lives of his men but hit an impasse. Even a senior investigator Mehdi appointed in the strictest confidentiality to uncover what had had happened made no progress. Mehdi made yet another effort to find out what had happened to his operatives and set up a team comprising two highly discreet personal assistants. With their help, he began the process of scrutinizing the credibility of his agents in Europe by sending each of them contrived messages in the utmost secrecy.

One day, Tibriz got a coded message classified as 'Top Secret,' according to which there was to be an attempt on the life of the Israeli ambassador to the European Union. Unbeknownst to Tibriz, he was the only address. No other agent received this coded message from Mehdi. On the day that was scheduled for the planned assassination, Mehdi's men, who were assigned to observe the complex where the Israeli delegation was headquartered in, noticed that security around the building had been heightened. The entire place had been surrounded by members of the Belgian security services and persons later identified as Mossad agents. Mehdi immediately realized the reason for this.

***

Tibriz realized he had been caught. Bound to a chair in a banana-like pose, he regretted his own indiscretion, the cause of his downfall and capture. He knew all too well what was about to befall him. Sheer torture. '*First, my toenails, then, my balls, and ultimately, what's left of my life… oh, how I'd wish it was the other way around, but I am no longer in charge.'*

Tibriz was kept waiting in this position for hours. Much to his surprise, nothing happened. The guard who was standing watch next to him even gave him some water. Then, the door flung open. He couldn't be more surprised to see his all-powerful boss, chief of special ops Mehdi Mohammad, entering the room. The look on Mehdi's face beamed pride and self-importance.

"I came to bring you kind regards from your wife and kids. I saw them this morning. She asked to show you their picture."

Upon being shown a photo of his wife from today's newspaper, Tibriz, who was perfectly calm until that point, began shaking all over. "What do you want from me?"

"I want you to save the life of your wife and save the future of your two kids," Mehdi retorted.

"What do I have to do?"

Mehdi smiled, but his eyes were as cold as ice. "I will show you three things, so you'll get the full picture." He laid a Parabellum firearms cartridge on the table by the torture chair Tibriz was tied to. "This is exhibit *one*. Now, here's exhibit *two*: a real Paraguayan passport under your name. exhibit *three*: a photo of a Paraguayan passport for your wife and your kids."

"What do I have to do to get all these riches?"

"Take out your handler. This will atone for some of the crimes you've committed against our homeland, help save the life of your wife and save us the trouble of placing your kids in two separate orphanages. As a bonus, you would also be saving your own miserable life, may blessed, merciful Allah forgive me for that."

***

The very next day, Tibriz flew to Lisbon for an urgent meeting he had set up with his handler, whom he met at their usual spot at the city's boardwalk, right by Fernando's café. A.K. approached him, smiling wholeheartedly but only briefly, for Tibriz pulled out his parabellum and noticed A.K.'s look of understanding right before sustaining three shots to his chest and falling onto the promenade's pavement.

***

Back at the headquarters in Tehran, Mehdi and his team celebrated their victory over the Mossad. The next day, a special envoy from Iran's president came to tell Mehdi he had been appointed QF commander as successor of the chief who had died a week earlier from cancer.

Mehdi knew the Mossad and figured its response for eliminating one of its top field operatives would not be late in coming. He just didn't know where and when the retaliation would come, or how hard.

Chapter Thirteen

The sight was as powerful as it was mesmerizing. A red pillar of smoke rose over the bazaar, only to be followed by blue smoke a few second later and another pillar of yellow smoke within a few seconds after that. These pillars of smoke soon converged over the *khana*, the Mohammadi family's commercial compound, to form a spectacular rainbow. Their store's indigo, saffron and ochre burnt to cinder in no time, and the now black smoke was all that remained of all those marvelous handcrafted carpets and rugs.

Mehdi received word of the fire during a QF meeting with the topic of 'preparing for an anticipated Mossad reprisal.' He called the meeting to a halt. "I have to catch a flight to Tabriz. No need to discuss the possible ways the Mossad might strike back in response to our killing one of their top agents in Europe. They just beat us to it."

***

The entire bazaar had celebrated the birth of Ali, Mehdi's elder brother. Suleiman, the proud father, had run through the market streets and told everyone about the new heir to the Mohammadi family. His wife Fatimah had been right beside him, handing out homemade sweets to the shopkeepers and stall owners, as well as to the visitors. The entire course of Ali's life was set at birth. Ever since he turned three-years old, he spent every moment he could spare in the khana, studying its secrets. He grew into a marvelous young man, tall, brown-eyed and with lovely, raven-black hair. He went to a local boxing gym twice a week and grew fitter. His lovely features and handsome figure won him the attraction of all the girls in Tabriz, who never tired from gazing at him from afar. After he graduated high school, the family sent him to Tehran to study business management, after which he went to a renowned college dedicated to the carpet trade. Upon completion of his studies there, it was only natural that he would join the family business, initially as a public relations and marketing manager.

Two years after Ali was born, his mother gave birth to Bahiz. The two brothers could not be more different. Unlike his elder brother, Bahiz was slim and introverted. He had to wear glasses at age six. The doctors advised Fatimah to administer all sorts of potions to make him stronger. He would spend his time thinking and playing elaborate games. He seemed to prefer those intricate pursuits to the company of other people.

"Bahiz will be our finance guy," Ali determined before the boy was even six. The boy made good on this prediction when he graduated in Tabriz, then in Tehran.

When the fire erupted in the khana, both brothers were seated in their respective chambers on either side of the complex. The smell of smoke and the shouts of the staff drove both Ali and Bahiz out, but whereas Bahiz ran out with everyone from the burning building, Ali disappeared. All attempts to find him failed. One employee said he had seen Ali running down the corridor and shouting he was going to save the carpet and that he'd be back soon. But he never returned.

Everyone knew which carpet he was referring to: a masterpiece three years in the making by a highly qualified weaver. Her as yet unfinished work had already been sold to the royal palace in Saudi Arabia for a huge fortune.

Concern for Ali increased as the hours went by. Several hours after the fire, the commander of the local emergency forces paid a visit to the family and told Suleiman solemnly, "We've recovered Ali's body. A concrete beam fell on top of him. He died on the spot."

The family's grief was enormous. Traditional and close-knit, the Mohammadis' loyalty and love for one another was known to all. Ali's death was a serious blow as he was the eldest, the heir apparent to Suleiman, designated to head the next generation of carpet weavers.

The bazaar went on sabbatical on the day of the funeral. All the other merchants closed shop and paid their respects at the Blue Mosque. The lamenting *muezzin* eulogized Ali, his cries sounding across Tabriz over loudspeakers everywhere.

Grandma Suheila insisted on attending the funeral, despite the urgings of her doctors that she should stay in bed. Her age and various ailments were plainly visible. She could barely walk, so she leaned on Suleiman and Fatimah. Amid the tears and cries that poured out everywhere, Suheila kept a stern face, shed not a single tear and retained her composure. Regal to the last moment, she did not even sigh.

Mehdi, clad in his Revolutionary Guard uniform, walked behind his parents and his grandmother, along with his brother Bahiz and their two sisters. He was surrounded by his bodyguards, some in uniform and some in plainclothes, merging with the crowd. Mehdi's face was blank, masking the terrible pain inside. His eyes beamed decisiveness and determination. The huge crowd of mourners looked upon him with great admiration as befitting a famous commander, one of Tabriz's finest men.

Chapter Fourteen

The Mohammadi home was situated in Tabriz's magnificent boulevard, which was renamed 'Imam Khomeini Boulevard' after the Islamic revolution. The family home was one of the city's finest, a testament to their longstanding wealth and prosperity. Their residence, which actually resembled a palace, was big enough for the entire family. Ali and Bahiz each had their own independent apartments, where they lived with their wives and children. Suha, Ali's widow, continued to live there along with their three children. Bahiz and Mehdi's two sisters each had her own room and her own enclosed space, in expectancy of their husbands to come. Suheila, the matriarch, had her own separate apartment within the family residence, right next to the living room.

The family's day to day life revolved primarily around the spacious living room, the large kitchen and the adjacent dining room, where, right at the center, stood a mahogany table with eighteen matching chairs. Beside it stood a smaller dining table, for those occasions when fewer members attended supper.

The living room floor consisted of marble tiles connected

by strips of triangular and square mosaic in blue and gold. Most of it was covered in the most marvelous carpets, the handiwork of generations of Mohammadi weavers. Thick crimson curtains with golden tassels covered the windows, complimenting the gilded chandelier that hang from the high ceiling

Both parts of the living room featured a sideboard with antique silverware, the work of generations of Persian craftsman, along with ancient ceramic and earthenware brought all the way from Uzbekistan, Armenia and other Asian countries. The northern cabinet had a golden goblet right at the center, atop an ivory stand. It was adorned with the designs of all sorts of animals. Family legend told that a Persian artisan had produced it two centuries earlier. Opposite, on the southern sideboard, stood, in all its glory, a golden goblet with two-headed figures, a gift from one of Persia's rulers to the chief of the Mohammadis back in the 18th century, in honor of filling the ruler's place with carpets that were especially woven for the royal household.

A three-legged Carrara marble table stood at the center of the family living room. Its legs were gilded, to match the red padding crossed by golden stripes of the armchairs and to match the curtains, as well.

The entire family was sitting on the armchairs, their faces somber, and sunken eyes bespeaking their lack of sleep. Seven days had passed since Ali died in the fire that wiped out the khana, but they were all still shocked and despondent.

"So, what do we do?" Suleiman, still head of the family, began their sad gathering.

Mehdi's absence was inescapable. Shortly after ali's funeral, he told his father he had to leave on urgent business. They didn't have to say another word. Suleiman knew how special the relations between Ali and Mehdi were, so he knew for sure that no other *business* could possibly force Mehdi to leave at a time like this except for something to do with Ali's death.

Fatimah Mohammadi, who seldom spoke, was the first to respond. The whole family marveled at the courage this newly bereaved mother showed and the determination her words attested to. "For seven days and seven nights Suleiman and I have wept for Ali. I remember his difficult, 24-hour birth. I told myself then and there that he was born under such pain, he would bring great joy into the world, and so it was. He brought us nothing but pride and joy, and all this is over and done now. We shall weep for Ali for the remainder of our lives, and we shall always see him before our eyes, but life goes on. Suha, Ali's dear wife, sitting here with us, and her three children, our grandchildren, light of our lives, you ought to know that Ali would have wished to see you continue with your lives, cherish, cultivate and preserve your wonderful family."

The widow, Suha, the small children and everyone else in the family wailed at what Fatimah had just said. Suleiman too, whose tears had seemed to have run dry by now, wiped his eyes on the white tablecloth.

"I would like to take this opportunity," Fatimah continued, "and tell you about the other families this fire impacted. Twelve people were taken to hospital, mostly due to smoke inhalation and injuries, except for one woman whose injuries were severe. They were all released from the hospital by now.

Let me tell you, it could have been a lot worse."

Heavy silence and darkness descended on the room as each person there succumbed to his or her own sadness and private thoughts. Bahiz, who, now that Ali had died had become the eldest, was the first to break the silence. "We have no choice but to continue in Ali's footsteps, for his honor, in his memory and for the family," he said. "I would like to report that the insurance assessors came by earlier, and that, following their visit, the insurance company informed me the business was under-insured. Consequently, what they are willing to pay us in damages is not worth twenty percent of the estimated cost of rebuilding our khana. I am not even talking about the carpets that burnt, they weren't even insured. Luckily for us, most of our carpets were not stored there but in our external warehouse," he concluded.

Suleiman woke from his musings. "I would like to tell you all I've been getting messages and calls promising us assistance and aid. All sorts of people and institutions are reaching out to us. For instance, a friend of mine, Mazay, offered us his own space at the bazaar for two whole years at a reduced cost. Thing is, we do not have enough funds to rebuild and buy new machinery. What's disappointing the most, is that we received no response, no offer of assistance, from either the government or the city. I'm afraid that if we decide to rebuild and buy new machinery, supplies and so on, we'll have to sell some valuable assets in order to afford going back to business as before." He looked sadly around the lavish interior of his home.

The Mohammadis continued its lamentations as darkness

crept in from the outside. No one rose to turn on the light or fill a plate from their packed dining table, which the family's cooks kept filling with dishes. "Troubles and appetite seldom mix," as the old saying goes.

Suheila finally broke the silence. "Come on, rise up, dears, trust Allah, and his salvation will not fail to come soon. All these years, our family went through its share of ordeals, from the great earthquake and the infidels' invasions, to the terrible plague that nearly wiped out the entire family. Thanks be blessed Allah, we have survived so much and withstood it all. We must have faith in God and in ourselves, and in this way, we shall come out of this stronger than ever."

After a short pause, the old matriarch added, "Know this, the Lord has given us the good as well as the bad. Why? Why would he bestow both? For if he had only done good for us, how would we know how to cope with the bad, should it arrive? God gave us bad news too, so that we'd always remember that after the bad occurrences, we also get the good. Come, let us all show Ali his death was not in vain, that we have sworn to follow his lead."

They could all tell how difficult it was for Suheila to speak out loud. She bowed her head and closed her eyes. However painful, her words nevertheless made an almost miraculous impact on the entire family. Everyone held their head high, rose up, shoulders straightened, eyes fully opened, and lo and behold, the main door flung open, and the house filled with light.

It was Mehdi, standing at the front door.

He quickly looked round the room and saw the astonishment

in everyone's eyes as he ran over to Suheila. Bending his knees, he kneeled before her and kissed her hands. She laid her hands over his head. "Bismillah, may God bless you," she whispered, her eyes filling with tears.

Mehdi ran over to hug his mother, whereupon he gave in to his father's embrace and shook hands with Bahiz firmly and proceeded to hug his excited sisters.

"You came just in time," Suleiman told him. "We were getting desperate."

"Did you really think I would leave you hanging?" Mehdi replied. "I had to go for the sake of a sacred cause, namely, to arrange the revenge for Ali's murder. Now that things are getting back on track, I am back, ready to lend my support to my beloved family and gain strength from you all." Everyone smiled again, for the first time that week. "Can I get some food around here?" he joked. "I haven't had a bite in two whole days. Besides, good food ushers in good news, too."

It was as though the maids had waited for this particular moment all along. The moment Mehdi came in, they began heating all the food and proceeded to lay everything on the great dining table, which once again united the whole family. As they haven't eaten since that morning, they suddenly remembered how hungry they were. After they dined, they returned to the spacious hall and sat on their big armchairs again, had sweet tea and helped themselves to some more delicious homemade food.

"I've come to share the following news with you," Mehdi resumed his update. "The Revolutionary Guard has sent its very best police investigators to uncover the reasons for the fire.

Their inquiry came to the conclusion that this was a planned arson. They tracked down several places where it was started on purpose, so they concluded it must have been the product of several men working simultaneously. I know who's behind it. However, I can say nothing more. I promise you all that the perpetrators will pay dearly for what they've done."

He paused for the short gasps he heard around him. "Another thing I would like to tell you is that our esteemed president has decreed that our family be compensated in full for all the damages, including a full reimbursement for rebuilding our khana. They will also foot all the bills for re-stocking and for purchasing new equipment and machinery. What's more, they will compensate us for all the carpets and make up for the earnings we would have lost for the next three years."

"What did I tell you all?" Suheila commented. "God has delivered us, in the flicker of an eye."

PART THREE

Chapter Fifteen

Darkness descended upon him. The world was gone. When he came to, Bonnie found himself lying in bed in his own bedroom, still in his clothes, his shoes on, covered up to his neck in a grey woolen blanket, although the sun was out, as it was about noon.

'*How did I get here? I remember the letter I opened by the dim light of the night lamp, while sitting on my favorite chair. But then, it was like a hammer hit me on the head.*' Bonnie recalled his legs getting too heavy to carry him; he had felt his back was on the verge of cracking, until he had managed to sit himself down with great effort. He relived the moment; he felt he could barely take his shirt off but could not get to his shoes.

He allowed himself a bit more time to compose himself and pull himself together. On his way to the kitchen, his eyes fell on the old bottle of scotch on the small coffee table in the living room. The night lamp was still on, despite the glowing daylight that flooded the apartment. Bonnie leaned against the wall. '*Now, how about a drink? No, better clear my head.*

Not the right time for that. Better have coffee so I can think straight,' he finally decided.

He had to lean against the wall and grip the odd chair before he could get to his kettle and turn it on. As luck would have it, the kettle was half full. As he waited for the water to boil, he filled a mug with three spoons of coffee and poured water over it. Then, he pulled up the nearest chair and landed himself. *'That's it, two more sips... now, let's get rid of these shoes.'* He removed his pants and continued to drink his coffee, still in his shorts. *'So, what now?'* He now remembered his sister had told him she wouldn't be coming back until that evening. Something about a few errands. He wasn't due back at the ministry for two days. His landline was on the floor. *'But where's my mobile? So typical... Well, that's just fine. What's next?'*

Bonnie reflected on the words of the kaddish, the Jewish prayer for the dead, which he had read out loud at his father's funeral from the cardboard the rabbi had produced from a ragged piece of plastic wrapper. Back then, he had recited it mechanically, not really referring to the words' meaning. He suddenly recalled the words 'an orphan's kaddish' as though they were right in front of him. *'Orphan? Really? From mother too? Could there be another white envelope hidden in one of those drawers?'*

He put this thought immediately out of his mind. Another memory flashed before his eyes now. One day, when he was four or five, his mother called him and put a mirror right in front of him. He immediately recognized his own blue eyes. "Just like your mother's," everyone always told him."

"Look at your left eye. Now, tell me what you see," Bonnie's mother asked him.

"Nothing."

"Under your pupil."

He looked closely and saw a tiny triangle. Its exquisite golden hue complimented the blue of his eyes.

"Now, look into my eye," she said as she removed the mirror.

Bonnie was taken aback. The same mark in his own left eye, he also saw in her eye, only hers was in her right eye.

'*I don't need to look for another envelope.*'

His body was too tired to struggle to remain awake. The hours went by. he couldn't help it. He had drunk nothing since yesterday evening except for several cups of coffee.

That evening, his sister Michal came by and helped him sort out more of the paperwork their mother had left. The way her brother looked scared her. She had never seen him like that before: grey-faced, white stubble and blank eyes.

She had always looked up to her older brother. Something made her suspect that her girlfriends who fawned over her weren't actually after her company but rather wanted to get to her attractive, clever brother through her. He was always highly sought after, by everyone. Very often, far too often in fact, she felt her life revolved around his. She took great pride at his achievements at school, in his social standing and his military career. Oh, how she wept in pride and excitement when he graduated officers' course. He was of course the best cadet. She and her mother were both concerned for him during his military service in Golani, a combat unit, so out of that concern, she had followed the daily Israeli defense news very closely, especially when they touched on military and security matters. When he was accepted to veterinary school, among the precious few out of the many who had applied, this seemed so natural, so typical and in line with his achievements up until then. *'Of course, he was admitted; if not him, who else?'*

Bonnie never looked like that. Michal had never seen him in such a state before that evening. This smart, handsome leader of men, renowned vet, acclaimed minister was lying on his couch, beaten and helpless. Bonnie was a wreck.

"What's wrong? Are you unwell? Shall I get you a thermometer?"

He didn't respond. *'Why is he lying there, all twisted in pain and blurry-eyed?'* Michal decided to take matters into her own hands. She turned the pot on, picked a fresh lemon right from the tree by the driveway, added three spoons of sugar, *'for energy'* and poured the tea. She laid a few pastries she had picked up at a stand near her home in town.

"You have to eat!"

By the time the tea got cold, she had cleared all the empty coffee cups around the house, retrieved the half empty bottle of whiskey and placed it back in the living room sideboard. Much to her relief, Bonnie sipped his tea and took a bite out of one of the pastries.

"Now, tell me what's wrong."

Bonnie's lips were moving, but she could hear no sound.

"Would you like another cup of tea?"

She could tell he was getting his strength back, so she waited.

"I do not have a father..." he said finally. Michal was taken aback. *'He's way worse than I thought.'*

"But, of course, you haven't got a father. He's been dead for three years now. Speaking of which, may I remind you the memorial service is in two weeks. We have to tell his friends. Those who are still alive, that is..."

"He isn't my dad."

Michal panicked. This vague memory of a distant relative of theirs came to mind. She recalled there was talk about someone she had never met being committed to a mental asylum out in the country for many years. *'It cannot be,'* she concluded after some debate. *'We had a stable family. Mom and Dad were sound people. As ordinary and upstanding as anyone can be. That can't be it. I must be need of some coffee too.'* She went over to the sink, cleaned one of the cups and made herself a black coffee without sugar.

"Would you please explain yourself?"

Bonnie pulled one hand from under his blanket and pointed at the small table by the standing lamp where the white envelope was.

"Read it."

Michal grabbed the envelope. Concerned. "What is this? Is this a letter from Mom? How did you come by it?!"

"I would like you to read it."

'That's the brother I know. He's back to his old, commanding self again. He's always ordering me about.' Nevertheless, her curiosity got the better of her. She found herself really anxious to know more. *'What personal matters were going on between Mom and Bonnie?'*

Michal opened the envelope and read the letter. This time, it was her turn to get herself a double scotch. But unaccustomed as she was to drink, it made her dizzy. Save for light white wine, and even that not very often, she barely ever had a stiff drink. She was in shock.

"What's this stuff about a biological dad?" She was talking out loud but was addressing more to herself than to Bonnie. "Mom had a fling with another man?! No way..."

Esther was an unassuming person. Her husband Avram and her two children were her entire world. She kept to herself, and the course of her life never went beyond her household. Her family was all she ever cared about. She did have the most amazing blue eyes but being complimented about that only made her self-consciousness. 'If it were up to Mom, she would have changed the color of her eyes. Maybe she would have preferred brown,' Michal had thought to herself.

The very thought that her mother, Esther Fiddlemann, could have had an extramarital affair gave Michal pause. Her entire life flashed before her eyes. 'It's true that Dad adored Bonnie. No wonder. He lived up to all his dreams. But all that was on the level. Very rational and conscious. Whatever emotions Dad had, they never ran very deep. Besides, he loved us equally. I never felt he loved either of us less or more. But what about Mom?'

Michal's mind was racing with all sorts of scenarios and flashing red question marks. One event from the distant past came to mind. 'Bonnie and I went for an evening walk in the village and got lost. How old was he? Maybe eight. I think I was four. Before we knew it, night had descended upon us. A few anxious hours went by before we heard Mom and Dad looking *for us with our neighbors. When we saw them from afar, we ran, arms stretched, crying... I'll never forget the look on Mom's face... how she ran and shouted joyfully. First, she turned towards Bonnie and gave him a great big hug. I felt cast aside, abandoned and dismayed. But then, Dad picked me up and hugged me. Mom's admiration for Bonnie was endless. But I feel the same way towards him, so why does this bother me so much?'* But then, Michal realized there was something else. She felt it all these years but couldn't put her finger on it. There was a kind of bond between mom and Bonnie. It went beyond kinship. A sort of fate that had brought them close, intimate. Some great secret. *'Now I realize it was one-sided. Mom kept it to herself all these years.'*

Michal began to feel sorry for her mother but also admire her at the same time. *'How could she bear such a burden all by herself all these years? She didn't share it with anyone. That much is clear. She certainly didn't tell Dad. He wouldn't have been able to take it. Was Mom being honest about it? Was she truthful? Was it fair of Mom to leave an envelope only for Bonnie? I wonder what really happened. What's the story with Mom and that guy? What a story! Well, at least Mom got to have a torrid affair... some fling that could have shattered her quiet little life. But didn't she ever share her secret with me? Would I have borne it? Where would my loyalty have stood? Had I known would I have told dad?'*

"So, Bonnie, what now?" Michal awoke from her thoughts and broke the hiatus of silence.

"I now realize why she showed me that triangle in my left eye."

'*Is he going mad on me again?*' "What triangle?" She asked him finally.

"The one in my eye," came his reply, in broken voice.

"What are you on about? What triangle? What eye?"

"It's a memory I've had for years. Once, when I was a child, Mom called me and showed me that I had a small triangular mark in my pupil, as did she. Only hers was in her right eye and mine was in my left eye. I never took it seriously as a child, but now, I am beginning to understand what she meant by it. She tried to get this message across, some idea I should bear in mind my entire life."

"What message?"

"That come what may, I should always bear in mind she's my Mom."

Bonnie and Michal went silent. Their strong kinship was nevertheless bothered by all sorts of questions and perplexing thoughts that hung in midair.

"So, does that make you my stepbrother?" Michal tried to break the silence with a smile.

"Never mind that, you and I are fine. But to think I had a stepdad all these years, and that Mom hid the truth from all of us. She and her triangle. Could it be that Avram was none the wiser?"

"Don't call him Avram. He's your dad!"

"He is not!"

Saying this was like a ton of bricks falling on top of him. '*If he isn't my dad, then who is? What do I do next?*'

"What do we do next?" He heard Michal asking him.

All of the sudden, Bonnie felt energized. He rose up, threw

his blanket aside, poured himself some scotch and heard himself telling Michal the following: "I am going to look for my father."

Chapter Sixteen

The government's regular Sunday meeting stretched longer. "I would like ten minutes of your time, please," Bonnie asked the prime minister at the end of the meeting.

"That's about all I can spare," the prime minister replied. "I've got a very busy schedule." He directed Bonnie into his office, which was next to the government's meeting room.

"What's this about? Oh, but first, please allow me to offer my condolences on the death of your mother. I couldn't make it to the funeral. You know, pressing state business."

"Thank you, prime minister. The issue I would like to put to you does have something to do with my mother's passing. In the week that followed her funeral, I discovered something that shook me to the core. I stumbled on the fact that the person whom I thought of as my dad my entire life was, in fact, not my biological father."

"That's truly amazing," the prime minister peered above his stack of paperwork. This was the first time he looked at Bonnie since they had sat down. "Other than offer you my sympathy, what more can I do to help you?"

"That's the thing. When I joined the special cabinet for

diplomatic and security affairs, I filled out all sorts of forms for my security clearance. I put my father's name, but since then, as I've told you, it has turned out he wasn't my actual father, so I thought it best to inform you of this."

"This is a truly curious turn of events. In my ten-year tenure as prime minister, I have yet to come across any similar situation. Let me look into it."

And thus, their meeting adjourned.

***

Israel's security service consists of several sections: The Operational Branch, the Arab Branch, the Counterintelligence Branch and the Administrative Branch, which consists, inter alia, of personnel and logistics. The 'service' is tasked with conducting security clearance and assessments concerning top classified positions in the civil service, defense industries and other bodies whose very function necessitates a security clearance.

This inquiry probed quite deeply and was also extensive, including background checks on the candidate's family. A large part of the probe relied on the details the candidates themselves filled out in the questionnaire forms prior to their security checkup.

***

Once a week, Israel's prime minister has regular separate meetings with the IDF chief of staff, the head of Mossad and the head of Israel's General Security Service GSS). These meetings consist of reports and updates provided by these figures and feature discussions of various topics under their respective purviews and responsibilities within the framework of Israel's security array.

At the end of his regular weekly meeting with the head of GSS, the prime minister addressed the following issue. "There's another matter I would like to discuss with you. Minister Binyamin Pladot asked to speak with me. He told me that a certain detail he filled in upon his appointment as minister turns out to have been incorrect. He never meant to deceive anyone, it's just that his circumstances have made a surprising turn."

"Prime minister, would you care to explain regarding what this is?"

"Certainly. It has emerged that the details the minister gave on his security questionnaire about his father were incorrect. He has since discovered he has a different father, who is in fact his biological father. The question I would like to put to you is as follows, does this new fact have any security implications? To make matters all the more complicated, the minister does not know who his biological father is."

"Yes, we do have a problem, and a serious one at that," the GSS chief replied, as befitting the practical and thorough man that he was. "We know, based on many years' worth of experience, that the personal background of any person's parents plays a major role, it makes an essential impact on the child. We're talking here not merely about a minister who is part of your security cabinet, but who is also a member of your select subcommittee on intelligence and terror within the security cabinet. Even when you appointed him to the subcommittee, I told you I wasn't too thrilled to have a minister of science added to the cabinet. It isn't enough to have a former career as an officer. It isn't even enough to be a veterinarian to merit being made a member of our most sensitive committees.

"We've already discussed this," replied the prime minister. "Luckily for you, you only have to deal with matters of security, whereas I have to deal with political matters on top of that. His appointment to the cabinet and to the subcommittee is the outcome of a coalition agreement without which I would not have succeeded in forming a government, and then I would not have been your prime minister. Question is, what should we do about it now?"

"I need three months to look into it."

The prime minister was a busy man. He would always peruse the dozens of documents in front of him during meetings and divide his time between them and the person he was speaking with. Whenever he would raise his head to look at his interlocutor, that was a clear indication of the importance of the issue they were discussing. The prime minister looked up from his paperwork. "What do I do in the meantime?"

"I must ask that you do not include him in the meetings, at least do not invite him to the subcommittee's meetings."

"You are wreaking havoc on my government. How can I refuse him?"

"You're the politician. If I were you, I simply would not issue the invitations to the meetings. He doesn't need to be aware of each and every meeting that's taking place."

"Sometimes it takes more luck than brains," the prime minister replied. "Minister Pladot has asked me for a leave of absence for three months, which I granted. So, you have the time you have asked for. I await your account."

Chapter Seventeen

Professor Shimoni entered his office, gave Tzila, his faithful secretary, the box of chocolates he remembered to get her at the duty free in Rio, gave her a fleeting kiss on the cheek, asked her casually how she was doing and inquired after her family. Then, he proceeded to his office and took his seat at his executive armchair.

"So how was Rio?" Tzila asked him.

"Excellent," he replied. "They succeeded in surprising me. They gave me an award for my contribution to the field."

Prof. Shimoni was one of the world's top geneticists. Apart from chairing the Genetics Department at Tel Aviv University, in addition to his highly prestigious position at Refu'ah Shlema, Tel Aviv's leading hospital, he was also a much sought-after lecturer, whose talks attracted crowds worldwide. His lecture at the University of Rio de Janeiro, entitled, 'The struggle between hereditary and the environment,' sold out within three days of publication. The professor had kindly turned down the university's request that he add two more lectures.

His paperwork was piled up on his desk on top of numerous emails. Tzila knew that on his flights, the professor always flew business; he would rather read a good book or listen to a soothing concert rather than go over dull emails. "That's my 'time alone', the only quality momentary lapse I have by myself, and I will not have it spoiled with work," he'd always tell her.

Whenever a highly urgent case would come up while he was abroad, and there were precious few of those, Tzila did allow herself to text him, knowing full well the sort of grimace on the other side of the line as, abhorring the intervention, he checked them.

Right at the top of the emails that had accumulated during his six-day absence, the professor noticed this message, highlighted in red: "the head of Israel's GSS requests an urgent meeting."

"What could I have possibly done?" Prof. Shimoni asked his secretary over the private line.

"I have no idea what they've got you for, but about the meeting, I told them that wasn't possible, since you're due in Oxford in two days' time. Nevertheless, they told me the matter was paramount and urgent and that the meeting could not be delayed. When I asked them what this was about, they said they would rather speak with you privately."

"So, what do I do, Tzila?" He knew he could always count on her good advice.

"Security always comes first. I arranged with the GSS's office that they come pick you up for the meeting scheduled for tomorrow at eight pm They wouldn't even tell me where it's at."

"What do I tell Rina? She'll murder me. I promised her we'd go to dinner tomorrow."

"Leave your wife to me. I know how to soften her up."

The next day, a limousine with dark windows was waiting for Prof. Shimoni outside the hospital at eight that evening. He produced his ID, and they let him in the back seat. He managed to catch a glimpse of the bridge as they were heading north, and surmised they had crossed the Yarkon River, just north of central Tel Aviv. Shortly thereafter, they reached a large stone edifice whose steel gates opened in the front to let them in. The car entered an underground parking and stopped right at the entrance to the elevator. The driver asked the professor to accompany him, and, after he had punched in a secret code, the driver pushed the button that sent it up. As they left it, Prof. Shimoni saw a spacious lobby featuring leather armchairs. He did spot artwork by modern Israeli painters. '*Whoever had them hang here sure knows about art,*' he told himself.

As much as he tried to play aloof, he was nevertheless excited about meeting the chief of what was considered to be the world's best intelligence organization.

"The head of the service is expecting you." The secretary led him into a spacious, modestly, albeit tastefully, decorated office, with paintings and other works of art by Israeli artists on the walls and at corners of the room.

The GSS chief relished the professor's keen interest in his collection of Israeli art. "Hello, professor."

He was of average height, and his hair was thick and black. '*He has brown eyes,*' Prof. Shimoni noted to himself. He also noticed when the chief rose from his chair to greet him that he wore black pants and a white shirt. When they shook hands, the professor was impressed by the sense of power and authority the chief instilled.

"I noticed you're an art connoisseur, so let me tell you a nice story. What's the difference between those who know art and those who are just full of airs?" The professor asked.

The GSS chief had no answer.

"The boors keep mentioning Tchaikovsky, but they have yet to see a single painting of his..."

The head of the GSS burst out laughing wholeheartedly, unveiling two rows of pearly white teeth.

'*Now I know he didn't invite me over because I had met some Iranian guy,*' the professor smiled to himself.

"It's time I introduced myself. My name is Yossi. I know you're a busy man. You have a six am flight to London to catch, but a question of national importance has come up, and I require your opinion."

"I would do anything for our country's security," sighed the professor. "How can I help you guys?"

"We require your expert opinion: what shapes someone's personality more, their environment or their genetics?"

Prof. Shimoni was about to faint, and surely would have, had he not pulled himself together quickly and helped himself to a glass of water right in front of him. '*The head of GSS, one of the world's most powerful organizations, is asking me about genetics?*' The professor was expecting to be asked about the chance encounter he had had with a member of the Iranian delegation to the Lisbon convention. He also expected he might have to answer a few questions about the project he had in the works with a team of scientists from Egypt. '*Could it be that Israel is doing so well security-wise that its defense chiefs have the luxury to pursue genetic and academic studies?'*

The head of Israel's GSS noticed his guest's uneasiness, "Don't worry, I am not about to embark on genetic research. We are, however, faced with a grave matter of security and we are in dire need of answers. I wish I could tell you more, but I can't. Surely you understand. Nevertheless, your assistance may prove vital, so let's proceed."

Prof. Shimoni cleared his throat. He felt the nation's security was resting on his shoulders. "Well, it's not a simple question. It's quite complex. The answer is open-ended. The current prevailing assumption is that genetics and environment alike have a similar impact on the way people conduct themselves. Nevertheless, this opinion is in dispute. A few years ago, a team of psychologists from the University of Minnesota published a study that gained a great deal of attention worldwide. They compared pairs of *identical* twins who grew up in two separate families with pairs of *regular* twins who grew up together in the same family. The results of the study showed that the identical twins had similar personality traits compared with the pairs of twins who had grown up together in the same family. The conclusion they'd reached was that the impact of genetics is greater than that of the environment. This study was met with a great deal of criticism. One of the claims was that it was based on curious statistic data and could not be regarded as an established study with any statistical significance."

"And what is your own opinion?"

"I am more inclined to think there is some correlation

between environmental and genetic impact on one's personality. That's what I tell my students."

"Let's move, for a moment, from the academic level to practical reality," the chief of GSS said. "What personality traits that originate in genetics can you attribute to someone?"

"I can cite several examples," replied Prof. Shimoni, "but again, let us bear in mind, by way of caution, that these are generalizations rather than compelling formulae we can live by. For instance, personal attributes such as an aggressive nature or the tendency to take risks are inherently genetic rather than environmental. It is true that even a person with a calm disposition can on occasion 'lose it,' as they say, but this is extraordinary rather than the norm. Even a hesitant person may come to a decision that comprises a major element of risk. Nevertheless, this decision is unusual. It does not contradict the fact that, essentially, this person tends to avoid risks on a regular basis."

"How interesting. Do you have any more examples for me?"

"My lectures usually take three hours, whereas I realize I only have fifteen minutes, so let me cite one other example to illustrate my point. Let's take fear. Being a coward is a consequence of genetics. But that said, this does not mean that environment cannot cause any person, even someone who is not a coward, to fear something. We have to make the distinction between this person's psychological element, which comprises, among other aspects, fear, and this person's conduct, which is driven by impacts from the environment."

"You've been most helpful, my dear professor. Thank you for your assistance. The driver is waiting for you at the entrance."

Chapter Eighteen

Bonnie, or "Minister Pladot", as the prime minister's secretaries called him, though they also snickered that 'his excellency the minister' was younger than some of them, felt encouraged as he left the prime minister. '*At least the powers that be now know that Avram Fiddlemann was not my real father and that I put those details in that questionnaire upon taking office quite innocently,*' he thought to himself as he left.

Minister Pladot informed the government secretary he was leaving on a three-month leave and proceeded to the formal apartment issued him by the government and took a few necessary items. Then, he was driven to his own house, where he told his chauffeur that he might leave, and he would call him if and when he would have need of him.

'*What shall I do next?*'

Bonnie sat in his comfy chair on the veranda, overlooking the Gilboa Mountains and tried to figure out his next move. '*Well, one option is for sure out of the question. I will not be left hanging. I cannot abide the doubts and lingering questions. That's not even an option. Besides, that's not what mother's will was all about,*' he told himself. '*Had she wanted me to keep living a lie, she would not have written me that letter. No doubt about it, she wanted me to have the freedom to decide for myself.*

He then thought to himself, '*even when I was four, when my mother Estée showed me that triangle in our respective eyes, she planned on writing that letter. Even then, she wanted me to know the full truth and to be sure this concerned my biological father, and that I would not doubt she was my biological mother. How do I begin my search?*'

The first name that popped up in his mind was Ofer Ben Ari. They were friends since elementary school. He recently had made headlines as the attorney who had devoted himself to the much debated affair from the late 1940's and early 1950's, when, allegedly, babies and very young children of Yemenite descent were forcibly, sometimes secretly, taken by the authorities and given to families of European descent, without the biological parents' knowledge or consent.

Prior to what has come to be known as 'the Yemenite Children Affair,' in 1949, the government of Israel decided to have as many Jews as possible brought over from Yemen. Israel had just been founded in May 1948. Thanks to a truly heroic feat, some fifty thousand Yemenite Jews immigrated to the newly formed state. Prior to their immigration, they were concentrated in transit camps from which they were flown over to Israel; sometimes, over one thousand were flown in one night.

Among the immigrants were numerous sickly babies and children. They were admitted to hospital on arrival, where some did die without any proper documentation. Years later, a great deal of effort went into locating records and the surviving children, who in the meantime had grown up and disappeared without a trace. Many individuals and organizations made it their mission to get to the bottom of what happened to the children. One of them was Attorney Ofer Ben Ari. Bonnie decided he was the man to turn to, all the more so as they were boyhood friends.

Once they got through the courtesy of exchanging pleasantries, as befitting longtime friends who hadn't met for many years, and after Bonnie had reminded his attorney and friend of his commitment to attorney-client privilege, which was unnecessary as Attorney Ben Ari was a professional, he decided to tell him the full, highly provocative story.

"So, what is it you want from me?" Attorney Ben Ari got right down to business.

"I have a personal matter that weighs on me very heavily. I am trying to cope with it. I could have received assistance from various authorities, which I am sure would gladly come to my aid. Nevertheless, since this matter is highly sensitive, and since I wish to resolve it as discreetly as possible, I decided to come to you both as a friend and as a lawyer bound by attorney-client privilege.

"I am glad you trust me so deeply," the attorney replied, "and I hope to justify your trust. Now, tell me what this is about, and we'll see how we may proceed from there."

Attorney Ben Ari was sitting in his luxurious offices on the nineteenth floor of an office tower in Ramat Gan, just outside Tel Aviv. He was looking, part amused, part puzzled, at his boyhood friend, the esteemed minister, as Bonnie, obviously made anxious by his situation, was choosing his words very carefully. This excited the attorney's curiosity, as well. '*How did it come about that of all the capable students in our class, it was he who had become an esteemed minister, Bonnie here, a real celebrity?*' he wondered to himself.

"So, what's this all about, Bonnie?"

"You gained a real expertise in locating missing persons and getting families back together, so I'm asking your help in finding my biological father," Bonnie replied and told him the gist of it.

"So, what do we have here?" Attorney Ben Ari did his best to recover from the minister's surprising story. "In fact, we have got practically nothing to go on. Aside from your mother's letter, which, for the sake of the matter we shall regard as a credible source, we have nothing. Do you have any thread we can use to pursue this further and conduct an inquiry?"

"I haven't got anything else, but I do remember that in the Yemenite Children Affair, you succeeded in establishing a biological connection between people using a DNA test."

"That's true. We used an app developed here in Israel to find a match between one of the deceased children and one of the families that was looking for their missing child. But this case is nothing like yours. They produced a DNA sample from the remains they found in a certain grave and found a match with a living family member who was one of the persons who sought my help. But in your case, we've got one DNA-donor, whereas we require two donors in order to establish a genetic connection between two people."

"So, what do we do? Doesn't Israel have a genetic bank with which I can run a test to compare a sample with my own DNA?"

"Well, in Israel, as opposed to certain other countries, a commercial company is prohibited from being in possession of a DNA bank, as important as such a bank indeed is. Israeli Police and several hospitals do have a DNA bank, but I am not sure they'll give us access."

"So, what's our next step?"

"Give me two weeks, Bonnie, and then I'll be able to report to you whether we can use the police bank or the hospitals' DNA banks."

***

Two weeks went by, and the minister and the attorney had another meeting.

"What news do you have for me?"

"None, I'm afraid. The police turned my request down, claiming their DNA bank is strictly for police investigations, so access cannot be allowed outside the police. The hospitals simply gave me the runaround and rambled something about medical confidentiality."

"Thank you so much for your assistance, my dear attorney. I must thank you for waving your fee as well. I'll get back to you as soon as I have something new."

***

At the meeting held at the headquarters of Israeli police in Jerusalem, the general manager of Israel's Internal Security ministry pulled all the stops in honor of the Minister of

Science. No doubt being approached directly by the Minister of Internal Security had its desired impact. Moreover, it was hinted to the general manager that this was concerning a security matter.

"The Department of Forensics is at our basement floor. They have their instructions concerning your request."

The head of the Forensics Branch was waiting for the minister in person and led him to the lab, where a young lab attendant gave him a cotton swab akin to a Q-tip. She asked him to leave an ample amount of saliva on the swab, which she then inserted into a hermetically closed plastic-wrap right after she wrote his donor ID number and other personal details. The lab attendant then told Bonnie the results of the test would arrive within a few days and promised to call the moment they did.

The head of Forensics called the minister several days later.

"Hello, minister. I wanted to call you and tell you in person. I actually do not know how to put it, as I am in the dark as to what you might expect, but the results of your DNA test came out negative."

"What does that mean?" The honorable minister asked, nervously.

"It means there's no match between the sample you've given us and the samples on record in the police's DNA bank."

***

The Director General of the Ministry of Health was more reserved. "Look, minister, in Israel, the hospitals operate independently of the Health Ministry. They don't like it when we bureaucrats meddle in medical matters."

"But this is not a medical matter," Bonnie replied. "This is an administrative issue, a procedural matter. Besides, let's not forget they do depend on the Ministry as far as budgets are concerned."

The director general grimaced. "First of all, access to bio-data banks is a strictly medical matter. Secondly, if you are alluding to pressuring them for assistance by bringing up the matter of budgets, forget it. One Deputy Minister already went that road and it did not end well. Anyway, let me see what I can do to help you."

Ten days later, the Director General of the Ministry of Health was on the phone again.

"Just as I thought, the hospitals are not too keen to collaborate. Apart from that, we have a practical issue. Turns out the hospitals have a tissue bank rather than a DNA bank. Producing DNA out of these tissue samples is an expensive process, and it serves no medical purpose. In certain sporadic cases, when there is a specific requirement for DNA, they do derive the DNA from the relevant sample. The bottom line is this: the hospitals do not have the technical capacity to draw the comparison you've requested."

***

The minister sat on the veranda in his comfortable chair and wondered what to do next. '*At least my father never got into trouble with the police.'* He tried to calm himself, realizing this was the first time he had referred to the mysterious figure as 'my father.' *'But that's hardly comforting,'* he told himself. *'The police's DNA has hundreds of thousands of individual samples, but there are millions more worldwide.'*

Bonnie went back to his parents' bedroom, where he has not been since he had completed going over his mother's papers. He combed her school-day diaries. *'That's a dead end,'* he told himself. *'Nothing but memorabilia from her youth.'* He found the office envelope bearing his mother's familiar handwriting. It said, "Personal letters." That was the envelope he and Michal had found in the dresser's bottom drawer. The disappointment he and his sister felt when they discovered the envelope was empty had gotten more intense since. *'What did it contain? Why did she keep those letters? And if she did keep them, why did she hide them? And when? So, what did she do with them?'* It was clear to Bonnie the letters held the solution to the questions that were engulfing him, but they were gone.

He went over to the dresser, picked it up and laid it on the sofa, in search of secret compartments. He pulled the drawers out and took the bottom apart. Nothing. He removed the back panel and checked the sides. Still nothing. Bonnie returned to his favorite chair, disappointed and exhausted. Right before he dozed off, he had this dim, flickering memory. He got up, went over to his own house, entered the laundry room, which was adjacent to the bathroom, where he found a pile of dirty clothes. He pulled his plaid shirt, which had been waiting a long time to go in the washer, out of the pile and looked through his pocket. *'Got it.'*

It was that same used envelope he had picked up from his mother's bedroom floor when he had put the papers together. Absent-minded as he had been at the time, he had inadvertently put a few papers in it without fully grasping their contents. He pulled out a few documents. The top paper had a copy of the following telegram:

"Please be so kind as to provide the details of the young man who was hospitalized in your ward on October 17th after a car accident on the road from Sithonia to Thessaloniki. I would like to pass on to him a personal item he forgot with me."

The letter, which was addressed to Hypocratio Hospital, Thessaloniki, bore the date 22 October 1979.

It was as though Bonnie was struck by lightning. He was covered in cold sweat and on the verge of fainting. He picked up the telephone in a trembling hand and called Michal, his sister.

"I am coming to see you!"

"Is something the matter?" Michal wasn't accustomed to spontaneous visits from Bonnie, let alone on a regular weekday afternoon.

"Yes! I'll tell you when I get there."

"But I am in the middle of my errands. Besides, I hear on the radio there are huge traffic jams. I was thinking of coming to see you anyway tomorrow evening. Can we put it off until then?"

"No. We have to meet," he slammed the receiver and hung up.

Just as his sister had warned him, Bonnie reached her

house, usually a drive of about half an hour from his home, only after an hour and twenty minutes. He was all hot and bothered coming in. Before he even sat down on the chair Michal offered him, he exclaimed, "I'm sure Mom had an affair in Thessaloniki."

"Are you trying to be funny? What will you tell me next? That Mom was the world champion in the women's 100-metre dash?"

"Here. Read this," he tossed the letter at her.

Michal read it. "I don't see what this means..."

"What don't you get? I was borne in June 1980."

"Wow!" That was the only word Michal was able to utter.

"I just don't see what Mom has to do with Thessaloniki," he said.

Michal was wrapped in thought. "Listen, many years ago, I got a letter from some woman in Thessaloniki. She asked about Mom and told me she was a distant cousin of hers. She also wrote that she was one of the guests at Mom and Dad's wedding, but unfortunately, Mom cut off all ties with her and never answered any of her letters. When I told Mom about the letter I had received from this woman, Mom told me she was a pest. That was the precise word Mom used, 'pest.'"

"Do you happen to have this letter?" Bonnie asked nervously.

"Why would I? I'm not in the habit of hanging on to letters that aren't important. But hang on."

Michal went over to her study and came back a few minutes later with an envelope marked 'Condolence telegrams – Dad.' She produced several of them from the envelope.

"Here. Got it!"

The telegram was brief:

"So sorry for your loss, may Avram rest in peace." The telegram had the sender's name: Claudia Panov, 46 Demetrius St., Thessaloniki.

"She didn't send a letter of condolence about Mom. I don't even think she knows Mom's dead."

Bonnie snatched the letter.

"What are you going to do with it?" she asked him.

"What do you think? I'm going to see her!"

"But Bonnie, you have to bear in mind that Mom treated her unkindly. Moreover, you mustn't forget that this Claudia person is no longer a young woman..."

Bonnie's drive back to his home in the village took precisely thirty minutes.

Chapter Nineteen

Claudia was waiting for Bonnie in her beautiful apartment overlooking Hagios Demetrios (the Church of Saint Demetrius) in the center of Thessaloniki. She was both expectant and wary ahead of the meeting, which Bonnie had established a few days earlier. He had called her, explained who he was and told her he had received her phone number from the Greek consulate in Jerusalem.

"How is Esther doing?" she asked Bonnie on the phone.

"She died about a month ago," he replied. He felt she was taken aback at this. He could almost feel the tears running down her cheeks.

"Yes, we're all in tears," he added. "I would very much like to see you."

She was excited to invite him over to her home and set the meeting for the following week.

He was now standing at her doorstep, and after the customary greeting and hello kiss, he handed her the gift he had brought over from Israel, a decorated wooden box with a bottle of oil from the Galilee, a wine bottle from the Golan and a box of the choicest medjool dates from Israel's Arava district, south of the Dead Sea.

"Tell me how she died." Claudia asked Bonnie. "She was so young... Oh, how I've missed her,"

"That terrible illness. Fortunately, it was only a short time from the moment the discovered she had it until she died. Mother didn't suffer a whole lot and she did die with her family at her bedside. She died three years after burying her husband."

The tears from Claudia's eyes made their wet way down the still beautiful face of a sixty-five-year-old woman.

"What's new with you? And with your sister? You look so much like your mother..."

While omitting his public career, Bonnie gave her a short summary of the developments in the family's life. "And how are you?" he inquired politely.

"I used to work at a travel agency until I retired a few years ago. Sadly, I never got to start a family of my own," she replied in a tone of acceptance. "But my greatest sorrow has been the estrangement between your mother, Esther, and myself."

All the time leading up to the meeting, Bonnie had had a hard time deciding how to navigate his meeting with Claudia to touch on the topics he was curious about. "Please tell me, what happened between you two"

"Your mother never told you? We are cousins. We were very good friends and kept in touch all those years. I even came to her wedding with Avram, which was the happiest occasion in my entire life."

"Did you see her since the wedding?"

"No, and this is one of the greatest mysteries of my life. After the wedding, I sent her a letter, thanking her for the wedding invitation and telling how happy Celia and I were at her wedding, but she never answered my letter. In fact, she never made any contact after her wedding."

"Who is Celia?"

"She was my best friend. The both of us threw your mother a surprise celebration right before she married. It was quite a feast. Unfortunately, poor Celia also died a few years ago."

"Where did this surprise celebration take place?"

"At the most beautiful place on earth, on Sithonia Peninsula, a two hour-drive from Thessaloniki." The memories overwhelmed Claudia, and she began crying again.

Bonnie tensed. "Do you remember when this party took place?"

"The only thing I remember is that it took place about a month prior to the wedding."

"Who attended the party?"

"What do you mean, who? You mother, Celia and I," Claudia was becoming intrigued. "Why are you asking me all these questions? Don't worry, there wasn't any other guest there. It was a bachelorette party... your mother would never have agreed to have more company, certainly not other men... we were naïve back then – and your mother even more than Celia or me. I can promise you she would never let any man lay a finger on her before her marriage."

"What do you recall about the party?" Bonnie was intrigued.

"I remember everything, even what each of us was wearing. I had this white dress with an embroidered pattern. It's still hanging in my closet. Every time I feel sad, I put it on, and would you believe it? I can still fit into it. My figure hasn't changed since those days. Would you like to see?"

Bonnie couldn't fully realize whether it was the dress she wanted to show him or her figure.

"Poor Celia had a red blouse open at the belly and short black pants. She always thought she had nice legs and nice breasts, but your mother was a real knockout... She had this Arab garb on, whatchamacallit?"

"You mean, a galabia?" Bonnie played his part in the conversation that was unfolding to be most amusing.

"Yes, that's it, galabia," Claudia recalled. "She had a terrific figure, your mother. May she forgive me, but I do believe she wore it without a bra. I can also tell you what fabulous dishes we feasted on. Maria prepared them for us..."

Before she got into all the evening cuisine, and before she remembered she had meant to show him something, Bonnie excused himself and said he had to go, or he'd miss his flight. Before he took his leave, he promised to keep in touch, and asked her, seemingly just out of curiosity, "By the way, have you ever heard of the Hypocratio Hospital?"

"Sure, it's the largest hospital here in Thessaloniki. I did my CT there only last week. Nothing serious, just a pain in my back. Why do you ask? You're not feeling well?"

"Oh, no, just a favor for a friend."

Bonnie and Claudia parted with a hug and a kiss.

***

Bonnie sat in the office belonging to the manager of 'Privat Investigos,' a detective agency, right at the heart of

Thessaloniki's business district.

"How may I help you?" the manager asked him.

"I am looking for the details of a seventeen-year-old guy who was hospitalized in Hypocratio Hospital on 17 October 1979 after a car accident."

"Do you have any more details about him?"

"No, but I would like you to limit your investigation strictly to a young man."

"Fine," replied the manager. "But we are talking about many years ago. That's a lot of work. Besides, there will be plenty of expenses along the way. It will cost you two thousand dollars."

"Agreed, but that is only part of the job. If you do track down the person I am looking for, we will proceed to the second part of the job. I am returning to Israel later today, and I await your phone call. I would like to add this case is sensitive, security-wise, so I need your written commitment to absolute confidentiality."

"That was clear from the start," the investigator replied. "I have a statement ready for my signature right away."

***

The call from the detective agency came two days later. "I think I've got the goods for you. My investigation uncovered that on 17 October 1979, a young man was admitted to the hospital after he sustained injuries due to a car accident on the road between Sithonia and Thessaloniki. There weren't many accidents in that area on that day, so according to the information you've given me, I think we have the right guy.

He would be nineteen, the only person driving. He was taken to Hypocratio Hospital that morning. When he was admitted to the emergency room, they found a raptured spleen, three broken ribs and a few additional injuries. He was rushed to surgery, was operated on, and according to his patient's chart, the surgery was over without any complications. I am also reading from the chart that he was hospitalized for five days, after which he was discharged in good condition pending further observation."

"What else does the medical record tell you?" Bonnie asked.

"Hang on, let's see. I can see here they made a histological test. I don't know what that means. In any case, the results of the histology show 'no suspicious findings,' that's what it says."

"Sounds interesting, but you haven't given me any details concerning the patient himself!" Bonnie was getting impatient.

"There's a problem. The patient's name has been erased. I cannot make it out. What I can tell you is that the patient's serial number is 8200/79."

"Thank you," Bonnie told him. "I'll call you as soon as possible."

The information he received from the investigation agency caused Bonnie's thoughts to spin very fast. '*Is this 8200 person his own life's mystery? Is he the reason his mother contacted the hospital? Why did they erase his name from the medical chart? Was this some accident? Was it done intentionally? And what should my next move be?* He was overcome with different emotions. On the one hand, he felt relieved for finding the first clues on his winding way to discover the truth. On the other, he was concerned and fearful of the secrets this truth was hiding.

***

"Now, let's proceed to the second stage," Bonnie approached the investigation agency's manager the following day.

"What do you mean?" the investigator from Thessaloniki asked.

"In the patient's medical chart, which you've read out to me, it was noted they performed a histology. It's important for me to receive the sample they conducted this test on."

"What are you talking about?! They ran this test so many years ago!" the investigator replied.

"I told you this was a special test," Bonnie replied calmly. "I need you to get me this sample. Prove to me you do indeed deserve to be called the finest investigation agency in the whole of Greece."

The manager smiled and grinned in satisfaction. "Let me check. I'll get back to you as soon as possible."

Chapter Twenty

The archive of the Hypocratio Hospital occupied the entire basement floor. Half of the archive consisted of an administrative library containing dozens of thousands of documents of medical records taken from the thousands of employee files pertaining to those who worked and were still working there. The other half of the hospital archive was entirely medical, chiefly devoted to the pathology department.

According to hospital guidelines, each and every sample from any histology carried out at the hospital had to be preserved in the archive. Accordingly, a small sample was taken from each tested tissue. This sample was frozen and preserved in a bloc of paraffin. These blocs with the tissues were stored in the archive. Each was assigned a serial number, and a card was kept with the details of each person the tissue was taken from.

Whenever the need arose to extract DNA, the relevant paraffin bloc was pulled out according to the serial number from the drawer it was stored in. A slice consisting of the donor's tissue would then be taken from the bloc to a lab where it was tested. At one time, the hospital put forth the idea to complete each procedure involving tissue testing by extracting DNA, but upon further inspection, as well as based on the procedures in other hospitals worldwide, powers that be at the hospital came to the conclusion that extracting DNA would be unnecessary. Aside from the cost, it was deemed useless, since only a small percentage of the tissue preserved in the paraffin bloc were actually ever used as a source of DNA. Likewise, the suggestion to upload the pathological findings to a computer was rejected on budgetary grounds, in the hope of better, more affluent times.

The keeper of the myriad items in the archive was Maya, the hospital's longest-serving secretary, a woman without an age, who seemed to have been working there since the beginning of time. Though her date of retirement had long since passed, she stayed on. "She is irreplaceable," the archive manager had told the hospital's management. Maya, so the rumors claimed, was capable of locating, blindfolded, any bloc of paraffin of the thousands there. She was also highly skilled in handling the rolodex with the test notes in the most precise and intelligent way. Everyone recognized and acknowledged the importance of her work and the grave responsibility she had, for any mistake in record keeping or identification might prove calamitous.

Maya had yet another trait in her favor. She was the aunt of Eleus, the manager of Privat Investigos investigation agency.

***

The phone call from her nephew Eleus completely caught

Maya by surprise. They haven't been in contact for years, more than twenty, in fact, ever since the row she had had with her sister, Eleus's mother, over the small olive grove at the foot of Mt. Olympus, bequeathed to both sisters by their father.

And after all this time, Eleus appeared in Maya's apartment, all smiles and pleasantries, with a bottle of her favorite kind of ouzo.

"What brings you to me?" She asked, puzzled. Deep down, she was glad for his visit. *'For a long time now, I've been thinking of mending fences with her... it's high time two sisters, each past sixty, would spend their golden years together.'*

"I heard you were about to finally retire," Eleus said, "So I thought of throwing you a small party and taking the opportunity of finally patching things up between you and Mom. She's always telling me how much she misses you."

The coast was clear. "I miss your Mom too. I've completely forgotten why we aren't talking anymore..." Maya opened the bottle of ouzo and one glass after another with her nephew. They spoke and did a lot of catching up after all those years of estrangement.

After her third glass, well, maybe her fourth, and once they had finalized all the details concerning Maya's retirement party, Eleus said, "I represent an English research fund that carries out tests on the ability of human tissues to withstand the test of time. I think you might be able to help me with this."

"What can I do to help?" She asked, elated.

"The fund people told me the hospital has old tissue that might help their research. They can contact the hospital through the usual channels, but this would take a long time, so I promised them I would look into the possibility of shortening the timetable."

"So, what do you want from me?"

"Only one little thing: two or three old samples of tissue."

"You know that tissues cannot be taken out just like that."

"Of course, I know it's not allowed. But then again, these are old samples no one needs, and they are required for medical research as it is."

"Are you sure that's what they are required for?"

"Dead sure. Have I ever lied to you?"

"Oh, no," Maya quickly replied, forgetting she and Eleus haven't spoken in over twenty years. "But what type of tissue are we talking about?"

"Don't worry, in fact, all I need is one sample. I'll leave you the serial number I need. Besides, I would like to tell you this fund is very generous. I shall gladly give you one thousand dollars out of the fee they're paying me."

The fifth glass of ouzo concluded the jovial, liberating meeting. Eleus left her a note with the serial number of the test, kissed her on the cheek and agreed with her that he would come for the sample in three days' time.

***

The investigator called Bonnie the very same day. "I've got good news for you. I believe I can get you the goods, but you have to realize this is a very complex operation, involving a great deal of effort and payoffs to all sorts of elements I cannot specify."

"Well done," Bonnie replied. "I'm impressed. How much?"

"Ten thousand dollars."

"Go for it."

***

"I've found a science convention entitled 'Cannabis – blessing or curse?'" the office manager told her minister. "It takes place within a week in Vienna. Registration did close a few weeks ago, but the managers told me they could always find room for Israel's Minister of Science, as our country is a world leader in cannabis research."

"Works for me. Make the necessary arrangements."

The manager of the ministry's office reported to the government secretary on the Science Minister's short visit to Vienna. Accordingly, El Al Israel Airlines reserved the minister a good seat in business class, and Israel's embassy in Vienna booked him a junior suite at the luxury Carlton Hotel in the center of town for a few days.

Prior to his flight, Bonnie discreetly received, from a friend who was a doctor, the details of an opulent clinic on Kundera Strasse at the city's center. This clinic's specialty was in testing and examining DNA samples. Renowned for exacting large fees for its services, the clinic was highly regarded for its strict adherence to discretion. The clinic even allowed certain clients who requested it to have the tests made under a code name, without the subject having to leave any identifying features.

As soon as the opening lecture of the convention ended, Bonnie rushed over to the clinic to keep the appointment he had arranged in advance. He settled the matter of payment and had a file opened under a code name. Bonnie proceeded to the examination room, where samples of his blood and saliva were taken. At the end of the medical procedure, he arranged with the clinic's management that the results would be sent over to Israel via a special courier within 48 hours once the tissue was received and matched with the saliva and blood samples he had given.

After his visit to the clinic, Bonnie returned to the convention hall to listen to the dreariest lecture by an Indian scientist on India's own cannabis research. At the end of the lecture, Bonnie rushed back to his suite to make a phone call, during which Eleus told him the tissue would arrive soon, along with two additional samples by way of a bonus.

"You can sell the two extra samples for ten thousand dollars each to other suckers," Bonnie told him. "Deliver my sample to Vienna, to the address and file number I'll provide immediately."

***

"I have the goods," Eleus reported the following day. "As soon as you transfer my fee to the bank account I shall give you, I'll send the sample to Vienna."

The following day, Eleus confirmed he had received he funds and told him he sent "the goods." Bonnie apologized to the convention's board and said he had to return to Israel on urgent business and caught the first flight from Vienna back to Israel.

***

Four days after his return to Israel, Bonnie received a call from an international delivery company and coordinated that the shipment from Vienna would be transferred to his home in the village in no time.

Seated on the same good old armchair he sat on as he had read the letter his mother had left him, the envelope that came by special delivery with a courier a few moments earlier was now resting on his knees. He was going through the same anxieties and fears that had enwrapped him when he opened *that* envelope.

He opened the decorated envelope in a trembling hand and pulled out a pink piece of paper with the clinic's letterhead in gilded letters at the top left-hand corner.

The contents were brief:

Test results:

The DNA test showed that the blood samples taken from x and the tissue we received from Hypocratio Hospital in Thessaloniki are identical.

Bonnie couldn't tell how long he was out cold. Once he came to, he found himself in the armchair. The envelope was lying on the carpet, which has seen much better days.

He restored himself using a glass of water and a cup of strong coffee. He tried to control his trembling voice as he called Eleus at the investigation agency in Thessaloniki.

"I received the shipment. What I still do not have are the details of the tissue donor from Thessaloniki."

"What? I haven't sent them to you? Hang on. Here. Got it.

Sorry for not sending it. Please make a note."

Eleus then proceeded to say the following, "The identity of the person the tissue was taken from is Mehdi Mohammadi, Iranian passport number 1421830828, D.O.B., 22 October 1961."

PART FOUR

Chapter Twenty-One

The toughest men referred to the place as "the bunker." Gentler folks called it "the villa." Both terms were correct. It did embody opulence and grandeur, featuring the most luxurious meeting rooms, state-of-the-art software, a well-equipped kitchen, a gym, a Wi-Fi system, an electronics lab, underground parking, guestrooms, a library and an archive. It had it all.

One snag though. It was a highly secure building. It was entirely underground.

One of the first decisions Mehdi took immediately upon assuming the post of QF Commander was to build his unit its own separate facility, designated for special purposes. The building proved useful for strategic, secret meetings, brainstorming, intimate encounters and certain investigations best kept under wraps and far away.

Back at QF headquarters in Tehran, the force did have its own large and well-equipped building, but Mehdi nevertheless preferred to have an exclusive, intimate installation, far from the hassle of Tehran, far from the people's families and everyday commitments, a place featuring the utmost comfort as well as the utmost security, while being cut off from the outside world.

Mehdi was aware of the conditions his organization was operating under. Security and intelligence organization worldwide had targeted QF, and these were highly formidable, well-funded forces with highly skilled operatives armed with the most cutting-edge electronics available.

Mehdi had Hezbollah in mind: here was a large organization, situated in Lebanon, numbering thousands of combatants and receiving aid to the tune of one billion U.S. dollars each year from Iran's Revolutionary Guard. Nevertheless, it was leaking like a sieve. However large and no matter how well-trained its personnel was, and despite its immense investments in intelligence and security, Mehdi knew that Hezbollah was completely exposed to its enemies, primarily Mossad and Israeli intelligence. That was the kind of exposure from which he wanted to spare his own organization the most.

The villa's location was carefully chosen by a team of experts, and Mehdi approved it in person. Some sixty miles south of Tehran was far enough to keep the hustle and bustle of the capital at bay and yet only an hour and a half's drive away. Another advantage was afforded by the relative proximity of the rather cozy QOM airport, only about ten miles from the villa.

The site for QF's secret base used to be a hill, which in fact survived, but its core was dug out and Mehdi had the villa built in its place. The dominant part of this structure was the ceiling. It too was built after consultations with the best experts in order to conceal the building's real purpose. The ceiling was made of a fifteen-inch thick layer of cement, over which lay nearly ten feet of earth, and over that, a good fifteen-inch layer of rocks.

The experts gave Mehdi their personal assurance the ceiling would be bomb-proof and that the villa itself would be protected from imagery and listening devices. The villa remained hidden even from the treetop dwelling bee-eaters, as well as from the other species of 'birds' circling over Iran's skies, constantly monitoring suspicious objects and sounds from below.

The hill itself retained its original vegetation: wild nut and ancient pine trees, which afforded it the perfect cover from any prying eyes and ears. The only unperturbed view the hill had was to the road going eastward, diverging from the Tehran-Qom road. After a little less than half a mile, the road led to a large steel gated barrier next to a large stone structure with the sign 'National Geological Institute. No Entry.' The road stretched for a further one hundred yards until it disappeared into the villa.

***

The data on the construction of the villa piled up on the desk of Mossad's 'Trident' outfit chief the moment the construction works began. An elite unit within Israel's Mossad, Trident was tasked with keeping tabs on Iran's nuclear program, codenamed 'Emad Project.' This meant that Trident was in charge of detecting Iran's nuclear facilities, mapping them, following their development and finding new sites. Each nuclear facility was then passed on to a separate desk with the task to study the site from each and every angle and perspective for any eventuality.

Trident pursued its target in numerous ways, from collecting information from open sources to ways even the wildest imagination could not fathom. As soon as the first report came in about major dirt works on a hill in the outskirts of Qom, Trident was in on it, as this triggered its alert. The outfit's think tank's working hypothesis was that the Iranians were planning to build another nuclear facility within the framework of Emad Project, akin to the facility they had already built near Fordow, on the other side of Qom.

Their assumption was fortified once it became clear that the same Iranian construction company that had built the facility in Fordow was assigned this new project as well, so Trident formed a new desk to keep track on it. Customarily for intelligence personnel, they gave it a new code name. As the project was entirely underground, 'The Mole' seemed a fitting tag.

When Trident's Mole Desk received the Iranian construction company's folder, complete with all the blueprints, they were happy to encounter an old, familiar name, known strictly by his Mossad code name. Since then, much later, in fact, this man was exposed by Revolutionary Guard security services and was executed by hanging. Thus, his real name may be divulged: Hossein Shirazi.

***

The construction company that was awarded the villa project was highly reputable when it came to building sophisticated sites. It even had a quite high security clearance, along with a security officer on the payroll, whose job was to assist the Revolutionary Guard in maintaining secrecy about the company's security-related projects. Its managers were screened and had to sign a confidentiality agreement. The entire staff, universally Iranian, was warned never to discuss its work, and, on occasion, were debriefed on security procedures and protocols.

Hossein Shirazi was this construction company's top foreman. A burly man with sun-burnt face, he had a long, thick mustache on both sides of his mouth that had turned grey, then white over the years. Shirazi was part of the select management team, the select few top executives who were part of each and every project the company was involved in. After the successful completion of the Fordow nuclear project, the company had sent him to Tokyo, as a bonus for a job well done, to an international seminar entitled 'The implementation of innovative technology in constructing complex projects.'

One free evening in Tokyo, Hossein entered a museum dedicated to the commemoration of the horrors inflicted by the atomic bombs on Hiroshima and Nagasaki. Awed and enthralled by these shocking images and terrible sights, he found himself standing next to a pale-faced man of average height who was regarding the same exhibits very sadly. This man shared his impressions and sense of horror at the artifacts. At some point, the two newly acquainted men decided to have dinner together in a nearby sushi joint, where, as the company was pleasant and Hossein had plenty of sake, which, as a devout Muslim, he was ignorant of alcohol's influence, he found himself confiding in his friend, "Tony," or, at least, that will be his name for the sake of this story, about his family, his work, and in general, about the project he had just finished in Fordow.

During his remaining time in Tokyo, Hossein and Tony went to several restaurants together, strolled the city's fine gardens and did not skip the treat of a typical Japanese sauna either. Tony told Hossein he was of German descent and a resident of Geneva, having married a local Swiss woman. He also told him he was in the international high-tech business and that he dedicated a great deal of his free time to volunteering at an anti-nuclear organization. "This is why I was so shocked back at the museum," he confided in Hossein.

Before they parted ways, Hossein told Tony that the following month, he would be vacationing in Istanbul, so the two arranged to meet again at a restaurant overlooking the Bosporus straits.

* * *

Hossein was busy eating a juicy fish with his hands as he watched Tony and could not help exclaiming, "This is 'The Sultan,' one of Istanbul's finest seafood restaurants, so why on earth would you order shish kebabs here, of all places?"

"I'm sure the fish is excellent, but I strongly believe all the fish here are saturated with radioactive residue. You know how I feel about this subject," came the reply from Tony.

"Truth be told, I too have my own views about radioactive radiation and the danger it poses to mankind," replied Hossein.

"But you make a living off this radiation."

"Why would you say that?" Hossein replied, offended.

"Didn't you tell me you were involved in the construction of a nuclear facility?"

"Yes, that's right, but that's my livelihood. Nevertheless, I do begin to mind it."

"Come visit me in Geneva, I have lots to show you and offer you."

Two weeks later, Hossein met Tony in the latter's luxurious offices on Geneva's rue de Marche.

After a few meetings and lavish dinners, Hossein agreed to cooperate with Tony in the framework of the latter's fight against nuclear arms. Hossein's consent to assist was bolstered after his new friend told him that the fund he chaired had de-cided to award Hossein the sum of one hundred thousand U.S. dollars, "in order to assist you in coping with the high cost-of-living in Iran," as Tony put it.

***

"I regret to disturb you during your vacation, Tony, but—"

"Call me 'Tony' one more time – and I'm out of here, on my way back to my vacation."

"Very well, Koby," 'Trident' chief smiled. "Actually, the

name Koby does suit you better, but I wanted to put you back in the thick of it."

"Any news?"

"Yee," the head of the desk, sitting right next to the Trident chief, said. "Our friends back in Iran are about to embark on a new project, north of Qom, this time. We're thinking they are constructing an auxiliary facility to the one in Fordow."

The Trident chief continued, "We have to get busy right away, just as we did back in Fordow, before any major progress in construction."

***

Tony arranged to meet with Hossein in one of the small tea houses in Tehran's grand bazaar.

Tony and Hossein were talking about their respective families, until he changed the subject of the conversation. "I know they are about to start working on a new underground facility north of Qom," he told Hossein. "My organization needs your help."

"I already know what you're talking about. I would love to help. At this point, I would like to take this opportunity and thank you for the generous financial assistance you've been giving me. It isn't simple to arrange the marriage of one's daughter in Tehran these days. Just think, I have two more daughters to wed..."

"We would always be glad to help. I'd like you to know I have another one hundred thousand U.S. dollars for you right here in my bag."

"Thank you so much for your financial aid, but all the same, I would like you to know I am helping your organization out of conviction. I totally identify with your cause."

"I'm sure," replied Tony. "We all admire you for all the assistance you've been giving us.

"Please thank your friends for me," Hossein replied, holding on to the bag Tony had handed him.

***

The very night the cement pouring phase was completed, Hossein arrived at the construction site. Armed with his own electric drill, he pierced a hole nearly one quarter of an inch in diameter through the layer of cement and inserted a metal rod nearly a foot and a half long, with a tip comprising a tiny hidden microphone. The other end of this rod had a connector to which he attached a three-yard pipe.

The following day, Shirazi showed the truck driver how to disperse the poured dirt not too tightly over the cement. He also had the driver alert to clogging the pipe's mouth. Just to be sure, Shirazi noted for himself, in secret, the driver's details and the truck's license plate number.

The rocks that were brought over to cover the dirt had been quarried from the nearby mountains. Acting as chief foreman, Shirazi asked his staff to leave a small space between the rocks, telling them he was considering adding a cement support beam. When they were done, he pulled the pipe so that it protruded from the layer of rocks, and he covered the remaining open space using a few leftover stones the workers had left nearby.

The elongated pipe, containing the cable, was connected to 'Charlie,' which Hossein received from Tony in one of their meetings. Charlie was a rock. It was identical in color and texture to the other local rocks. It also weighed about the same. The only thing that set it apart was its name, uttered in admiration by those in the know, which, in this instance, were the scientists at Mossad's electronics lab. They had built this cleverly sophisticated transmission device that specialized in hooking up with satellites over three hundred miles above ground. The transmitter was hidden within the cavity of a stone that had been brought specially from the mountains of Qom. When the device was inaugurated, they decided to name it 'Charlie' in honor of a friend who had died on duty.

Hossein placed Charlie among the thousands of other rocks at the site. No one would have ever distinguished between it and the other rocks. Its tiny antenna all but disappeared within the roots of the nut tree that grew nearby. Charlie maintained radio silence, suspended until its activation code would be sent from the sky.

***

The meeting took place at the Trident chief's office. In attendance were also the desk head and three of his senior staff.

"So, either our friends over in Qom are fooling us, or were fooling ourselves," the head of the desk began.

"What's bothering you?" the Trident chief asked.

"Something about the Qom project just doesn't add up."

"Care to specify?"

"We're treating the Qom project as a nuclear site, but I have a nagging suspicion we are misdiagnosing, that this might be something else."

"And what makes you think that?"

"We're working under the assumption it's an auxiliary serving in parallel to the facility in Fordow, but the findings we've collected thus far do not seem to support this claim."

The head of the desk proceeded to specify, "Look, first of all:

A. The facility in Fordow has six entrances and exits leading to and from the underground facility, but our facility only has one entrance and one exit.

B. Three of all the entrances at Fordow are specially to allow trucks in, whereas the Qom facility features an entrance exclusively for regular vehicles.

C. The Qom facility does not have an emergency exit – which is simply impossible for a nuclear site.

D. The entrance to Fordow features spacious parking, including employee buses, whereas the Qom site doesn't. This suggests the latter is not designated for a large crowd.

E. The Qom facility is not connected to high voltage power lines. This, too, is not possible regarding a nuclear site.

F. The security measures at Fordow include high, double wire fences, minefields, watchtowers and so on. Our site at Qom also features tight security, but they are more localized, not tailored to a major site.

G. The site at Qom is too close to the main road so it constitutes both a safety and an intelligence risk. This is not like
the Iranians."

"I'm sold. So, what do you suggest?"

"I am sure the Qom facility is going to be the scene of
something big but not part of the nuclear program. Therefore,
I suggest we turn over the responsibility for this site to the Ops
Branch, so they use their own means to get to the bottom of
what's going on out there and take full charge of the activity
there."

***

The meeting between the Mossad branch chiefs was short.
The head of Ops Branch assumed, as authorized by the head
of Mossad, responsibility for the site near Qom and received
all the relevant intelligence, including Charlie.

Only a few days passed until the head of Ops made two important decisions. The first was to position a static 'Janus' type
reconnaissance satellite over the Qom site for a limited period
of three months. The second was to augment the technical intelligence with human intelligence, also known as HUMINT.

Janus was built in Israel, according to specifications the relevant space industries received from a collaborative effort of
Israel's array of intelligence agencies. Smart and modular, it
could easily be configured for various specific designations.

In accordance with Mossad's request, the specific Janus
satellite to be positioned over Qom was fitted with a special

algorithm capable of analyzing in real-time the meaning of vehicular traffic above ground. The data collected was immediately relayed and rephrased in the form of operational commands.

This algorithm was designed to trigger Charlie, buried a little over three hundred miles below the satellite, whenever the suspicion arose, based on the traffic below, that something out of the ordinary was taking place at the Qom facility. The controlled activation of Charlie was designed to limit its exposure to the Iranians' means of detection and to minimize its activity as much as possible.

As soon as all the necessary modifications were made, the satellite was launched and positioned at its predesignated coordinates, some three hundred miles above target, all-seeing and unseen.

The Janus-type satellite continuously related images of what took place below. The view it kept transmitting to the control facility was fantastic: the sacred city of Qom, Kavir National Park, Namak, a blue colored salt lake, the mountain range that dominated the scenery and numerous objects on the ground, viewed directly from above at a resolution of nearly twenty inches.

The observation staff at the control center back in Tel Aviv kept a 24-hour surveillance of the traffic along the Tehran-Qom road, placing particular emphasis on the access road from the main highway to the facility. Apart from the vehicles, they also saw numerous animals, some unfamiliar, as they crossed the road. An amateur naturalist on duty swore he saw a real live tiger crossing the road near the facility one night.

The satellite produced fascinating imagery, but the moment for Charlie to shine was still long in coming.

Chapter Twenty-Two

The flight from the Baghdad airport to the Tehran airport took about forty minutes. The Boeing aircraft taxied to the point where the passengers got off to be taken to customs and checkpoint by bus. Many of them were Iraqi Shiite pilgrims on their way to the holy places this sect of Islam reveres in Iran.

Standing in line at the control point were Mahmoud and Fatimah, his wife. Tall and solid, with thick black hair and one long eyebrow across his face, he handed both their passports to the officer as Fatimah stood right behind. The clerk gave him Fatimah's passport and asked them to pass through one by one, separately.

"What's the purpose of your visit in Iran?"

"We married about a month ago. My wife and I vowed to consecrate our marriage at the great mosque of Qom," replied Mahmoud.

"And how long do you plan on staying in Iran?"

"We intend to spend two days in Tehran and five days in Qom."

The checkpoint officer gave Mahmoud a piercing glance, took notice of the black beard that graced his face, as befitted a devout Muslim, and was equally impressed with the black hijab that covered the entire face of Mahmoud's wife. And so, he stamped their passports.

The following two days, the two spent in Tehran, where they visited the grand bazaars and strolled the city's broad avenues. After the two days in Tehran, they hired a car and drove about sixty miles south to the holy city of Qom, where they stayed at Hotel El Zahra in the center of town. The couple consecrated their marriage at Jamkaran Mosque, one of the world's loveliest mosques and took in the atmosphere of the Shiite Muslims' most sacred city.

One morning, they travelled farther south to Fordow, now world-renowned since Iran's previous president, Mahmoud Ahmadinejad, had announced to the world that Iran had built a large underground uranium-enrichment facility there.

Early into their excursion, the couple were stopped by a police car. When they told the officers they were headed to Fordow, they were instructed that foreigners have no business being there, and it was suggested they turn back. Mahmoud and Fatimah heeded their advice and back they went to Qom, where they continued strolling about and marveling at the city's numerous shops catering to the many thousands of pilgrims seeking all kinds of Islamic artifacts and souvenirs.

The following morning, they asked the hotel receptionist for advice how to get to Kavir National Park, one of Iran's finest, with Namak Lake, which, apart from being a truly magnificent natural treasure, also constitutes one of Iran's major freshwater reservoirs. The hotel clerk suggested Mahmoud and Fatimah take Route No. 7, travel north and after about six miles turn east and follow the signs to the access road leading to the park.

And so the two took to the highway, passed the turn to the park and continued onwards for about three more miles, where they exited the main road and took a lane leading eastwards, at the entrance of which was a sign, 'National Geological Institute. No Entry.' They ignored the sign and continued all the way to the stone structure with the sign 'National Geological Institute.' Next to it, right by the steel barrier were men in black uniforms carrying Kalashnikovs.

"What are you doing here? Didn't you see the sign?" The guards darted toward them.

Mahmoud and Fatimah, embarrassed and apologetic, replied "We must have missed it; we want to get to Kavir National Park."

"Hold still!" One of the guards shouted at them, drew his gun and aimed it at them, while another guard went over to the nearby structure and returned a few minutes later.

"You're in luck," said the guard. "We could have arrested you for a blatant violation of security and ignoring the signs, but we decided to let it slide. You can go. Go on, get, before we change our mind. If it's the park you want, go back to Qom, and after about three miles on Route No. 7, turn left. Now, keep watching for the signs! Now scram!"

Grateful, they turned their car round and hurried away. They did take Route No. 7, and indeed took the left turn after about three miles according to the signs. They reached the great lake after about twenty minutes.

On a remote corner of Namak Lake, Fatimah removed her

hijab for a brief moment, letting the cool breeze stroke her lovely face. Her green eyes shone as she smiled at Mahmoud right before she pulled out a satellite phone from her bosom and punched one code word 'negative.'

Then, she removed the batteries from the device and handed them over to Mahmoud, who in turn threw each battery a yard apart and threw the device about three miles farther still, into a thundering waterfall that spilled into the lake.

Mahmoud was now relieved, as well. They were through with the most dangerous part of their mission. If he could, he would have kissed Fatimah's lovely full lips, but the security briefing they had received prior to their mission outweighed his passion. "Never do anything foolish you might live to regret," their instructions cautioned, and so they obeyed. '*Someday*,' he told himself.

"Our people have ruled out the possibility this site could be nuclear," the Ops team summed up the situation at the new Qom site. "Nevertheless, it's still interesting to see what it is the Iranians are planning there."

***

Mehdi convened the high command for a special meeting in the villa's lavish conference room. At the same time, the Mossad control center began to literally flash and buzz, with various alert lights turning on and off in an array of colors, as computers came to life and auto-keyboards began typing. The controller on duty called the squad commander, who in turn called the head of the team, who called the head of the desk, who finally called the Trident chief.

The villa's parking lot suddenly got crowded with an unusual number of Mercedes and utility vehicles. The Janus-type satellite calculated that the day had come and dutifully woke Charlie, issuing the command to begin working.

***

QF's twelve senior commanders were seated around the long desk at the conference hall. Alert, they gazed at their much-admired chief in awe but also with no little fear.

"We are gathered here today," Mehdi began his address to the high command, "to greenlight operation 'Queen of Vengeance,' on which we have been working for several months now. This is the most complex and audacious mission we have ever embarked on. It is designed to deal a decisive blow to the Zionist entity once and for all and teach Mossad a lesson they will never forget."

He stood upright, his eyes burning bright as he spoke with the intensity and vigor of a conductor rallying his orchestra.

"The purpose of this operation is to take revenge on the Jews, on the Zionists and on Mossad for being so cruel, for hunting down our brave fighters and for hurting innocent people, killing them and setting their property on fire. The plan I would like to take you through is to hit Israel's embassy in Lagos, Nigeria, and kill as many Israelis as possible. Israel has turned this embassy into the hub of its activity in Africa. They are using their embassy as the base of operations designed to strike everywhere there's friendship towards Iran across Africa. To that end, the Israelis are instigating internal revolutions and are encouraging opposition leaders. They have resorted to any means, including bribes of key officials, even leaders, and physically harming their opponents."

Mehdi continued, "The Zionists are focusing special attention on controlling the Bab-el-Mandeb Straits. They secured an alliance with Saudi Arabia, the self-proclaimed "protector of the holy sites," in the framework of which the Saudis are supposed to secure the eastern part of the straits whereas the Zionists, the western part. Now, control of the straits means endangering Iran's oil exports and ensuring Israel's free passage, all the way to the position they've already occupied in the Gulf of Aqaba. To that end, the Saudis have intervened in the civil war in Yemen, and Israel, for its part, has bolstered its own embassy in Lagos, where Mossad has a major station, in charge of conducting the war against the Islamic State across Africa.

"We shall turn the straits, also known as 'the gate of tears,' into the Zionists' sea of tears. The waters of the straits will be saltier that the Dead Sea. The blood we shall exact from the infidels will indeed justify calling it the 'Red Sea.' We are determined to put an end to all these interventions. Operation 'Queen of Vengeance' will do just that."

Mehdi concluded his message and looked at the senior commanders' adoring and humbled eyes, fully aware of what 'lonely at the top' means.

***

Charlie recorded Mehdi's entire speech and had it relayed by the Janus-type satellite, complete with simultaneous translation from Farsi to Hebrew, to the computer screens at Mossad HQ. The original text in Farsi was catalogued and archived straight away. The staff at HQ followed the speech very closely. When the recording concluded, everyone present were surprised to read the following message on the screen: "**Good luck! Charlie and Janus**"

Even during the recording, the Mossad chief was called to the Ops room. As soon as it ended, he requested to be put through to the prime minister over the secure line. When the prime minister picked up, he okayed the hastily requested, urgent meeting.

Chapter Twenty-Three

The prime minister was sitting at the head of the table, with the Minister of Defense to his right and the science minister to his left. The chief of the IDF general staff was sitting next to the defense minister, and next to him sat the intelligence affairs and strategy advisor. The head of the Mossad was sitting left of the science minister, and next to him sat the head of the General Security Service (GSS). This was Israel's top echelon.

The meeting was taking place in room X, whose exact location, four floors below the basement of the Mossad building on a hill north of Tel Aviv, was known to few. There was a small antechamber right at the front, accessible only by an elevator, whose entry code was known only to the head of the GSS security department, who had led the group into room "x" earlier.

Prior to their entry into the room, each of the participants, without exception, was asked to leave his cellphone with the head of the GSS security department. The cellphones were disconnected from their batteries and placed into the safe at the lobby.

The door leading from the antechamber to room "x"

featured hidden magnetometers that monitored the participants without their knowledge. The room itself comprised a unique electronic system constructed by a select team of electronics engineers from the GSS operations department. This system foiled any means of gleaning information on the goings on in room "x" through wiretapping, taking images or any type of surveillance.

The participants were all seated when the prime minister began. His message, like what everyone else were saying, was not recorded, but rather taken down by the GSS security department in his own hand. He later filed the protocol in a specially dedicated safe whose combination was known only to him. A backup code was kept by one of the members of Israel's security community, who was chosen jointly by the head of the Mossad and the head of the GSS.

"Gentlemen," the prime minister began, "we are gathered here today to discuss one issue and one issue only, namely – the removal of Iran's Islamic Revolutionary Guard Corps commander. I now call upon the head of the Mossad to provide us with a short briefing."

"We've had IRGC Commander Mehdi Mohammadi in our sights for many years now," the head of Mossad began his review. Mossad began compiling a file on him back when he was a junior university student in Thessaloniki, where he was also an operative for Iranian intelligence. He rose in the ranks all the way to the top thanks to his unique skills, uncanny ferocity, and extraordinary valor.

"At some point, Mehdi caught the attention of the CIA, who soon discovered it was he who had shot dead point blank one of their top agents in Europe. MI 6 also initiated a file on him, a little belatedly, after they found out it was Mehdi who was behind the elimination of one of their own, whose body surfaced in the Bosporus.

"Our own security services have a bitter score to settle with Mehdi. He had one of our best field commanders, whose name is still a secret, eliminated. On top of that, he has masterminded numerous operations against Israeli targets worldwide.

"Today's meeting was called urgently when we received accurate intelligence according to which he is planning a major terrorist attack on one of our important embassies in Africa.

"Our joint efforts with the GSS Operations Department led to the conclusion it is high time we rid the world of this mass murderer."

"Now that we have heard from the Mossad," concluded the prime minister, "the concise message of the head of Mossad brings this matter before your approval. I would like your vote on the removal of the commander of Iran's Revolutionary Guard Corps by show of hands."

Everyone present raised his hand.

The minister of science approved the elimination of his own father by raising his hand in agreement.

PART FIVE

Chapter Twenty-Four

It was Friday afternoon. Bonnie told his driver he could go and asked him to return the following Sunday at five am to make it back to the government meeting in time, beating the morning rush hour, as Sunday is a regular business day in Israel.

A week earlier, the prime minister and the head of Israel's General Security Service met to discuss the inquiry into the matter concerning the Minister of Science. The head of the GSS told the prime minister that he still believed the minister's presence in government meetings was ill-advised, but given the political constraints the prime minister had to deal with, the final decision was, after all, the prime minister's, as was noted in the report by the head of the GSS.

After he saw his driver off, Bonnie called his sister, thanked her for the dinner invitation and apologized for not being able to make it due to an urgent matter that had come up.

'*I need some time to myself*,' he thought, '*some quality me-time*'.

After a brief mid-day nap, he poured himself a cup of coffee and continued to sip while lounging in his armchair on the veranda. '*The front grass lawn needs pruning; it's been a while since I last tended to it. All those yellow patches in the center and the edges growing wild. It won't do. Avram would never have let it get to such a state.*'

Bonnie awoke from his musings in a second. Ever since the '*revelation,*' he had ceased referring to Avram as '*Dad.*' He suddenly realized that in his mind, the word '*Avram*' had replaced the word '*Dad.*' '*Well, at least the trees Avram cultivated round the grass seem fine. The tall avocado trees seem fine. Full bloom. Should guarantee fine pickings after the wet winter we've had. Ah, the scent of those two lemon trees. Even the bees and other insects like them,*' Bonnie paused to take in the buzzing orgy of nectar and honey.

The flowerbeds that served to demarcate the grass from the fruit trees were Avram's domain. He had had a green thumb; a true lover of earth and nature, his love was always requited. Bonnie began longing for the view of Avram's bent back pushing the old grass mower over to the tree stump he had cut each year. How he had loved to adhere to plant rotation each season, so the house had had fragrant, colorful flowers all year long.

'*Dad or no dad, he was a good man. He loved his family. Perhaps he loved me just a bit more.*'

The back yard was the domain of Bonnie's mother, Esther. '*She loved animals so much, she kept a small henhouse and a goat for milk.*' He continued his stroll down memory lane. '*The red-tailed rooster wasn't the most dominant creature there, though it sure woke the entire household up at the crack of dawn, but rather the hen, Kat, as I had come to call it.'* The ever-busy hen with the languishing comb gave him his daily treat each morning. *'The morning egg always waited for me at the same corner. I would always thank Kat and hand the egg over to Mom, who proceeded to make me my favorite breakfast in the whole wide world.'*

'But then,' he recalled, *'one day, the usual egg wasn't there, and Kat wouldn't look me in the eye. When I reached the usual corner, it was, lo and behold, empty.'*

"Mom! No egg this morning!"

"Don't feel down, son," she had calmed him down con-solingly, "Kat deserves a day off two, you know. Talk to Dad, he knows all about workers' rights."

The following morning, Bonnie ran over to the henhouse, fully anticipating finding an egg, but he was equally disap-pointed. 'Nada,' as his grandfather would have taught him to say. This repeated itself each morning, until, on the eleventh straight day, not only was there no egg in sight, the chicken had disappeared as well.

"I will get you a new one, I promise." But this wasn't enough to console Bonnie the child.

Three more weeks went by, and Bonnie went to the hen-house to feed the chickens. *'That sight drove me to tears. Even now, it's still exciting. There was Kat, proudly stepping out of the bushes, her comb held high, leading her eleven newly hatched chicks.'*

It was getting colder now, as it was nearly evening. *'Better get myself a blanket.'* He went up the hill through the village main street, which was in fact the only street. On his way, not far from his own house, stood his old preschool. *'That must have been Avram's day. He was the only dad who came during the holidays and so on, as all the other dads were working in the fields or cowsheds and chicken pens. The other children had their grandmas and grandpas come, since the parents were up to their necks in the grueling agricultural chores.'*

Avram used to sit among the kids in his white shirt and glasses, both cheeks of his buttocks spilling over the small children's seats there. Little Bonnie was embarrassed by his father's attendance, all the more so as the other dads were burly, suntanned men with stern faces. But then again, those dads never made time to rejoice with their kids.

'That business with the mongoose did save face for Avram,' Bonnie remembered. The orchard not far from their home had a family of mongooses burrowed deep inside a hole in the ground. One morning, Bonnie and his family were sitting down to breakfast when screams came all the way from the henhouse. Avram rushed outside, Bonnie immediately behind him, only to see a mongoose holding Kat in its mouth. Avram began running after the mongoose and grabbed it right at the mouth of its burrow. The mongoose was so scared, it dropped Kat, which, save for a few scratches here and there, survived the ordeal intact

Bonnie, who was very proud of his dad, told all his friends about his act of bravery. *'Yeah,* dad,' he repeated the word, for he had referred to Avram as dad for most of his life. *'Maybe I was being too hard in him.'*

The village road that meandered between the houses ended

near the last house and turned into a dirt road that crossed wheat fields laden with sheaves of grain. It was almost harvest time. The fields stretched as far as the hill, which Bonnie came to know as 'Squill Hill,' for they bloomed each year right before the first rain. In this capacity, they were harbingers of fall. The large bulbs retained their moisture by shrinking over the summer months, so the moment the first real rain came, they quickly shot their long, white, scented flowers as far up as possible.

A stone structure stood at the top of the hill, crowned, as it were, by a blue dome. It consisted largely of a tall white tomb that faced south. The Muslims had consecrated it long ago, believing Sheik Al Hamid was buried there. He was a known commentator of the *Quran*.

The tomb was sacred to the Jews, as well, who believed it was the burial site of one of the prophet Hosea's disciples. Hosea, whose own tomb was in Safed, was among the 'twelve prophets of the Bible.' Devotees of both religions, emboldened in their belief as to its significance by virtue of its facing south, embraced the site. For the Muslims, this meant it pointed to Mecca. For the Jews, Jerusalem.

Quite surprisingly, both faiths coincided rather than clashed. The followers of both persuasions respected their counterparts and shared the site. The Muslims would come to worship during the holy month of *Ramadan*, whereas the Jews usually came during *Shavuot*, the equivalent to Pentecost. An ancient oak tree grew right next to the domed tomb. The Jews had a legend, according to which the oak was planted by one of the priests at King Solomon's temple, who had been tasked with bringing over to the then Kingdom of United Israel the cedars designated for the Temple. The Muslims, on the other hand, said the oak was planted by one of the successors of the Prophet Mohammad, whom he had sent to conquer the land for Islam.

Certain botanists, cynics and true to form, claimed that the oak tree was only a few hundred years old. Nevertheless, they still gave it the respect they believed it was due and crowned it 'one of the three oldest trees in Israel.'

It was this oak that Bonnie was walking towards now. He and the tree were old friends. Whenever he was need of solace or peace of mind during a time of tough choices, he would make his way to the tree and draw the serenity he required, which the tree seemed to impart along with its wisdom of years. Upon his arrival, Bonnie cleared some space off the acorn-covered ground, rolled over the coat he had carried with him, laid it out and stretched across. '*The earth is still warm.*'

Whereas the fields reminded him of Avram, Squill Hill reminded him of his mother. She was the one who had introduced it to him early in his childhood. Each springtime, they used to cavort among the anemones that had taken over from the squill. '*I miss her so much.*' He recalled their parting on her deathbed, her constant love and support throughout his life, and dwelled on that letter inside the white envelope. '*That letter... It changed my life.*'

The letter certainly had disrupted his life and had him embark on a quest to regain his peace of mind and the secret of his very existence. In the wake of this pursuit, he had traveled all the way to Claudia in Thessaloniki, then to that enchanted house in Sithonia, where, right by the bay, he had come into being.

The tree's serenity flowed into him. As he began smiling, those feelings he would have from time to time, of anger and disappointment over his mother's behavior in that secluded villa, changed into acceptance and he was even pleased for her. '*After all, I always believed each and every person has the right to break with the norm. at least once in their life, and do something out of the ordinary, some act that would change the course of the rest of their lives.*' Bonnie realized that had been his mother's choice.

'*But what about me? Did Mom have any right to conceive me there by that splendid bay? She had to live by her decision her entire life, so now it's my turn? And what about my father?*' This was the first time he ever referred to that Iranian man as '*father.*' '*It is safe to assume he doesn't even know he has a child, let alone an Israeli son and a cabinet member of the Zionist government of Israel at that... and had he known, would it have made him anxious? Curious? Indifferent?*'

A faint sense of excitement crept up Bonnie's back. '*Come to think of it, who is this man my beloved mother spent the night with at that glorious place? What sort of person is he? What does he actually look like, as one cannot really tell from those doctored photos of his that made the papers once in a blue moon. What is the color of his eyes?*'

Bonnie knew Mossad had an extensive dossier on Mehdi. '*The file they have on him surely has in store up-to-date images.*' Nevertheless, true to form, Bonnie decided not to entangle

Israel's intelligence service in his own life story. '*I must get all the answers myself.*'

The rustle of the oak's leaves grew louder. '*What are they telling me? Yeah, sure, I could not avoid the question.* "I didn't seem to have any other choice," he spoke out loud, partly to himself and partly to the green foliage. '*I had to raise my hand in favor of eliminating him. For starters, objecting would have been met with all eyebrows raised. Besides, truth be told, I didn't see the connection at that moment. It still hadn't registered that the objective of the hit was my own biological father.*'

'*What now?*'

'*Can I really give my consent to the elimination of my own father? What would Mom have to say about that?*' He recalled the desperate letters his mother sent to all the hospitals in Thessaloniki in her attempt to retrace that fling, the escapade of a lifetime. His anger, frustration and disappointment have given way to wondering, acceptance and empathy.

'*Who am I to cast my vote to have the love of my mother taken out?*' Bonnie closed his eyes, his certainty and resolution engulfed by the warmth and love of the old oak's leaves.

Chapter Twenty-Five

Mehdi set the operational basis for operation 'Queen of Vengeance' at Kuala Lumpur, the capital of Malaysia, and for good reason. Although it was far from the ultimate objective at Lagos, Kuala Lumpur had its own advantages.

For one thing, Malaysia was a country consisting of two territories separated by a waterway. One part was in the Malayan Peninsula, and the other comprised the northern part of the island of Borneo. Malaysia had a border with Indonesia, Thailand and Singapore. Mehdi considered these unique traits and multiple borders an advantage.

Very early on, when the decision was made to embark on the operation, Mehdi also determined to keep it as far away as possible from Iran. '*I do not trust the intelligence coverage by Iran's intelligence services. I've witnessed Mossad penetrate my country's most sensitive places, only to be discovered far too late after the fact, rather than in time.*'

He also immediately dropped the idea of establishing an advance post in an African country, for he knew that everything in this continent was for sale and that Mossad and other intelligence agencies had the whole of Africa covered and leaking like a sieve for them. Europe had never been an option to begin with, as Iran was not well-liked there, not one bit, let alone its subversive activities, thereby rendering European intelligence services that much more suspicious and alert when it came to any step taken by Iranian nationals.

Malaysia featured yet another advantage: it had a large majority of Muslims and a standard anti-Israeli policy. '*Such a hostile atmosphere will make it even harder for Mossad to operate there*,' he thought.

Operation 'Queen of Vengeance' was a personal issue for Mehdi. If it were in his power, he would have called it operation 'Vengeance of Queen Suheil,' but he knew better. '*Giving it a personal touch would not go down well with the powers that be*,' he reasoned. '*Besides, this name would be too long*.'

Another thought that gave him pause was '*Why is it that they assign names to military operations, anyway? There is probably some reason that has to do with psychology, an image thing and morale. Fact is every organization does it.*'

He decided on this operation the moment he learned about the fire at the family khana. He didn't need any proof to know it was arson. Likewise, he didn't need any inquiry to learn who the perpetrators were.

'*As sure as the sun rises in the east and fish swim in water, revenge will come, and it will come down hard and painful. This will be the vengeance of Suheila and Ali, and family and me personally. They went too far this time.*'

***

The two Turkish merchants came to Mydin, Malaysia, by flight from Bangkok, Thailand, and from Mydin, they boarded a connection to Kuala Lumpur via Singapore. They checked into a room in a small hotel in the center of Malaysia's capital city and entered a real estate agency they happened to see, the third they had encountered.

"We're looking for an office we can rent for a year," the two told the realtor, who seemed drowsy. "We come from Turkey, where we have a spice business, and we would like to set up shop here."

The realtor could not be less surprised, as Malaysia was one of the world's largest tea exporters, as well as a major producer of spices, notably fine, world-renowned pepper. The two new clients and the realtor proceeded to arranged for a meeting the following day, during which he would show them a selection of options.

The two merchants went to town, supplied themselves with maps of the city at the local tourism bureau, and found the capital's large flea markets quite impressive. "Almost like the ones we have in Istanbul," they told the realtor the following day.

They spent most of that day looking at various properties until they made their choice and informed their realtor. It was a rather shabby-looking office over on Raja Solan Street, a far cry from the famed 'Petronas Towers,' known primarily for their height and unusual architecture. '*Better far from the madding tourists and electronic surveillance*,' the two merchants thought. They picked up two workmen from one of the markets and asked them to have the office cleaned and fixed up. They also picked up a few old pieces of furniture still in pretty good shape at one of the flea markets.

The two merchants had memorized their instructions: no contact with Iran's embassy in Kuala Lumpur, no contact with any foreigners, especially friendly ones, no new offices, for they might be under surveillance or monitoring, no custom-made furniture.

The office was relatively secluded, but just to set the minds and the curiosity of the occasional passer-by or distant relative at ease, they hung a sign in the local language and in English, 'Tea and Spices Export Office.'

As soon as they got organized, they sent Mehdi a coded message via a satellite phone, updating him of the beginning of the first stage of the operation.

The phones Mehdi and 'the Turks' used cost a fortune and were the first of their kind in the Revolutionary Guard, as they featured a special type of software: a unique scrambler whose designers swore could not be cracked. Any message relayed using these phones was scrambled according to a highly complex algorithm, as was any word uttered over the phone. Everything was also simultaneous unscrambled so that it might be intelligible too.

In addition, the two 'merchants' and Mehdi agreed on code words for emergency situations, which were also supposed to be relayed via the scrambler.

'*This time, those bastards will not get the better of us,*' Mehdi told himself.

***

The operation's core personnel comprised only three people, who also finalized its principles: Mehdi, the chief; Zephyri, one of the 'Turks' and one of QF's most skilled ops men; and Mustafi, the other 'Turk,' QF's top specialist on explosive devices.

Mehdi knew them both personally. He had already worked with Zephyri on a number of operations in Europe and Africa and had come to appreciate the latter's courage and loyalty to both the organization and to Mehdi himself personally. Zephyri was a man after Mehdi's own heart: silent and professional. He couldn't be more suitable to this operation.

As for Mustafi, it was rumored he had a special sense of smell for explosives, that he could discern a mile away between a fragrant rose and TNT secreted within a seemingly innocuous postal envelope. Mustafi himself knew that an explosives operative does not get a second chance, and he taught his subordinates this all-important lesson, which life had taught him.

One morning, Tehran police called him to inspect a parked motorcycle near the address of one of Iran's top nuclear scientists. He ordered the premises be sealed off and asked they wait for him. This was the exact same time his wife was in the midst of giving birth in their bedroom. Through his wife's screams and cries, he called one of the members of his team and asked him to go and inspect the motorcycle for the police. But the friend who took over for him lacked three things: a keen sense of smell, minimal caution and the blessing of Allah, and so his body shattered along with the suspicious motorcycle, their fragments scattered for miles.

Shocked, Mustafi promised to take revenge. This appealed to Mehdi, as he was fond of vengeful people, knowing full well that they exact the most ferocious and most determined payback. This was exactly the sort of man he was looking for to man Operation Queen of Vengeance.

∗∗∗

According to principles of the operation, as laid down by the three, the entire building that housed Israel's embassy in Lagos, Nigeria, had to be completely demolished by means of a powerful explosive device. Furthermore, boobytraps had to be placed en route to the embassy, and finally, the highest possible number of casualties among the embassy staff and everyone around was a highly desired outcome.

The plan had another ace up its sleeve, which shall be revealed later on in the story, so as not to reveal too much this early, for it constituted the basis for the whole operations.

The three had a steel-hard pact to maintain the highest compartmentalization. This meant they would not rely on assistance from Revolutionary Guard HQ or any other official Iranian body. They further pledged not to communicate with Iran's embassy in Kuala Lumpur in any way, and to adhere to the strictest precautions.

One month after Zephyri and Mustafi established their outpost in Malaysia's capital, they met with Mehdi for lunch at a restaurant downtown. Keenly aware their adversary could easily use cellphone as listening devices and even relay the recorded conversations via satellite, each removed the batteries from his own cellphone.

During their meeting, they concluded it was time to move on to the next stage of the operation. They also agreed to purchase satellite images of Lagos from a specialized company headquartered in Geneva, Switzerland, with an emphasis on high-resolution images of the city's main buildings. As well as purchasing an accurate map of the city's roads.

At Mehdi's suggestion, they agreed to send his own personal photographer there under the guise of an innocent tourist. He was to take photos of the Israeli embassy building from every angle possible, as well as the adjacent buildings within a radius of about five hundred yards, just to be on the safe side. The rest of their meeting focused on concluding all the other technical details of the planned operation.

Their last decision, right before returning the batteries to their cellphones, was to meet up again a month later, also in Kuala Lumpur, as far away as possible from Tehran.

***

On the morning of April 21st, Mehdi received a call from Revolutionary Guard intelligence chief, telling him of the news. Essentially, this was merely routine update passed on to a select group of seniors.

"We received a report that earlier this morning, at half past six local time, a hit was carried out at Kuala Lumpur. We have no further details at this moment. We'll keep you posted when we have more information."

Mehdi, a courageous man with ice in his veins, felt his

knees shaking. Ever since the news of the family khana set aflame, he had not felt so helpless and beside himself as he did just now. '*Where did we go wrong? How could Mossad play us like that again?*' he asked himself.

Two hours passed until he received another routine update from his intelligence chief, who wasn't in on operation Queen of Vengeance.

"The Malaysian security authorities are reporting that earlier today, at six thirty am, two gunmen on a BMW motorcycle shot a man dead right on Kuala Lumpur's main road. Their target was Fadi al Batsh, chief rocket engineer for Hamas."

Mehdi received this update with mixed emotion. '*I am so glad none of my men were involved. Nevertheless, the target of this hit must have been different. There's no doubt in my mind.*' He ordered Zephyri and Mustafi to leave Malaysia's capital city "this instant."

Chapter Twenty-Six

As soon as Bonnie was appointed minister of science, he was called over to the government secretary, who explained to him what the ministerial post entailed and what it included as far as its authority was concerned. He further told Bonnie that in accordance with previous government decisions, cyber was under the minister's purview.

Bonnie, or we might call him by his full, official title, his excellency Minister Binyamin Pladot, was perplexed about his responsibility for cyber. '*It has become such a buzzword,*' he told himself, '*but what does it actually mean?*'

Well-versed in such matters, the government secretary noticed the minister's embarrassment and self-awareness at being clueless about this subject and told him he would schedule a meeting with the official in charge of cyber in Israel in order to get better acquainted with this issue and with what was required of the minister as part of his post.

The following afternoon the esteemed minister spent with the cyber official, an electronics engineer by training and a long-serving intelligence man until he retired.

"Cyber," explained the expert, "is about a virtual world,

which nowadays encompasses most human activity. Its importance in the framework of our modern world keeps growing. Information security is a basic element of cyber, being essential to preventing information getting destroyed or stolen by hostile elements and being used by them. Without such security, any unwarranted party is capable of paralyzing power stations, disrupting airports, undermining emergency services, and, in fact, sabotaging any internet-based activity throughout any country."

The expert continued his review. "Being in control, in the lead, when it comes to cyber, is essential for any government and any branch of government, as well as for any business. Information security, an integral part of cyber, is also vital to individuals, for without it, anyone could break into bank accounts and empty them, invade our privacy and wreak havoc on our daily lives."

At the end of his review, the cyber official and the minister concluded they would meet with the heads of cyber in Israel's intelligence organizations as early as possible to broaden the minister's knowledge and to increase his involvement in the field. During one of these meetings, in the course of updating the minister, one of the cyber chiefs told him about a pilot they were about to launch at a particular date. They were going to hack into Tehran's traffic lights system.

*

International cyber conferences were as frequent as they were common. Their stated objective was to enable countries, organizations and individuals exchange information in the framework of this field, and the Israeli minister of science took part in many of them. A cocktail party was held during one of these meetings that took place in Geneva, Switzerland. The minister happened to come across the cyber chief from Iran, who probably didn't recognize him. Nevertheless, as diplomatic protocol and prevailing norms dictated, they exchanged calling cards. When Bonnie returned to his hotel, he pulled out the Iranian official's card.

***

A week after that conference, Bonnie went to Thessaloniki to visit Claudia. On his way to his apartment, he bought a cheap cellphone in a small shop and inserted another SIM.

Claudia was glad to see him and thanked him for the visit and for the box of Israeli dates he brought her, "Ah, you remembered how much I loved the dates you brought me once." She seemed older than her actual age and far from her best. She told Bonnie she had spent a long time in the hospital and that her medical condition is not good.

Indeed, this was not the same Claudia as before. Walking was difficult for her; she bent over and could not sit or stand upright, and when she spoke, she was faint and erratic. It saddened Bonnie to see her like this. Nevertheless, one could still tell how beautiful she had been in her youth and how glad the visit made her.

Before they parted, he asked whether he could leave his cellphone there so that he could receive a message from an acquaintance of his, "on official business." Claudia gladly obliged.

He sent a text message from this cellphone to the number on the Iranian cyber official's business card: "I would like to meet Mehdi Mohammadi."

He then connected the cellphone to the charger, hugged Claudia goodbye and off he went. He wished her the best of health and returned to Israel.

A week later, he returned to Claudia's apartment. At the entrance to her building, he met a neighbor who told him, sobbing, that Claudia had passed away two days earlier. At his request, the neighbor let him enter the apartment using the key she had. She walked in with him and noticed the sad look on his face as he sat in the armchair he recognized from his previous visit. "Yes, she was a dear soul," she muttered in somewhat broken English and gave him a glass of water.

Bonnie noticed a white dress with fine embroidery on a hanger in the open closet. The neighbor followed his gaze. "This was Claudia's favorite dress," she told him. "She asked me to give it to my niece after she was gone."

Before taking his leave, he picked up his cellphone, explaining he had forgotten it on his previous visit. One quick look at the screen was enough for him to see he had received no reply. He said his goodbye to Claudia's neighbor and went off to the nearby park, where he took out the SIM card and discarded it, then removed the batteries and threw them separately into the lake at the center of the park.

He couldn't help feeling sad as he rushed to catch his flight back to Tel Aviv.

***

Ten days passed. Bonnie had another business trip. London this time. He took a taxi to Piccadilly Circus between meetings, where, in an old office building, on the second floor, he found the office with the sign, 'Electronic Reporting Centre,' and walked in. This office provided various services, including anonymous email boxes. In exchange for a hefty fee, one could send and receive messages without either party's true identity ever coming to light. The inbox was available on a daily basis, using a unique, one-time coded password that was deleted the moment the message went through. The staff at the Centre took great pride in the fact that although the odd cyber expert did manage to track the Piccadilly address of the actual premises, no one had ever managed to crack the code and uncover the identity of anyone involved in the message exchange itself.

Bonnie leased an inbox and got a message through to the Iranian cyber official. He noted it was addressed to Mehdi Mohammadi. His message said as follows:

"Don't go out into the streets of Tehran this coming Tuesday between eleven am and 12 o'clock."

The following Tuesday at precisely eleven am all hell broke loose. Tehran was in a traffic frenzy due to the failure of its entire traffic lights system, which remained fixed on red, rendering all vehicles at a standstill. Infamous for its traffic jams and impossibly overcrowded roads, Tehran ground to a halt and remained paralyzed. Police cars, ambulances, official cars and dozens of thousands of vehicles of all kinds simply could not move an inch. The city's control center, the local police and the engineering department all attempted to get to the bottom of the malfunction, but to no avail.

At twelve noon precisely, the traffic lights came back to life, but it was only after long, grueling hours of endless traffic that the situation improved, but it was already late at night.

The following day, Bonnie received a message via his London service: "Beijing. The Fifth cyber conference. Hotel Nuo."

***

China was outpacing the rest of the world. Knowing full well that leadership in cyber meant controlling the flow of information around the world, the Chinese government guided its specialists to focus less on what 'cyber' meant and more on controlling it, citing it was for anyone to arrive at their own interpretation, but being at the top of that field would lead them to dominance over each and every facet of data, resulting in global dominance. With this in mind, China invested billions of US dollars in cyber, both directly in thousands of Chinese cyber R&D companies and through knowledge and know-how acquisition from foreign sources, not always in ways that were above board.

Following instructions from the top, Chinese cyber experts attended each and every conference, wherever it would take place. Such conferences served not only the Chinese but also anyone and everyone involved in the cyber sector worldwide. Over time, these conferences had grown into lavishly decorated street fares attracting all those who wished to buy, sell, exchange, spy, steal, learn or whatever.

The Chinese are great believers in 'the bigger the better,' and the global cyber conference at Beijing certainly lived up to the expectations of those who knew this, with some ten thousand participants, practically anyone who had any stake in this field. They put in an appearance, which was acknowledged by the hosts, who offered them an imperial hospitality that was hardly what a people's republic should have entertained, but for the fact that it was, after all, China. Beijing's finest hotels likewise regaled the conference goers with a royal-like program of entertainment, an expensive personal gift for each guest in the room and fabulous yet free meals. The Chinese went out of their way to endow the conference with a festive, buoyant atmosphere, fully intending it to work in their favor.

Israel, considered a world-class power in the field of cyber, was an honored, prominent and sought-after participant, whose delegation included dozens of representatives, led by none other than Science Minister Binyamin Pladot. Even prior to his departure, citing he had heard this was a good hotel, the minister had asked his office manager to book him a suite at Hotel Nuo in the center of Beijing.

"I feel like indulging myself after all the hard work I've had these past few days," said the minister. "Please let the Chinese organizers know they can accommodate the other members of our delegation in all the other hotels according to what's available.

***

It was five o'clock when Bonnie heard a knock on the front door of his lavish suite at Hotel Nuo and opened the door, only to have one of the hotel staff serve him an envelope. Bonnie received it, tipped him and went back inside. He opened the envelope as he sat in the armchair at the suite's sitting room, only to find one sentence in English: "Six o'clock at the bar."

Bonnie took a seat at a side table at five to six, making sure he put some distance between himself and the few others at the hotel's bar. Even before receiving the Chivas Regal he had ordered, a man of average height sat next to him. The man sported a fancy suit. Bonnie also noticed the cyber conference badge on the man's lapel, with the name 'Mazi Nazimi.'

"I see there's no point ordering you a glass of whiskey, but perhaps I might order you something else?" Bonnie asked.

"Thanks. I'd love a bottle of soda," the stranger replied in a reserved voice. "I understand you wanted to meet. What about?"

"Who is *us*?" replied Bonnie. "I asked to meet with a particular person. I know for a fact he is in Beijing."

"This particular person is busy today, so he asked me to inquire what this is about."

"I have a highly personal matter to discuss with your man, and I believe a meeting will prove very important for him."

The man's face remained blank. He was obviously examining Bonnie's intentions and trying to figure him out. Bonnie also took notice that the bar, which was nearly empty when he came in and sat, was now packed. For a moment there, he considered smiling, as it was clear to him the entire meeting was being recorded, complete with images and even close-ups of his face.

The man glanced at Bonnie and then suddenly got up and left the place without a word.

Bonnie realized there were fewer people at the bar now. '*Time for another shot,*' he told himself.

Not long after he had made it back to his suite, Bonnie heard another knock on his door. '*Good thing I have some spare change,*' he thought as he received an envelope from the hotel's errand boy through the open door.

"Eight o'clock in the lobby." That was all the note said.

Chapter Twenty-Seven

The weather in Beijing had changed. A cold front was upon the city, complete with a storm. At five to eight, Bonnie stood in the lobby, berating himself for sticking to his habit of always coming five minutes early to any appointment. There he was, in his thick, black, warm coat, his head covered in a Chinese fur hat with slits for the eyes, ready for what he was sure would be an excursion out of the hotel.

Bonnie did not have to wait long. *'Here's another person with a habit of showing up five minutes early,'* he realized, looking at this man wrapped in a similar coat. The man asked Bonnie to follow him, then opened the back door and invited him into a Mercedes with dark windows waiting right outside. *'Ah, so he's the driver.'* The passenger Bonnie met in the back seat was wearing a huge coat and sunglasses though it was already dark outside. Sitting far away from Bonnie, he kept silent. The driver started the car.

And then, during the ride, the man turned to Bonnie in perfect English with a note of apology, "Do you mind if I search you?"

Not the least surprised, Bonnie acquiesced.

It was a thorough inspection, complete with a mobile magnetometer.

The Mercedes pulled up near a restaurant. Bonnie could make out its name, 'Jia,' as well as other Mercedes cars parked outside and uniformed Revolutionary Guard men patrolling the entrance.

Not only was Jia fancy and expansive, it featured a high ceiling, black marble floors, red tables and gilded curtains. The high ceiling was covered with blue silk carpets with red stripes crisscrossing them. The place was packed with diners who were the epitome of the wealthy. Bonnie did not fail to notice the men in the crowd who kept watch, always looking around.

A beautiful hostess greeted Bonnie and the other man. Her long-gilded dress, adorned with Chinese dragons in fabulous colors, complemented her ivory face and small, full, bright red lips. The tall man who had accompanied Bonnie leaned over to her and whispered something in her ear, upon which she smiled, showing pearly white teeth, and instructed Bonnie and the other man to follow her. The hostess led them to the far end of the restaurant, where she pointed at a highly decorated oak door and quietly stepped away.

The man who accompanied Bonnie knocked on the heavy door. This was followed by a murmur of reply from inside, upon which the host invited Bonnie in and made himself scarce too.

Bonnie found himself in a beautifully decorated and furnished room with an exquisitely carved nut-tree dining table superbly done with Chinese carvings. It was set for two, featuring fine glittering bone china and handmade silver and gold cutlery.

Once Bonnie got used to the dim light in the room, he noticed a man that seemed tall even though he was sitting across the table. One glance, and Bonnie was on the verge of fainting. He did not need a second look to know this was his biological father.

Bonnie tried to breathe normally, despite his excitement and trembling. *'Ever since that letter, I simply lost my peace of mind. I've been searching for a safe haven for all this time.'*

Mehdi Mohammadi was sitting in front of him, stiff and frozen, his eyes firm. *'He doesn't have a clue.'* Then, for an instant, once he noticed Bonnie's blue eyes, a thought did run across his mind, but he cast it aside. His entire body language bespoke power and resolve.

"Are you all right?" he asked Bonnie as he realized the other man was about to keel over.

"Yes, I am fine," came Bonnie's reply as he thanked Mehdi for the glass of water, he poured him from a crystal carafe.

"What brings the science minister of the Zionist government here to meet me?" Mehdi asked in a cynical tone, while demonstrating he was well-informed. "Since when is it that you people are willing to meet us *'terrorists'* from Iran?"

For Bonnie, Mehdi's cold tone and stern face were a source of strength that helped him focus. He had yet to regain his voice, and his hands were still trembling, but he was able to get hold of himself. He produced the pink slip of the report he had received from the institute back in Vienna and handed it over to his father.

TEST RESULTS
"The DNA test showed that the two blood samples taken from X. and the sample delivered to us from Hypocratio Hospital in Thessaloniki are completely identical."

The strength and resolve Mehdi exhibited faded like dew in the sun. It was now Bonnie's turn to pour Mehdi a glass of water. '*I sure hope he doesn't faint on me now.*' Mehdi did not thank him for this gesture. His body shrank and he lowered his head. Both men were now sitting across from each other. Nothing but silence passed between them over the beautiful table.

Mehdi's face was pale as marble, whiter than his beard. Bonnie's face was white too. He had never been paler.

Suddenly, Mehdi got up. He did not say a word. He left the room while still clutching the pink slip of paper Bonnie handed him.

Alone in that room, Bonnie was shocked. He agonized, then couldn't hold himself any longer. The weight of this encounter overpowered him, and he burst into an uncontrollable tumult of tears and audible sobs.

The hostess came in, anxious and nervous. Concerned, she turned to the grown man who was weeping like a baby. "May I be of assistance?"

Bonnie managed to collect himself enough to gesture he was fine. He helped himself to another glass of water. The large carafe contained enough water for a third glass.

The hostess left Bonnie to fix her makeup, rendered slightly less perfect by a tear she could not help shedding. She dried her left cheek and upon returning to her guest noticed Bonnie had left her two one hundred-dollar bills for the dinner no one had actually eaten. Looking forward to his flight back to Tel Aviv, he hurried back to his hotel.

Chapter Twenty-Eight

Upon the return of the large Iranian delegation from the cyber conference in Beijing, Mehdi convened a meeting at the Revolutionary Guard HQ in Tabriz, inviting dozens of the organization's senior commanders. As supreme commander, he took his usual seat and asked the head of the delegation to Beijing, Nazem Nazarat, to summarize it for them.

Nazarat began by greeting Mehdi: "On behalf of myself and the other members of the delegation, I would like to thank our glorious commander, Mehdi Mohammadi. He worked tirelessly behind the scenes to promote the goals of the revolution. He has met, in secret, with various persons and elements, and has opened unto us doors hitherto closed. He has followed his own course and vision for our homeland."

Everyone there except for Mehdi rose to their feet, clapped and cheered for their brave commander.

"The conference," Nazarat continued, "honed our understanding of the importance of the world of cyber. We must boost our foothold in this field in both security and means of attack. Unless we are able to foster better information security, we remain exposed to the enemy's unrelenting attempts to uncover our secrets and disrupt our every move. By the same token, we have to establish an attack system capable of penetrating any data system our enemy may have, reveal its plans and foil them."

Mehdi was finding it difficult to follow Nazarat, as his own mind drifted and he was somewhere else. Halfway through Nazarat's discourse, he rose from his seat, thanked everyone present and excused himself, citing some urgent personal matter he had to attend to. He drove from HQ directly to his parents' house.

*****

Grown and a man's man in his own right, Mehdi was nevertheless always happy and excited to come home to his mom and dad. He never married. "I am married to the revolution," he told his mother when she expressed her concern or gave that reply to anyone who took an interest in his personal status. His parents' home was his haven, a source of refuge. Along with *maderbozorg*, his beloved grandma Suheila, the *khanom*, (lady or Mrs.), his loving parents, brothers and sisters, and numerous cousins, who multiplied over the years, were his entire family.

When she was still alive, Suheila never asked Mehdi about his marriage plans. Over the years, his mother Fatimah, also, came to terms with the situation and ceased presenting him with all sorts of potential brides among Tehran's elite families.

Nor did Mehdi's marital status present any issues with the organization he commanded. The leaders of the revolution and their supporters ruled out the possibility that Mehdi, a virile he-man, could have any 'extraordinary' sexual predilections. They accepted without any doubt his total devotion to the cause and understood as a matter of course that he simply hadn't spare time for leisure or personal relationships.

Mehdi avoided the company of women altogether. There was one woman, but for a moment, whose memory stayed with him for the rest of his life. His entire perception of his own sexuality revolved around that extraordinary recollection, the moment allotted him by Allah, back in that little patch of heaven on that Greek peninsula.

Even as he was recovering in the hospital in Thessaloniki after his car accident, his entire being was immersed in that heavenly encounter, that torrid night with a godsend. "There are those," he was reminded of an old Persian saying, "who spend their entire life to make their mark, whereas some make their eternal mark in the flicker of an eye."

'*Did I really make a mark in such a short time?*' he thought to himself. '*Or perhaps it was a bit longer? Either way, for me, it was eternity.*'

Meeting that fellow with the blue eyes back in Beijing had thrown him into a mental loop that had left his soul bare. '*I don't need any piece of paper to verify what was so plain in a split second to the naked eye,*' he reasoned, convinced some mystic bond tied that guy and him from the fringes of the conference together.

'*What I need now is some downtime, some reckoning of my own to do,*' he had realized at the meeting back in HQ. It was the very first time in his life he felt he could not take part in a professional discussion, let alone contribute. He upped and left and went home directly, thinking he might find solace at his parents' home. But then again, he had another reason to visit, one that was utterly plain and simple.

***

The khana was just completed at that time. It has been two intensive years since that terrible fire, and the family had devoted itself to having the complex rebuilt. Suheila did not live to see it built in her lifetime, but true to her last words and testament, they honored her and her memory by naming the new family complex, 'Suheila Hall.'

Her death was hardly a surprise. Towards the end of her life, she was afflicted by all sorts of ailments; however, she bore them all with dignity, not matter how much she suffered. She hoped to live to see the khana restored but died one year after the great fire. Her death was a sad event, but the mourners nevertheless took solace in her memory and in their great privilege of having known her.

"The great *poetess* of carpets and rugs," the commander of the Revolutionary Guard began his eulogy to her. He had come especially to the funeral of his beloved maderbozorg, grandmother. A magnificent blue carpet hung behind him, featuring her name in gilded silken letters.

The restoration of this building, which, in fact, meant it was rebuilt, constituted an opportunity to introduce large scale changes. The team of architects that was chosen included heritage specialists, highly proficient in preserving traditional architecture, as well as modern architects, who originated creative solutions for contemporary requirements.

The complex itself had two stories, in line with the tradition of that specific bazaar and the bazaar spirit and culture in general. It consisted of polished red Zagros stones, brought all the way from those splendid mountains, where a special quarry produced the marvelous, beautiful bricks, renowned throughout Iran.

The first floor was divided in two. One space constituted a large exhibition hall where visitors could view the wares on sale, complete with an open space where the weaving ladies demonstrated their art and skill to the general public. The other part of this level was the actual sales floor, which constituted an integral part of the grand bazaar the Mohammadi khana was part of.

As part of their route, the many visitors to the entire market of Tabriz would pass through the khana's open space and make their way by the piles of carpets and rugs, while being regaled by the calls and cries of the loud sellers.

The khana's second story no longer had the warehouses and weaving and production halls. They were relocated outside the grand bazaar to specially dedicated venues. Instead, the second floor of the khana now had board rooms. The central office, adjacent to the lavish conference hall, was where Suleiman, Mehdi's father, sat, managing the family business and steering it youthfully and forcefully despite his advanced years. Bahiz's room was next to his, as he was in charge of promoting the business. Another board room was situated next to his. For the time being, it remained unoccupied, although it was sumptuous and spacious, "for future's sake..." Suleiman dreamt of a new generation of directors to see the family business flourish through a long and prosperous time.

The second floor also featured sales rooms for exclusive clientele. This applied to large-scale buyers and certain connoisseurs who flocked from every corner of the world to marvel at the carpets and rugs and gaze at the Mohammadis' exquisite wares, which were, indeed, world-renowned.

The center of the second story featured the 'Museum of Carpets,' dedicated to the memory of Suheila. Its floors consisted of large marble tiles in gray-blue that hailed from the Alborz mountain range, famous the world over for its beauty and unique palette. The law prohibited quarrying there, unless, that is, you were part of the supreme commander's family.

The museum's main wall had a bright marble stand with a picture of Suheila, whose blue gaze dominated the entire space. A tribute to the contribution the Mohammadis' made to Iran's carpetmaking industry, it boasted artifacts that were centuries old, having miraculously been spared in the fire. Suheila's own contribution was highlighted as well: her unique, exquisite, patterns, the fine weaving together of silk and wool and her color scheme. These were a tribute to her rich imagination, astounding creativity and wondrously skillful weaving.

***

Suleiman stood at the entrance of his office and waited for Mehdi, his son. Following their warm embrace, the proud father led him to the sumptuous lounge, where his other son,

Bahiz, was already sitting. The three Mohammadi men enjoyed their family reunion and had countless cups of sweetened tea their loyal, long-serving servant prepared them.

Mehdi sang the praises of the newly built, impressive khana complex. "I couldn't get a good enough look during the opening with all the crowds, but I got a good glimpse now and really must commend you for a wonderful project you've built here." He then bid Bahiz and his sisters farewell and walked over to the museum with his father. He turned to Suheila's corner, bowed his head before her impressive portrait that hang next to Ali's, which had a black frame. For a while, he dwelled deeply in his prayers and thoughts.

On his way out, Mehdi got a chance to greet a group of students from the weaving faculty at Esfahan. In reply, they told him they had come especially for a study tour of the museum.

"Do not have any meal today!" Suleiman warned him. "Your mother has been busy all day with her special *horshet sabzi*."

"Don't worry," Mehdi replied, smiling, "as if I could forget Mom's beef stew with herbs."

Back at home, when he passed through the kitchen, he did his best not to lose himself in the intoxicating scents and smells of cooking as he surprised his mother Fatimah with a hug, seizing the moment her back was turned. He whispered, "I am going to be busy for a few hours" and went up to his own small piece of heaven.

The southern side of the family home had a short and narrow staircase that led to a spacious rooftop balcony. Realizing that the rest of the family made little used of it, for they had the entire spacious mansion to deal with, Mehdi embraced it from the moment he had first discovered it many years ago. The views of Tabriz lay before him, with all the city's might and splendor. He could see the teaming streets, palatial houses and the minarets of the mosques. He viewed the entire surrounding from the same level as the minarets that towered over the multitude of people below.

Over in the corner of the roof, there was a small chamber with an electric kettle for tea. The rooftop had a partial ceiling, and along with the ever-temperate breeze from the bluish far-off mountains, this was enough to stave off the city's usually warm air. The pleasant haven had two old chairs and a hammock, now holding Mehdi's outstretched legs.

He shut his eyes and let the swaying overpower him. Thus, the commander of Iran's Revolutionary Guard gave in to his thoughts, dreams and troubles. He was wracked with both certainty and doubt.

'*Surely Suheila's blue eyes, which I've seen only this morning in her portrait at the museum, are the same as those of that Israeli fellow I met at that bar in Beijing. They were without a doubt carved out of the same rock. But what does this have to do with me?*'

But still, Mehdi was also plagued by doubt. '*How could it be, that among all the people on earth, I would be related to a minister in the government of Israel?!*'

And yet, certainty once more, for '*the tears I saw in his eyes were real. And no doubt my excitement ever since my encounter with him is real. Who better than I knows what he must be going through... It's like something out of a novel or those movies...*'

He doesn't even know what's going to happen.'

His thoughts lingered. '*I doubt whether he can contain this terrible secret he is up against. Surely, he must resolve this. He has to get to the bottom of the mystery that has overwhelmed his life, too.'*

As he swung back and forth, the heat and his fatigue caused Mehdi to doze off. He was awakened by the sound of knocking on the rooftop's door. There stood his mother. Her concern for him was obvious.

"I am fine, Mom," he said, feeling as if a great, big iron weight had been lifted from his shoulders. It came loose. '*I have to see him,*' he resolved.

Chapter Twenty-Nine

The phone rang on Friday evening.

"Hi. My name is George. I am a tourist. I came from Armenia with a group of Bahai pilgrims. We're touring the Bahai gardens in Haifa and I would like to see you. I have something to deliver."

In the afternoon of the following day, Bonnie drove to Haifa. A waiter in a café near the entrance to the Bahai gardens led him to George, who in turn handed him a sealed envelope, which he opened the moment George was gone.

"I'll be waiting at the Hyatt Regency Paris on the 17th of this month" was all the message said.

***

"I'm about to go on a five-day private vacation in Paris," the minister of science told the chief of security at the prime minister's office. "No security. No bodyguards." Still, protocol, as well as security procedures, dictated he would disclose that he would be staying at the Hyatt Regency in the 17th *arrondissement*.

Once Bonnie finished checking in at the reception, the clerk gestured to a remote corner in the lobby and told Bonnie someone was waiting for him there. A large, bald man rose to greet him. When they sat down, the large man asked Bonnie whether it would be okay for him to take a three-day tour outside France. Bonnie feigned surprise but inwardly, he was hardly taken aback.

"Where am is supposed to be going?"

"That I cannot tell you," the large man replied. "All will be revealed tomorrow."

The following day, Bonnie came down to reception with a small traveling bag. He told the clerk his plans had changed and that he was going on a three-day trip to the south of France. He requested, and received, a hotel safe where he deposited his Israeli passport, Israeli banknotes, a book in Hebrew which he had begun reading on the plane, as well as any other item that might be associated with Israel.

The large man was waiting for him in the lobby. He greeted him and asked him to accompany him outside, where a rather simple-looking car with a French license plate awaited them. He asked Bonnie to take his seat in the back, next to another man who was already there. The car proceeded in the direction of one of Paris's airports.

Early on, the man sitting next to Bonnie produced an Iranian passport. It was green and it had the title 'Republic of Iran' embossed on the front. The man handed it to Bonnie, who was surprised to find a recent photo of his inside along with his personal details. '*It's for me! It's issued to me*,' Bonnie realized, leafing through, and discovering there were several stamps there, indicating a few journeys already made over the past year, for example to Turkey, Abu Dhabi and various countries in Europe. Needless to say, Bonnie had made no such visits. One of the stamps indicated that the bearer of that passport had entered France a few weeks earlier.

Inside the passport, Bonnie also found a flight ticket for Iran's national airline. Much to Bonnie's amazement, the destination was Tabriz, Iran. He also found a few Iranian banknotes, but the sums meant nothing to him.

When they arrived at Charles de Gaulle Airport, the large man bid him farewell in good English and wished him *bon voyage*. The officer at the passport counter examined the Iranian passport Bonnie handed him, saw the entry stamp to France, stamped the exit date and let Bonnie through to the Departures terminal.

The flight to Iran was on time. Shortly after takeoff, Bonnie was cordially asked to move from coach to business class. Five and a half hours afterwards, the uneventful flight ended. The plane landed at Tabriz airport.

It was afternoon in Iran. A car waited by the airplane stairs to take Bonnie to the terminal. The person who was there to attend to him indeed fast-tracked his arrival and his check-in through customs and passport control.

The car then took Bonnie from the airport to the Espinas Hotel in the center of Tabriz, where the reception desk gave him a key and informed him that *they* would come to pick him up the following morning at ten o'clock.

Tired as he was, Bonnie was nevertheless unable to sleep. His hotel room was spacious and lovely but simple and unadorned. The coffee table had a bowl of fresh cut vegetables, fresh sandwiches and an assortment of nuts and seeds. He also found a note inviting him to sample the minibar, which, as he discovered upon opening it, featured a large selection of fresh juice, mineral water and sodas but no alcohol. He helped himself to the snacks and the non-alcoholic beer, which he actually found quite pleasant.

He was overrun by troubling thoughts. '*How will the meeting go tomorrow?*' Ever since his first encounter with his 'biological father,' as he referred to him at this stage, his excitement had cooled off a bit but was still high.

The car was there at ten o'clock that morning. Bonnie was summarily taken to a fancy-looking, spacious house in the outskirts of Tabriz, where the car entered underground parking. Bonnie stepped into an elevator with an attendant who brought them all the way to the eleventh floor. The attendant pushed a buzzer and bid farewell to Bonnie before the elevator door opened.

Bonnie entered an apartment with a modestly decorated living room complete with thick Persian rugs and two armchairs. Mehdi Mohammadi was sitting in one of them. He got up, shook Bonnie by the hand and invited him to sit. They sat opposite each other. The silence was heavy. Mehdi was pale, tight jawed, his lips so tight they were white and his ears alert like those of a predator about to prowl. Bonnie, too, was nervous. He felt his jaws were tightening, as well. His back and neck were aching, and his stomach turned.

Mehdi spoke first, breaking the silence.

"We have matters to resolve," sounding very tired, he told

Bonnie in English.

"Yes," Bonnie agreed, in a slightly less tired voice than Mehdi's.

They exchanged blue glances, unsure how to proceed. Bonnie came to his wits first.

"Have you seen the message from Vienna?"

"I did. But what is it that you wish to tell me?"

"I came to tell you I am your son."

Mehdi was stunned by the direct reply. His blue eyes grew darker. The edges on either side of his mouth got deeper. His body tensed up. "What do you base this on?"

Bonnie was struck by terrific fatigue. His face, sun-kissed by years of horseback riding in the valley, turned gray. His shoulders sank and his entire body betrayed how weary he was. But after a while, he recovered enough to reply. "I showed you the results of a genetic test."

"This proves nothing," Mehdi retorted. Nevertheless, his eyes conveyed some curiosity, maybe even a dash of empathy. "What's your story?"

"It's a long story," Bonnie felt slightly encouraged by Mehdi's now softer tone and body language.

"We have all the time in the world. That's what we're here for," Mehdi answered as he poured them both tea from the nearby pot.

Bonnie sipped the tea carefully and began.

"My mother's name was Estée. She died two years ago in her home in a village in the Jezreel Valley. That's in the north of Israel. Subsequently, after tidying up, I found an envelope in a drawer by her bed. It was addressed to me personally."

He took another sip from his tea and lingered a bit. "Inside this envelope, I found a letter in my mother's own handwriting. She told me my dad was not my biological father."

The emotional turmoil that seemed to have subsided climbed from the bottom of Bonnie's stomach and went to his head. Mehdi noticed how overcome with emotion he was and quickly poured him a glass of water.

"And what did you do with this piece of news?" he asked Bonnie.

Bonnie felt Mehdi's vigilance. "Well," he said, "I decided to look for my father and track him down. I discovered my mother had been to Thessaloniki, Greece, during the time that matched her being pregnant with me. So I went there and met a woman called Claudia, a friend of my mother's. Based on the information she gave me, I went to a breathtakingly beautiful peninsula, Sithonia, saw the hotel and got to know where I was conceived."

The further along Bonnie went with his story, the faster he recovered, gaining strength from the close attention of the man across from him, his biological father. When he was done, silence descended on the room once again.

This time, it was Bonnie who broke it.

"Would you like me to go on?"

But Mehdi was no longer there. His mind took him to the dreams, the memories, of that godsend creature from Sithonia, whose image he had kept alive in his innermost thoughts all these years.

And then, Bonnie watched with anxiety how the tough commander of Iran's Revolutionary Guard suddenly collapsed right before his eyes. Mehdi seemed to have shrunk. His head fell, his eyes grew blank, and he began to tremble all over. He could not help it. Years of denial, repression and emotional blocking out were taking their toll and finally gushing out. Mehdi never cried. As much as he might want to, he simply did not know how. Rather, he uttered all sorts of yelps and moans. Then, in a gesture that stupefied them both, he laid his head on Bonnie's shoulder. Bonnie himself was beside himself with surprise, joy and perhaps even sadness.

"If only you knew how much I loved your mother..." was all Mehdi was able to utter.

After long moment of silence, Mehdi regained his composure and seemed to have returned to the image of power and fortitude. And then, as though nothing had happened, he asked, "But how did you manage to obtain my DNA?"

"Someone got hurt in a car accident and was admitted to the hospital. It's not much of a leap from that point."

"Tell me," Mehdi asked apprehensively, "is the Israeli Mossad in on this?"

"No. only two people in the whole world know the story, you and I."

**

The hours went by. It got dark as the day progressed. '*So, what do we do?*' each of them thought as they looked at each other pensively.

"We need to bide our time," Mehdi reassumed his role of responsible adult. He rose from his seat. Quite spontaneously he went over to Bonnie, who, likewise stood up, and the two embraced long and hard. Their identical blue eyes exchanged a long, wet glance.

"I would like you to have dinner tomorrow night with me and my family," Mehdi said as he turned towards the door.

***

The following day, Bonnie took the elevator down to the hotel's mercantile floor at the lobby. He entered a menswear shop and bought himself a white button-down shirt and black trousers. He then went to the nearby gift shop, wondering what present to bring that evening. *'I'm always so lousy at presents.'* He eventually succumbed to the warm and adamant recommendation of the lovely shop girl and bought a handwoven prayer mat.

"I am sure your hosts do not have such a beautiful piece," she told Bonnie, but inwardly, she commended herself on a good sale: *'another tourist sold, and at such a steep price.'*

***

The car brought Bonnie to a splendid house on a swanky street in Tabriz. There was Mehdi, waiting up front. Much to his delight, Bonnie saw that Mehdi, too, was wearing a white shirt and black trousers. *'Good match,'* he commended himself, *'I hope I did well with the prayer mat too.'*

After they shook hands, Mehdi whispered to him, "I told them you're an American who came to Tabriz on business.

They do not need to know anything more than that."

Mehdi led his guest into a luxurious living room with a floor of black marble tiles separated by mosaics in blue and gold. The heavy curtains were all crimson with gilded tassels hanging by the windows. Bonnie also marveled at the side tables laden with artifacts and at the thick rugs with a quality matched by that of the gilded chandelier. Ashamed of the prayer mat, he hid it behind his back, while figuring out how to bow out gracefully.

The family was already seated at their cushioned armchairs. Mehdi presented to Bonnie Ali's widow and their three children, his brother Bahiz, Bahiz's wife and their four children, his two sisters, Shahnaz and Yasmin, who came with their fiancés, and, finally, his mother Fatimah and his father Suleiman, who both got up in Bonnie's honor and shook hands with him.

Bonnie felt quite queasy at the sudden realization he was shaking hands with his paternal grandparents hit him.

Throughout his entire life, Bonnie had an acute absence of grandpas and grandmas. He had never had the pleasure of a grandpa coming to preschool and tell tall tales. He did not recall one Passover dinner at his grandparents, whereas his fellow preschoolers, afterward, school friends, would always be telling him about a present *their* grandparents have given them. He did not understand what they went on about.

Avram's parents died before he was born, so he never got to know the people who had raised his father. He had a faint memory of his maternal grandfather, in particular the poor man's *unsuccessful* attempts to teach him Russian. '*And here*

I am, shaking hands with and receiving a warm hug from my newfound grandad and grandma, so late in my own life,' he could not help thinking.

Dinner dragged on and on. So many dishes and such exotic tastes. Laughter and chatter filled the spacious dining room, and Bonnie fit right in. But he wasn't really there though. He kept picturing Estée with Avram, sitting right there with him, sampling the dishes and having such a wonderful time. *'What would they have said about my new grandpa and grandma?'* he asked himself.

When dinner ended and he bade farewell to his wonderful hosts, Mehdi asked Bonnie to come up with him to what he referred to as "my own patch of heaven." There, on the spacious balcony, overlooking Tabriz's night sky, lit by stars and city lights, the two sat and drank the sweet tea that Mehdi prepared for them. Bonnie felt very much at ease. He hadn't felt this happy and content in years. "I had such a lovely time with your family," he told Mehdi.

"They loved you as well," Mehdi replied, and continued, "So, you're going back to the Zionist country tomorrow, right?"

"And you're going back to your plans to bring about our destruction, right?"

They both burst out laughing. Such a liberating laugh.

"Iran doesn't wish to destroy anyone," Mehdi declared.

"So, what does Iran want?"

"Respect and security."

Bonnie went into deep thoughts. *'Everything I thought about Iran I have to reconsider now. It's not just an enemy, but also home to dozens of millions who want nothing else but to live their lives in peace and security.'* The Mohammadis' warm hospitality and getting to know them in person had made an impact. Their kind and affable ways got the better of him. His own family was not the same. His mixed emotions towards his biological father also became clearer to him, as did his unfolding affinity. *'We don't just have the same eyes, we also seem to have the same character. I have a newfound appreciation for him.'*

Bonnie suddenly surprised himself when he asked, "May I be of assistance?"

Mehdi, too, found the question surprising. "Only if you wish," he replied.

"I'll be glad to help," Bonnie replied, taken aback by the rollercoaster of his life.

"I told you Iran does not wish to destroy Israel, only to protect ourselves, so any information in that regard will help. As minister of science you know what I mean."

"I will surprise you," Bonnie told his father.

Much later that night, after establishing their secure, well-concealed modes of communication, the father drove the son back to his hotel. Their parting was emotional: an embrace and a promise to each other they would meet again soon.

***

The following day, the large man picked Bonnie up from the hotel and took him to the airport. He was once again cleared to depart quickly and efficiently and rushed into the plane so quickly, it seemed the flight was waiting just for him. Once the five and a half-hour flight back to Charles de Gaulle Airport in Paris landed, Bonnie returned to the Hyatt Regency, where he quickly gathered his stuff from the hotel safe, checked out and hurried back to the airport, where he went through customs again, this time using his real Israeli passport. He spent three hours waiting for the El Al flight back to Israel. Prior to boarding, he destroyed the Iranian passport, flushing the myriad pieces of paper down the drain at various stalls.

"So, minister, how was Paris?" his secretary asked when he returned.

"Quite all right," he replied, and went over to his desk to go over the paperwork that had piled up.

Chapter Thirty

The Revolutionary Guard's special staff, dedicated to the promotion of Operation Queen of Vengeance, convened at the villa near Qom. Commander Mehdi Mohammadi was seated, per usual, at the head, together, also as usual, with the heads of the ops and intelligence sections, the chief engineer and other top brass. Mehdi thanked them for their efforts in drawing up the plans for avenging the blows the Zionists had dealt them and asked the ops chief to review the final plan of action.

"The Israeli embassy in Nigeria," the chief of operations began his review, "is a real fortress. This five-story building consists of various wings. We've managed to obtain the blueprints, which I would like to present to you now."

He proceeded to show the slide displaying the comprehensive plans of the structure, pinpointing in great detail the exact locations of even the basements and parking spaces.

"Not only this, we also have the building's functional composition and the uses the Israelis are making of it. The front of the building is used for the administrative tasks of the embassy and the departments that are in contact with the local authorities. This is also where the consular office is situated."

Mehdi's chief of operations then pointed to another wing. "As far as we are concerned, the interesting part of the building is the back, where the local Mossad station is located. In fact, the word *station* is diminutive, as it unjustly underplays Mossad's activity throughout Africa. This wing concentrates their entire operations on this continent. This is where all the operational commands are relayed to the various teams. The back wing is also where the Mossad intelligence and cyber unit is located. They have at their disposal a satellite system that is operated via an array of antennas on the roof of this building."

He paused and continued. "I forgot to mention that the embassy's diplomatic mission is also up front. The connection between the diplomatic mission and the operational stations is minimal, if any."

The ops chief moved on to the next item. "The building's basement is used for various functions, such as the embassy's archive, small printshop and various warehouses. The most important section there is an open space they use for training special forces, complete with an adjacent, specially dedicated room for counterterrorism equipment."

"As you can all see," he was edging towards conclusion, "we've obtained a great deal of information on the embassy building and the activity there, but we are still unable to determine the use the Israelis are making with several rooms in the basement. We do know they guard them and use special security means."

He then made his final remark. "Hundreds of people work in this building, some of them are local. None of them have any access to the back section. Entry is exclusively allowed to Israelis, who enter this separate wing using a special code. Now, I suggest we hear from our friend Yazdi here, our highly qualified team engineer."

"I would like to thank the people from ops and intelligence for working so well to provide us with everything we need for this operation," engineer Yazdi Shirazi began. "My guidelines were to destroy the entire building, but, as you just saw, the most important part is the back, so our operational plans are to allow a zero chance for this wing of the building to survive the explosion."

He took a moment before continuing. "We had long discussions with our team of explosives experts. After consulting with them and studying the building's blueprints, we have concluded that we need an explosive charge of half a ton. If attached to the building, it would be enough to destroy it entirely."

The ops chief then brought his presentation to a conclusion. "As you can see, the building is surrounded by a tall cement fence. Entry is limited to an electric explosive-resistant steel gate. Resistant, that is, to conventional explosives. The compound and its surroundings are covered by special motion cameras that relay the images online to a control room within the building and, at the same time, to a special control room at Lagos Police. No doubt the Jews know how to take care of themselves.".

"Shirazi is correct," Revolutionary Guard Commander Mehdi reassumed the helm. "Nevertheless, we are just as clever. I would like to finalize this meeting and provide you with two updates. First of all, the explosive charge is ready and is kept hidden about two hours' drive from the embassy. Second, our *modus operandi* is tight. We will show these Jews, the Nigerians and the whole world who's really clever. At this stage, we've decided to share the final operational details only forty-eight hours prior to the mission."

He then added, "I thank you all for a job well done. I want you to convey our thanks to all our good people who have worked on this holy operation."

***

The prime minister was sitting at the head of the table, with the minister of defense to his right and the science minister sitting to the left of the prime minister. The chief of the IDF general staff was sitting next to the defense minister, and next to him sat the intelligence affairs and strategy advisor. The head of the Mossad was sitting left of the science minister, next to the IDF chief of staff.

"On today's agenda," the prime minister began, "is the removal of Iran's Islamic Revolutionary Guard Corps commander Mehdi Mohammadi. We have already authorized this in our meeting several weeks ago, but the details of the mission suggest that innocent lives may be lost due to its operational complexity. The attorney general insists that under such circumstances, the cabinet has to approve the operation with the members' full awareness of all the details and steps. We have here with us our Mossad chief to provide a complete, detailed outline of the operation and the risks it poses."

The head of Mossad gave a comprehensive report of the mission and the risks that it involved, including the possibility of innocent bystanders being injured or even killed. At the end of his presentation, he concluded, "the sanctity of human life is paramount among the values of Mossad and its activities. We turn to this option only under special circumstances and out of necessity. Hurting innocents is out of the question in terms of our code of conduct, but in the particular case we are discussing here, this operation is necessary to save the lives of dozens, perhaps even hundreds, of innocent lives that might fall prey to the savagery of this proxy of the Iranian regime. Under these circumstances and in the absence of any alternative, we have proposed to the prime minister to stop this mad Iranian mission by removing the snake's head."

Silence descended on the room, broken only by the prime minister. "Who is in favor of authorizing the removal of the commander of Iran's Revolutionary Guard according to the principles laid out by our Mossad chief?"

Everyone present raised his hand.

Chapter Thirty-One

"I, Binyamin Pladot, son of Avram Fiddlemann of blessed memory and son of Esther Fiddlemann, may she live long, do hereby pledge, as member of the government, to remain loyal to the State of Israel and to its statues, to faithfully execute my duties as minister and uphold the decisions of the Knesset."

Bonnie recalled the immense excitement he had felt standing on the podium in the Knesset, Israel's parliament, and taking his oath of office. He remembered how much he had missed his father, who had died not long before then and did not live to see the day his son was appointed minister in a government of Israel. As he stood on the podium, he had sought his mother's loving eyes. She was sitting in the section reserved for honored guests, along with his sister, with tears in her eyes.

'*How things turned around*,' he couldn't help but wonder.

***

'Lady' the mare loved her rider. Their 'affair' had lasted twelve years, during which he would give her favorite morning treat, a special brand of hay, mixed with alfalfa, and she, in turn, would stride along and gallop sure and steady. She liked the way he rode, light and respectful of her, and he liked the way his mare was devoted to him, cooperative and always in sync.

When he became a member of the Knesset, Israel's parliament, Bonnie asked Udi, his friend and neighbor, to have Lady join his stables. Every so often, when he returned to his house in the valley, Bonnie's first went over to Udi's shed to reunite with the mare. She, for her part, did not have to see Bonnie with her own eyes. She simply knew her best friend was on his way to her. She had such a lovely, acute, bloodhound sense of his presence. She would suddenly stomp impatiently, and there he was.

"Even my own faithful dog doesn't care for me as much as your Lady cares for you," Udi complained at the sight of Bonnie and Lady exchanging neighs of joy. Bonnie began preparing her for their ride, cleaned her hooves, brushed her mane gently but firmly, exactly the way she liked, put a thick blanket on her back and then the special saddle he had bought in Marrakesh, Morocco.

The moment he mounted his mare and put his feet through the stirrups, Lady trotted out, ever so lightly, out of the stables. The horse needed no direction, knowing full well, after dozens of hours of riding, it was the fields and meadows they were going to. The valley was a patch of green fields, cotton fields before they bud, clover, green wheat just before harvest, and long stripes of yellow daisies and wild mustard in between.

Lady simply loved to ride, ever so softly, through dirt paths, driving flocks of white egrets, yet careful not to trample a slow-crossing turtle. Bonnie breathed in the fields and savored the blue of the far-off mountains: the Carmel range to the south, the Galilee mountains to the north, and the Gilboa up ahead.

This was Bonnie's natural habitat. Here, he could commune with himself and his Lord. It was here that he made his life-altering decision.

***

The leaders of the Islamic Republic of Iran decided on a lavish, impressive parade for that year to broadcast to the whole world the country's might and offer the downtrodden masses something to be proud about despite their harsh economic crisis. Powers that be first thought the supreme leader should be the one leading it, but then they thought better of it and decided to bestow the honor on their commander of the Revolutionary Guard, who would also be assigned a seat right on stage near all the other heads of the country.

Ankalaev, one of Tehran's main streets, was chosen to host the parade because of its length, width and central location. A few weeks prior to the occasion, it was sealed off and traffic having been forbidden, makeshift seating, complete with roofs, was set up to accommodate some two thousand spectators. A dignitaries' booth was erected at the center of these platforms, complete with a throne-like box with a red canopy and gilded tassels.

Security was so paramount that even trash cans five hundred yards away were removed and relocated, as were all the trees within three hundred feet of the honorary platform. Much to the chagrin of the local residents, this was indeed a necessity to prevent any risk of snipers. Trees that were farther away were closely trimmed. Iran's security services made careful background checks of everyone living within some three hundred yards from where the country's top leadership was to sit. Moreover, the residents of the houses at closer proximity were driven out of their own homes for forty-eight hours prior to the parade. When given advance notice of this, they were obliged to surrender their keys to the security detail and prohibited from entering their own apartments until they were told otherwise.

The special force assigned to command the parade went into emergency protocol forty-eight hours before take-off. All the platforms were double-checked again, including the customary sweep for mines and explosive devices. They were then marked in blue tape, armed guards were posted, and parking was prohibited for the following twenty-four hours. The day prior to the parade, security force snipers took their positions in the apartments above and were given strict instructions to shoot anything or anyone suspicious – and ask questions later.

The morning of the parade saw helicopters patrolling the street very low as thousands of security men took their places along the planned route. At ten o'clock that morning, three hours before the parade was due to begin, the security detail from the 'special branch' sealed the platform and encircled it, barring anyone who was not due to sit there from getting close.

The person in charge of securing the parade, an experienced veteran of such events, had a simple rule, 'be concerned now so that you can have peace of mind later.' He and his men thoroughly inspected each and every aspect of the security arrangements until they had exhausted every query. The final drill concluded without a hitch, and everyone hoped for the best.

***

On the eve of the parade, Mehdi was sitting comfortably in his apartment in the center of Tehran in his shorts and t-shirt. He glanced at the fancy uniform hanging outside his closet, laid out on a clothes hanger in the center of his living room, exactly as his bodyguard, after thoroughly inspecting the uniform down to the last button, had brought it over.

Mehdi planned a quiet evening for himself, a welcome respite after the past few hectic days, ahead of the parade the following morning. He didn't care for parades. '*All that noise, the rigorous security arrangements, standing for so long, saluting at attention... all that hassle just isn't my thing,*' he told himself. '*Nevertheless,*' he thought, '*it can't be helped.*'

The telephone rang. He had three by his side. One of them was red. Only the President of Iran had the number, strictly for the utmost emergency. The second landline for operational matters was known to a select group of senior Revolutionary Guard commanders. Mehdi's third line, a personal cellphone, would vibrate whenever someone would use a special one-time code that was designed to self-destruct immediately after the message or call was accepted. *'Why is it vibrating now?'* Perplexed for a short while, Mehdi approved receiving the message, opened the screen and saw the following line: "**Do not show up for tomorrow's parade.**"

The message remained on the screen for three seconds before the code, the SIM card and the message itself self-destructed. *'I know who it's from. The only person in the entire world I gave the code to.'* Mehdi could not stop thinking about him ever since had they met. He could barely contain his emotional outpouring from then on. The only other person who had ever caused his emotions to surge in such a way was the blue-eyed young man's mother.

'Miss the parade tomorrow? I couldn't possibly...' but then, Mehdi did pull himself together, picked up the phone and called his deputy, Mosati Ahizi.

"How are the preparations going?"

"Everything is going to plan, sir. We are going to have a great parade, sir."

"What about security?"

"We conducted a general inspection of all the security matters and found everything to be in order, sir. We are assured zero risks and zero problems. The entire route is secure as of now, sir, by a large security detail. Everything is looking good, sir."

"Very good, Mosati! But I want another inspection done first thing in the morning; pay special attention to the podium area, especially where the dignitaries are going to sit."

"Yes, sir. Everything will be done according to your orders, sir."

After a deep, uneventful night's sleep with no dreams, Mehdi woke and took a morning shower to freshen up. As he stepped out of the tub, he slipped and hit his head on the sink. Crawling on all fours, he made it to his living room and pushed the alarm button. One of his 24/7 bodyguards burst into the room and saw the commander lying on the floor, blood gushing from his head.

Mehdi's personal physician came soon thereafter, and, after he had bandaged his head and run a few tests, he told his patient, "I think you might have a slight concussion. It's best you stay home today."

Although notoriously stubborn, Mehdi put up no fight and told his stunned doctor he would indeed do as he was bid. He then called his deputy Ahizi. "Do not be alarmed, but I had a small accident and the doctor said I was not to leave the house. It cannot be helped. You will have to take over for me at the parade today. You will take my seat at the dignitaries' podium."

"Yes, sir."

'He sounded different just now. Is he worried or excited at the prospect of sitting there with the leaders?' Mehdi thought when he replaced the receiver. A strange sensation he could not shake gripped him.

***

As soon as he got off the phone, Ahizi called his wife. "Don't wear the black hijab you set aside for the parade. Wear the white one, the one with the golden stars I brought you from Esfahan."

***

All the units due to attend the parade were waiting in a large assembly yard at the far end of Ankalaev Street, according to the order of their appearance. The dispatcher was standing on a small platform at the other end of the street. He was holding a megaphone and wearing an earpiece that enabled him to communicate with the marching formations.

At precisely twelve-thirty, the dispatcher ordered the band to set out. No less than thirty musicians in white uniform and pineapple-colored sashes, holding wind instruments and drums followed their jaunty conductor, who also sported a hat that matched his sash.

Exactly sixty seconds after dispatching the band, the dispatcher ordered the flag bearers, all three hundred of them, to follow suit. They held the poles in their strong arms and waved Iran's tricolor national flag alongside the Revolutionary Guard flags, which were yellow. Each unit that participated in the parade had its own uniquely colored flag, as well, so that the combination of the multitude of colors was indeed spectacular.

A tall and burly flag bearer led this parade of flags. The flag-pole he was brandishing was particularly long, over eight feet. Its lower end had a special holster within the custom-made belt that was tailored to this man. The tall end of this thick pole featured the flags of both Iran and the Revolutionary Guard.

The dispatcher sent forth the third outfit eighty seconds after the flag bearers went on their way. This third installment of the parade comprised elite, bearded, Revolutionary Guard commando soldiers in speckled uniforms and carrying short-barreled Kalashnikovs. The muzzles had already been removed the previous evening to prevent any possible risk. Their assigned route was a four-mile march.

The parade's fourth unit was the Revolutionary Guard's ballistics outfit, complete with green trucks towing missile wagon and carriers. The missiles' fuses had been removed. Those with a keen eye could discern that the missiles had been painted over recently. The anti-aircraft unit followed ballistics. It, in turn, was followed by the other units, which were still in for a good two hours of an arduous parade after being dispatched.

The band passed in front of the dignitaries' podium to the sound of loud cheers. Sixty seconds later, the flag bearers marched passed Iran's top-level officials at exactly one o'clock, precisely on schedule.

When the band reached the podium, the chief flag bearer called them all to salute, which they all did in honor of the Iranian people and the Islamic revolution. That very second, he leaped with surprising agility from where he stood in front of the platform and crossed the ten yards that separated the men under his command, still holding their flags, from the platform. Before anyone could get a chance to realize what was going on, the flagpole exploded a few inches away from Deputy Revolutionary Guard Commander Mosati Ahizi.

Except for Ahizi, who bore the full blow of the blast so that very little remained of his shattered body, few others were injured. Even among those, the injuries were minor at the most.

What a commotion this blast caused! People began fleeing in every direction. The parade ground to a halt. The valiant commandos, who were nearest to the explosion, simply stretched out on the road in fear. The ballistics detail fled, leaving their vehicles behind. The anti-aircraft crew likewise fled the scene, trampling those right behind them. Hundreds of thousands of civilian spectators were caught up in the ensuing stampede.

The only people who seemed to be entirely out of place were the members of the band. They simply kept on going, passed the platform, continued on with their route and on with their drums and trumpets, their noise rivaling that of the sirens of the ambulances that rushed to the scene.

Mehdi followed all this from his own room, on TV in real time. He was probably the only person in the whole of Tehran who was not surprised by the turn of events.

His operational line buzzed. "I am sorry to inform you that your deputy, Mosati Ahizi, was killed in the attack."

Mehdi got off the phone. *'I owe someone my life.'*

Chapter Thirty-Two

The Revolutionary Guard's entire high command, some fifteen seniors, was called up the following morning. They were all summoned to an emergency meeting. All, that is, but one. The very evening after the parade that had ended so abruptly, Mehdi ordered the Revolutionary Guard security services to arrest the chief of security and interrogate him for the enormous blunder that had brought the catastrophe about.

Mehdi was sitting at the head of the table and the chief of operations was sitting next to him. Mehdi's head was bandaged. His face was frozen and there was a foggy look in his eyes.

"Trouble," he began saying, "tends to come in pairs, like a team of oxen towing a plow or pigeons in their coup. But before we delve into all that, let us take a moment and stand in silence to honor the memory of our good comrade, the valiant, heroic Commander Mosati Ahizi."

Everyone stood up in honor of the fallen Revolutionary Guard deputy commander, whose body was torn to pieces right before their very eyes. In their heart of hearts, they blessed Allah for extricating them from a similar fate. Then, Mehdi sat back down, and they followed suit.

"Yesterday's terrorist attack was a serious blow to our homeland and to our righteous fight against the forces of evil that wish to crush the revolution. Immediately after this ferocious assault, our esteemed president called me. He lifted my spirits and asked me to pass on to you and to all our valiant men his sincere condolences and heartfelt commiserations for this terrible tragedy. I promised him we are standing firm, we have not lost our spirit, and we shall carry on all the way to victory."

Mehdi then added, "Immediately after the attack, I ordered the appointment of an investigation committee to look into all events leading up to it, as well as the conduct of our men afterwards. I instructed them to complete their inquiry and deliver their conclusions within seven days. In the meantime, I asked the chief of our ops department to give us a short review of what we've managed to examine thus far."

The head of the Revolutionary Guard Ops Department began his presentation looking very low as if frozen in gloom. "Yesterday, immediately after the terrorist attack, I assumed personal responsibility for the tragedy, although I was not personally responsible for security-"

Mehdi cut him off. "I immediately rejected his assumption of responsibility. As much as it is an ethical and moral step, it was not merited in this case. I assure you that those responsible for what happened will pay dearly. Please carry on."

"This is merely a preliminary review. The inquiry is in its initial stage. No doubt, the enemy has succeeded in surprising us, and by 'enemy,' I am referring to only two possible agencies that can be taken into account, CIA special ops or Mossad.

This attack has all the hallmarks of a Mossad operation."

"We must also admit this was a highly professional attack, meticulously carried out. The deputy commander was the only casualty, not including the perpetrator himself. There is no doubt that the one sitting right at the center of the podium was the designated target, and the fact remains that none of the dozens of people sitting in his vicinity were injured. Only a first-rate professional organization could execute such a highly focused operation.

"We were also surprised by the M.O. We thought of dozens of possible scenarios, but it did not occur to us that a plastic explosive could be concealed in such an unforeseen way. Our R&D department continuously gathers data from any terrorist attack worldwide in order to draw lessons from it, and there is no precedent for concealing an explosive device in a flagpole.

"Another issue we are carefully looking into is the identity of the flag bearer who took his own life in this attack. Thus far, our inquiry indicates that his personality and the environment where he lived are not in line with the psychological profile of a suicide bomber as we know it. We shall forward you our findings once we complete our investigation."

Mehdi thanked his ops chief. "As I have told you, trouble comes in pairs. In this case, the catastrophe of the attack on the parade is coupled with operation 'Queen of Vengeance.' The small team and I had decided to execute the operation three days after the parade. I regret to inform you that this mission we have been working on for so long has been postponed. Last night, while I was grieving and hurting for what had happened at the parade, I received word from our people in Lagos, Nigeria, that dozens of local police officers, together with persons identified as Mossad agents, have pounced on the figure who was designated the '*smoking gun*' of the entire operation, arrested him and uncovered the explosive charge that was already fully operational for detonation against the Israeli embassy."

***

One word threw the entire system in turmoil. A spy satellite way up in the sky, some three hundred miles over Tehran, picked up the phrase '*Thanks.*' Much like the other material it had picked up, it was relayed in the original Farsi. All the material received was simultaneously translated, along with other similarly collected data, into Hebrew, using a special software developed by Israeli computer experts.

All this material was compiled and further relayed to the Mossad intelligence, interpretation and control center some-where in Tel Aviv that is operational 24/7. There, systems analysts, intelligence-savvy team members and special ops personnel worked on it tirelessly.

When they came across the term '*Thanks,*' they were be-side themselves. They used all sorts of data analysis and inter-pretation programs to determine that this message came from Revolutionary Guard HQ in Tehran. According to procedure, any material that came from that particular location was to be immediately sent to the relevant branch chief, whose duty was to monitor the Revolutionary Guard.

This branch chief then convened a special emergency

meeting of all the best and the brightest within the department dedicated to Iran. They concluded that the '*Thanks*' message was sent to Israel!

At this point, they updated the head of the department and forwarded him all the data and the resulting conclusion. He in turn quickly informed the head of Mossad, who was of the opinion this turn of events was so unusual the data has to be shared with the chief of Israel's General Security Service (GSS).

A joint meeting of Mossad and GSS focused on the burning questions: who sent this troubling message, why was it sent, and to whom at what address in Israel. Ever suspicious, the people from the GSS were of the opinion this was a serious matter.

In line with the GSS recommendation, a joint taskforce was quickly assembled, with the directive to report to both service chiefs and apprise them of the progress of the investigation on a daily basis. Dozens of analysts, the very best both organizations mustered, worked to crack this case wide open. Mossad and GSS also employed cutting edge electronic and software means – but to no avail. The mystery of the identity of the person within Israel, for whom the message of thanks was meant, and from Iran's Revolutionary Guard, remained unsolved.

***

Tammy joined the IDF shortly after turning eighteen, as is compulsory for her fellow young Israeli men and women. After basic training, she was assigned to the State Archive, and upon the successful completion of her security clearance and after signing the Israeli version of the Official Secrets Act, she began serving as assistant filing clerk at the government archive's 'Top Secret' section.

Hundreds of messages arrived each day to the government secretary. After being sorted, addressed, and handled, a copy would be sent over to the archive to be filed and preserved. Some of these messages were digital, and some in print. Tammy's job was to file the digital and printed messages properly. She would scan the digital messages and file them in the recently established digital archive, whereas typed or written messages were first digitized and then filed in both the general archive and the digital archive. Documents Tammy did not know where to file she set aside and, on occasion, asked her superior, Mira, where to file the unidentified material.

Another uneventful day was drawing to a close with a few documents remaining to be filed. A document that came by email was at the top of the pile. It was empty, except for one word, 'Merci.' The bottom of the page had unclear figures. Tammy glanced at her iPhone and saw that she might be running late for her weekly Pilates class, so she rose from her desk and hurried to the lesson, promising herself she'd get it done the following day.

Come morning, Tammy took the curious piece of paper and went over to Mira's office. Her superior was sitting there with David, a veteran clerk at the archive, and had her morning coffee with him. Tammy welcomed their invitation to join, as she really could use a cup of strong Joe.

"Look," she told Mira as she sipped her coffee. "I have this file with only one word, '*Merci.*' Where shall I file it?

"It is probably some thank-you note a new immigrant from France must have sent the prime minister. File it in the general folder," Mira replied.

"But why French, necessarily?" David intervened. "It could be Farsi."

"Why Farsi? '*Merci*' means thanks. That's the first French word I learned in the course I took at the French embassy," she told him.

"I bet it is Farsi," David would not relent. "You people are always talking down and belittling everything and everyone from the Orient, so I will have you know that Farsi is one of the world's oldest languages, and the origin of many terms in European languages, as well as Hebrew, for instance, names of fruits, colors, all sorts of things. You'll be surprised how many words came to us from Farsi."

"Nevertheless," Mira retorted, "the word '*Merci*' is still in French."

"No!" David insisted. It first came from Farsi. It means "*Thanks.*"

And at that moment, Mira had her own 'eureka' moment. She rushed over to the office of the man in charge of security. "You were looking for the word '*Thanks,*' weren't you? Well, I think we've found it!" She tossed the piece of paper onto his desk.

***

There was no end to the excitement among the members of the special joint team. They forwarded the numbers at the bottom of the page to be processed at the IDF unit akin to NSA in the USA. They soon sent their reply, "These are code numbers. They were recently used on two occasions: one, in a phone call from Paris to Tehran, and the other, a few days later, in a call from Tehran to a phone within the prime minister's office in Jerusalem, Israel."

The joint team further learned that the translated message arrived at the control desk somewhat garbled. But it was the original that arrived in its entirety at the State Archive.

Chapter Thirty-Three

Bonnie felt like he was walking inside a narrow, dry strip of land with huge waves on either side, about to engulf him whole, much like the story of how Moses parted the Red Sea and allowed the Hebrews to cross safely. But unlike those ancient Israelites, he knew he wasn't going to make it safely to the other side. He was in for a life-changing turmoil.

Ever since he had returned from his meeting with his biological father, Bonnie had known his days were numbered. He somehow managed to spend his so-called *'borrowed time'* running the Ministry of Science, which he headed, encouraging investments in the high-tech industry, endorsing entrepreneurs to advance surprising new ideas in the fields of cyber and computing, touring academic and research institutions, and generally striving to promote science in Israel.

From time to time, Bonnie was also invited to attend the meetings of the government's select security and diplomacy cabinet. It was during one of those meetings that the members of cabinet were informed that the Mossad had not succeeded in eliminating Mehdi Mohammadi, but that they had succeeded in foiling the major terrorist attack the Revolutionary

Guard had been planning to mount against the State of Israel. Bonnie, Minister Fiddlemann, always kept silent during these meetings, avoiding any involvement in the matters on the agenda, a large part of which was related to the Iranian threat on Israel.

After his day at his ministry, Bonnie would return to his hotel suite, which the Science Ministry made available to him during the working week, which he spent in Jerusalem, Israel's capital. Bonnie preferred to spend most of his time there, agonizing all by himself in his hotel over the impossible predicament he was in.

Bonnie found himself spending a great deal of his time thinking about his biological father and what he must be going through. '*I wonder how much he laments the impossible situation fate threw both him and me into.*' After all, he had spent a lifetime not even knowing about his biological father until destiny had intervened, forcing a rude awakening.

'*I feel this great affinity with this man, of whose existence I didn't even know for nearly four decades,*' he realized all of a sudden. '*These past few months since I discovered him have been filled with such emotion, such longing,*' he thought as he took in the months he and Mehdi spent trying to make up for years of not being in touch. What made things all the more terrible and perplexing was the oath of office to which he had pledged when he was appointed minister in the government of his beloved homeland.

Those nights at his cold and impersonal hotel were rough on Bonnie. He spent many a night tossing and turning, mulling over the impossible dilemma thrust upon him: '*I know I cannot keep up this double life for much longer.* He spent his weekends at his home in the village, where, whenever his troubled soul kept him from falling asleep, he would pour himself a glass of wine, venture out onto his porch and share his turbulent temperament with the night sky and the nocturnal creatures: from the foxes, whose lantern-like eyes peered at him through the bushes, through the rodents' nightly foraging and the sounds of the mongooses. All this did take the edge off, a little. Once, he even caught a glimpse of a female Indian crested porcupine leading her three little offspring and teaching them the art of plucking spice roots in search of delectable grub.

Bonnie's true nighttime companion was the barn owl. It had built a nesting home in the oak tree his parents had planted when he was born. The nest featured a round hole and a front sill like a tiny bench. The barn owl that elected to make this its home was truly beautiful, sporting white, heart-shaped feathers on its front and a golden-brown back. It slept most of the day, and when darkness descended, it came out of its nesting hole, turned its head full circle and yawned, announcing it was good and ready for the new day. Then, it stretched its wings, squinted in a yellow gaze and looked for breakfast, seeking out a mouse that happened to hop in the grass in search of a mate. The barn owl would then pounce like lighting, grab the poor prey with its sharp claws and take it up to the nest, where it would dine to its heart's content. Once done, the barn owl would return to its sentry, perched on the sill, watching its neighbor down below.

Bonnie wondered what the barn owl might be doing

when he was away in Jerusalem. He knew very well what it was doing when he was back at his own deck. High above his head, sitting by the glow of the porch light, fearless, it looked straight into his eyes with its own sad and wise eyes, as if he were an open book.

Bonnie would watch the barn owl until he regained his composure and inner peace, and then he would return to his own bed, ready to face the rest of the night.

***

Minister Binyamin Pladot was summoned to Yakir Yavnieli, head of security at the prime minister's office. A tall, silver-haired man, Yavnieli cut an impressive figure. Smiling warmly, he rose to greet the minister and shake his hand. Bonnie noticed another man was there, peering at him behind his glasses. This man had a pointed face and thin hair.

"May I present Zelig," Yavnieli made the introduction, without telling Bonnie what this man's job description or even title was. Zelig held out his hand for a polite, faint shake.

'*His name sure matches his appearance,*' Bonnie told himself.

"On occasion," Yavnieli explained, "we hold a security briefing here for ministers and other seniors. This is why I've asked you here today."

They exchanged further pleasantries, followed by a direct question the security branch chief put to Bonnie, "So, how was Paris, minister?"

"Paris is always fun, although five days is too short for a visit. I wouldn't mind spending more time there had I not been so swamped with things at my ministry."

They continued to chat, and finally, Yavnieli asked him, "Do you have anything to add?"

"No," replied the minister. "Everything is hunky-dory."

Bonnie took his leave smiling. He avoided shaking hands with Zelig, who did not utter a word during the minister's entire exchange with Yavnieli.

Six days later, Bonnie was summoned to another meeting at the security chief's office. This time, an additional man was there besides Yavnieli and Zelig. "I would like you to meet Amitay," the chief said.

Contrary to Zelig, Amitay was an impressive man in dark pants and matching striped shirt and with a stern look and piercing gaze. Very early on, Yavnieli apologized for having to leave early in the meeting, but an urgent matter had to be attended to, leaving Bonnie with those two, which made the minister uncomfortable.

"May I know who you two are?"

Zelig responded adamantly, "We ask the questions here."

Amitay, 'the good cop,' responded in a pleasant manner. "We are investigators on behalf of the General Security Service. We'd be happy to show you our credentials."

Bonnie felt a chill running up his spine. "No, that will not be necessary. I believe you. How may I be of service, gentlemen?"

"May I know what you were up to during those five days in Paris?" Zelig asked.

'This here is another Zelig from the one I met before,' Bonnie thought to himself, observing the man's prominent, bespectacled, forehead. Zelig's jaw tightened, as did his eyes. Bonnie could swear he seemed taller, too.

"What does one do in Paris?" Bonnie feigned 'whimsy.' "I was here and there, like any tourist..." He gave them a list of Paris's most familiar tourist attractions.

"Cut the BS," Zelig frowned. "Consider your answer before you give it. Tell us exactly what you were doing in Paris for five days."

Bonnie could feel his apprehension tuning into a clear sense of danger, paralyzing him with fear as it crept up his spine. 'He can't be called Zelig,' he warned himself, 'He probably goes by a different name.'

"I've already told you. I may have forgotten a few details... Maybe I haven't been to Notre Dame, perhaps it was the catacombs or the crypt at Île de la Cité."

"You're lying!" the other investigator pounced, the one who was supposedly, 'the good cop.' "We know you were in Paris for only three days. Where were you during those two other days?"

Bonnie was stunned. The pressure of the interrogations was too hard for him.

"I have but one question for you," Zelig assumed the lead again. He put the following sixty-four-thousand-dollar question to Bonnie: "**Who in Iran's Revolutionary Guard owes you? What did he thank you for?**"

Bonnie collapsed. He, the epitome of an upstanding citizen, panicked. He was in shock. The sweat pouring down his face was a sure sign for his investigators they were close. They knew full well even the best, most experienced liar could not control their sweating.

They paused the interrogation. They lifted Bonnie and took him through the cargo elevator down to their car in the basement of the security branch building. The car, whose windows were dark and sealed, drove for an hour or so. Bonnie, in his state, on the verge of blacking out, could not follow the route. He did not even try.

The car entered this basement of a house that seemed completely deserted. They asked him to get out of the car, and he obliged. Zelig and Amitay led him down a narrow corridor into a shabby looking room and asked him to take a seat in a chair that looked very old and worn out and left him by himself.

About fifteen minutes later, a man in black trousers and a white shirt came in. He placed a typed statement in front of Bonnie.

It said as follows:

Attn., the Prime Minister,

I, the undersigned, Minister of Science Binyamin Pladot, hereby inform you of my resignation from the Knesset and the government, due to personal reasons. My resignation is effective immediately.

Yours sincerely,

Binyamin Pladot

"Kindly sign this," the man in the white shirt told him politely.

Bonnie did not hesitate for a moment. As soon as he signed, an immense sense of relief descended on him. The man took the signed letter and left the room.

Then, a young man entered, and asked Bonnie to follow.

He led Bonnie into an adjacent room that had a bed, a small toilet, a desk and a chair. There were no curtains. '*This room is obviously below the ground,*' Bonnie quickly realized.

Bonnie spent the following three days alone in this room. The young man, never exchanging a single word with him, brought in a small lunch three times a day.

Three days after he was first brought there and had signed his letter of resignation, Bonnie was taken to the room where he had been asked to sign. Zelig and Amitay were already there, waiting for him. They greeted him and sat right in front of him, motionless and silent.

"Save your breath, I will tell you everything," Bonnie beat them to the punch. A recording device was placed on the desk. Out came the camera, into plain sight.

Bonnie talked for three days and three nights straight. He barely touched his food. Water seemed to be enough for him. He did not refer to his interrogators and did not even notice they took turns and had continuous shifts in the course of those three days. He did not speak to them but only to himself and about himself.

Bonnie spoke about his days in preschool; his kindergarten teacher's name was Eve. He recounted everything from childhood to the very last moments of collapsing the other day, when he realized his double life had been exposed.

He spoke into the recording device the same way he communed with the barn owl back home, speaking to someone or something that listened. The more he spoke, the greater he became relieved. He felt his life was beginning to make more and more sense. The words displaced his distress, his suffering, his sense of loss and dead-end.

Once he was done, his head slumped into the chair as he fell asleep. This was the first time Bonnie had slept soundly ever since he had opened his mother's letter to him. When he awoke in bed, he found himself in the sealed room. They told him he had slept twenty-four hours straight.

Upon waking, he got to take a decent shower and was given fresh clothes they had brought over from his hotel suite. Here were Zelig and Amitay, sitting across from him in silence. Depression and sadness dominated the room. Not a word was uttered, not a single question asked. His two interrogators had seen their fair share and heard many a good story, and yet, here they were, affected by his story. Zelig asked Bonnie to sign his confession, which was made into a transcript that captured its spontaneity. Bonnie did not even bother to go over the saga of his life. He signed it and made a parting gesture with his head as they left the room. Then, he was taken back to his small chamber, where he slept, or, more like a groundhog, hibernated for another twelve hours.

The following day, or perhaps the very same day – Bonnie had already lost all track of time – he was called back to the adjacent room, where he was given another piece of paper.

This time round, it was the following document:

Penal Code 1977

Article 113 – Disclosing a state secret without proper authorization with the intention of undermining the national security is punishable by lifelong incarceration.

A 'State Secret' – an item in reference to which the national security requires strict confidentiality.

Article 114 – Whosoever engages with a foreign agent without a plausible explanation is subject to incarceration for fifteen years.

A foreign agent – one who is reasonably suspected of having been sent by a foreign country or on its behalf or at the behest of a terrorist organization or foreign country to collect intelligence or perpetrate any action that might undermine the security of the State of Israel.

Amitay walked into the room after a short while. He was alone this time. "We have a court order granting us leeway to prevent you from seeing your attorney for fifteen days. But seeing as you have given us a full confession, we have no objection to you meeting with an attorney."

Initially indifferent to the proposal, Bonnie thought about it a little and decided to seek council with an attorney he had met many years prior. This man had assisted him in registering the land rights and entitlements according to the deed for his parents' estate. This attorney, who was highly embarrassed to even come to the meeting, heard the amazing story of his one-time client.

Once the attorney regained his composure, he turned to Bonnie with enthusiasm, "Listen, it's all going to be fine." He proceeded in this tone, which lawyers adopt all too often when they wish to impress their clients and convince them. "We shall prevail upon the court and persuade your panel of judges that you broke no law. At the very worst, this is an infraction, a misdemeanor that does not justify your being held in custody."

Bonnie, who had regained his senses and calm, as well, asked him, amused, "And how are you going to accomplish that?"

"What do you mean, '*how*?' I'll simply prove in court that you had no intention of undermining the country's security and that you have a reasonable explanation for meeting the commander of the Revolutionary Guard. I do not know a single judge who would not accept the merit of my arguments..."

'*Your arguments, but they aren't mine*,' Bonnie thought to himself, bid his attorney farewell and promised to give him his reply soon.

***

The day after his meeting with his attorney, Bonnie asked for an audience with his interrogators. They were surprised to see him sitting upright, serene and full of confidence and focus.

He spoke to them for two hours, and the more he said, their eyes opened wider and wider still. Once he was done, they were so stunned, they could barely speak. Zelig was the first to overcome his shock.

"We will have to clear this with the chief," he said quietly as he and Amitay left the room.

Epilogue

Bonnie had arranged with Mehdi they would meet by the frog pond at the Bois de Boulogne, one of Paris's famous parks. He turned up early.

A singer nearby, surrounded by a group of young adults, was holding a guitar.

"The falling leaves drift by the window/" the singer played and sang *Les Feuilles Mortes*.

Bonnie saw his father approaching. They went over to a large poplar tree, a few yards off the pond. They shared a warm embrace, but before a single word was uttered, Bonnie pulled out a 9mm Beretta gun with a silencer and shot his father.

Even before the father's body reached the ground, Bonnie put the muzzle into his own mouth and pulled the trigger. Both men fell onto the ground that was covered with leaves.

But the singer didn't notice any of this. He played on, echoing Yves Montand's famous rendition, in French:

"*Les pas des amants désunis*" – "the footsteps of disunited lovers" "when autumn leaves start to fall."

The End

Made in the USA
Monee, IL
21 June 2022

98352953R00169